Half fearful, Suzie look[...] eyes, and then he bent his head and his lips brushed the side of her mouth in the gentlest of caresses. His hands slid into her hair, and she turned her head a little so that he could take full possession of her mouth, but his lips touched hers again in the lightest of kisses and then her cheek.

'I never could keep my hands off a beautiful woman,' Nat said.

'Does that mean you've had many beautiful women?' Suzie faltered, and then could have bitten her tongue for the naïveté of the question.

But as he looked at her his eyes changed, and the laughter disappeared. There was no teasing when he eventually spoke.

'I'm sorry. That was a cheap line. Don't look so embarrassed. You had every right to ask.'

She couldn't meet his eyes now. 'I'm sorry—I——'

'No,' he interrupted quickly. 'Don't be. I get to meet a lot of very attractive women, who make it clear that they are . . . well, available. But there have been very few that I *haven't* been able to keep my hands off.' The smile in his voice encouraged Suzie to look up. 'As you see, I haven't yet been able to take my hands off you. But then I've never met anyone quite like you before, and I can't yet believe my luck . . .'

INNOCENT PRETENCES

BY

LUCY KEANE

MILLS & BOON LIMITED
ETON HOUSE   18-24 PARADISE ROAD
RICHMOND   SURREY   TW9 1SR

*First published in Great Britain 1988
by Mills & Boon Limited*

© Lucy Keane 1988

*Australian copyright 1988
Philippine copyright 1989
This edition 1989*

ISBN 0 263 76223 8

*Set in Plantin 10 on 10 pt.
01 – 8902 – 63940*

Typeset in Great Britain by JCL Graphics, Bristol

Made and printed in Great Britain

CHAPTER ONE

EYES wide with fear, a smudge of dirt on one cheek, Suzie half scrambled, half fell down the last few feet of the rocky path and ran out into the dirt track that snaked through the ancient rock city. Surely there must be at least *one* European tourist she could call to for help?

Vividly, a conversation she'd had with Katrina only a few weeks previously flashed through her mind. 'You'll be OK on your own if Bob turns up, won't you?' Katrina had asked. 'If he can get the time off he's going to try to spend a few days in Jordan, and he wants to take me round a bit with him.' Why on earth had she agreed? She should have known she wouldn't be able to cope. It was all very well for Katrina—she was adventurous by nature, and used to spending her holidays abroad.

She could feel a scratch down her left leg, and her hands were streaked with sweat and dirt. She had lost her camera, but at least she was still wearing her money-belt with her passport and a few remaining traveller's cheques inside it. Now, almost sobbing for breath, she glanced helplessly round the theatre that had been cut into the curiously brick-coloured stone centuries ago. It rose in deserted tiers to her right, its long, curved seating empty of even one human figure. Behind her, and in front of her, towered the massive ledges and rock cut walls that formed the famous tombs of the rose-red city of Petra.

Intent only on outdistancing her pursuer, she had been counting on reaching the track in time to attract attention. Now she had finally reached the valley floor, there was no one.

Her panic increasing, she began to run in the direction she knew led towards the Siq—the long, narrow channel between towering rock walls that for centuries had been the only access to this legendary hidden city. But even as she started she could hear the sound of someone sliding over a patch of uneven chippings on the path she had just descended, and a man's voice shouting to her. Visions of being raped there in the middle of the road filled her mind. Suddenly there seemed to be a horrible inevitability about it. She had been very foolish ever to accept the offer of a guide—and foolish young tourist women often got what they deserved. She knew that, if someone didn't appear quickly, she'd be very lucky indeed to get away.

She was so caught up in her own fears, she almost ran into two riders unexpectedly rounding a sharp bend in the track. They had been hidden from her by a sheer wall of rock and, blind and deaf to everything but her own panic, she hadn't been aware of their approach.

They were Arabs: both wore headcloths secured round by a black headband in the Jordanian fashion, and their horses—the second a fine grey—were hung with brightly coloured trappings. The two men were probably locals who supplemented their earnings by posing for tourists' photographs.

Both riders reined back abruptly, and Suzie only just avoided colliding with the leading horse. The man said something in Arabic, presumably to quieten the animal that was now sidling and tossing its head.

Panting, speechless and uncertain, Suzie gazed up at him. *Two* Arabs! Was this falling from the frying pan into the fire? The first man had the dark, chiselled, hawk-nosed features of a good-looking bedouin, and a small moustache. The black and white checked cloth covered his hair, and shaded his brow and the sides of his face. He was wearing jeans and a light-coloured shirt, and on his wrist an expensive-looking gold watch. His hands on the the reins were darkly tanned and strong.

Suzie glanced quickly at his companion. He was similarly dressed, although he wore no watch, and his headcloth shaded most of his face.

The first man was speaking to her, his words heavily accented. 'You are all right? Have you lost your friends?'

Suzie, trying to regain her breath, found herself unconsciously grasping at the reins he held.

'Be careful—she is nervous!' he warned.

The second rider laughed and urged his horse forward. 'I'd say that just about described both of them, wouldn't you?' The remark was addressed to his companion, and at that moment the mare threw up her head, pulling Suzie off balance. She let go of the reins to find herself sitting unexpectedly in the dust, the mare dancing temperamentally beside her. The sudden fall almost knocked the breath out of her.

The second rider halted inches from her, and she was startled to find herself staring, breathless, into a pair of unexpectedly grey-green eyes. She hadn't thought there were any Arabs with light-coloured eyes. He leaned from the saddle and stretched out a hand.

'Don't look so scared! It's OK. Whatever you were in such a hurry to get away from—it's gone. Or are we keeping you from your tourist bus?' His English was perfect, educated, without the slightest trace of a foreign accent.

'No—I . . .' She gasped, and hesitated, embarrassed to find herself so near to tears. This man sounded so normal and ordinary all of a sudden. She couldn't trust herself to explain.

He gazed at her speculatively, his hand still stretched out to her. 'Come on. Get up. I think we can guess what happened—especially as you're dressed like that.'

The blood rushed to Suzie's face. She was all too conscious now that the blue and white print sundress she was wearing revealed far too much of her shoulders and back—modest though it was by European standards—for a country that still veiled many of its women. Stupidly, she had assumed that historical sites would hardly prove likely hunting grounds for predatory Arabs.

To cover her confusion, she reached up to grasp his hand and let him pull her to her feet. But there was an appraising glint in those grey-green eyes that reminded her too clearly of her recent experience—somehow she knew she wouldn't escape this one if he turned out to be like the guide. 'Didn't anyone warn you that female tourists are considered the natural prey of every Jordanian male over the age of six?' The other Arab laughed, black eyes glinting in the dark face, and his companion, with a grin at his friend, continued, 'That includes Fahad here. It's just as well you can trust me.'

She looked at him in astonishment. 'Aren't you an Arab, then?'

Both men laughed, and exchanged glances before he replied, 'Sure. My name is Ahmed. I just happen to have an English mother.'

Fahad said something incomprehensible in Arabic, which did nothing to wipe the grin off the face of the grey-eyed Ahmed. Suzie, her cheeks still burning, dropped her eyes and brushed a stray wisp of brown hair from her face nervously. She knew she must look a mess, but her appearance was not now her main concern. She was beginning to wonder how she was going to extricate herself from this new encounter.

It had begun to dawn on her that her first reaction to the two horsemen might have been an accurate one—she might now have got herself into a worse predicament than before: she could hardly hope to fight off two of them. What a fool she was! Ready to be lulled into a false sense of security at the first sound of an English accent. She had no more good reason to trust this curiously light-eyed Arab than she had had to entrust herself to the so-called 'guide' who had caused her precipitate flight from the rocks a few minutes earlier.

Not for the first time since getting up that morning, she wished, with mingled desperation and annoyance, for Katrina. If Katrina had only stayed with her as originally planned when they had booked the holiday, she wouldn't now be in this mess. When you were twenty-one, not long financially independent, with scarcely any experience of foreign travel, you were easily lured by the glamour of the tourist agencies' advertising. And, while sitting at home with their glossy brochures, you could persuade yourself without much difficulty that you had a sense of adventure.

The reality, of course, was very different.

What on earth had posssessed her to come to Jordan, of all places, when she had scarcely ventured abroad further than France on her own? Family holidays didn't count—you had no responsibility and no difficult decisions to make.

She swallowed painfully and began to back away. At least there had been no sign, as yet, of the 'guide'. It she could just get away from these two, she might meet some other tourists. They *must* be somewhere! After all, she had come with a busload of them, and it wasn't yet time to leave. She glanced at her watch; the hands showed two o'clock. Her reaction must have shown very clearly on her face. The one who called himself Ahmed said quickly, 'What's the matter?'

She looked up at him, blue eyes wide with apprehension. 'What time is it?'

Ahmed glanced at his wrist automatically, and then shrugged. 'Sorry—forgot to put my watch on. Fahad?'

'Ten to three.'

'Oh, no—my bus leaves in five minutes from the entrance!' As soon as she had said it, she realised it was a bad idea to have given them so much information: it made her too vulnerable.

Fahad shrugged. 'There is no way you can catch that one,' he said. 'It takes about fifteen minutes to walk down the Siq. Are you alone?' She wondered just how much of a threat there was in that question, but looking at his face she couldn't tell.

'You came with a tourist party?' Ahmed asked, when she hesitated.

'Yes—I—my friends will be worrying about me,' she lied.

'Do you think they'll delay the bus?'

'They might,' she said hopefully, wondering if she could meet his eyes. She knew she wasn't a good liar, but she began to see a way out of the present difficulty. If she could only persuade him that her non-existent friends would be waiting for her, it might ensure her safe return to the site entrance; once there, she would surely find other tourists. She didn't know what she would do if the bus hadn't waited for her, but perhaps she might meet some English or American sightseers prepared to take her back to Amman.

'Can you ride?'

Surprised, Suzie found herself looking Ahmed straight in the eyes. She wasn't sure she could interpret their expression. Was he laughing at her? But his smile seemed nothing more than friendly, and his question sounded serious.

She shook her head. 'No. Why?'

'A pity. It puts a last-minute bid for escape on horseback out of the question.'

The word 'escape' wasn't lost on Suzie. He knew she was trying to evade not only the man who had been pursuing her, but himself and his friend as well. She knew that the flush on her lightly tanned skinned had deepened—she could feel herself growing hotter. Now was the time to get away, before the situation became impossible. A polite, rather cold goodbye might let them know that she wasn't interested in their company. It might help her play for time, if nothing else.

But before she could summon up the resolution to open her mouth, Ahmed spoke again. 'Where did you come from—Amman?'

Without thinking, she answered, and then could have kicked herself—with every exchange she was becoming more involved with them. 'Yes.'

'You were with a tourist group, and you're going back to Amman?'

She nodded reluctantly.

'So what are you going to do?' He managed to make the question sound like friendly interest, no more.

Suzie shrugged, in an attempt to appear casual. 'I'm going back to the site entrance. My friends might have decided to wait for me, after all.' She made a move to pass the grey standing patiently beside her.

Fahad spoke again in Arabic to his companion, and Ahmed said, 'He thinks you will be safer with us.'

'No, thank you. It's quite all right.' Suzie found herself reduced to a rather stilted politeness almost against her better judgement; you had to be forceful and decisive if you were going to get anywhere, but it was so difficult to be rude to people who were persistent. Why couldn't they just take the hint and leave her alone? 'I don't want to take you out of your way. Thank you. Good——' Before she could get out what she hoped was going to be a cold dismissal, Ahmed burst out laughing. She looked at him with surprise and some apprehension, and took another sideways step or two in the direction of the Siq.

'Only an English girl could make a speech like that!' he exclaimed, when he could trust himself to get the words out. Fahad was grinning from ear to ear. 'How old are you?'

he continued. 'Sixteen? Seventeen?'

Belatedly, Suzie adopted the attitude she should have had from the beginning. 'I don't think that's any of your business!' she snapped. 'Now will you please get out of my way?'

The horse had shifted across her path; she couldn't tell whether Ahmed had deliberately encouraged it or not. She was beginning to feel frightened again, but was determined not to show it if she could help it.

'What's your name?' It was Ahmed again.

'That's none of your business, either—stop your horse doing that!'

Ahmed was grinning, and this time he was fully in control of the horse's movements at it sidled towards her. He halted it instantly, only inches from her, and bent down towards her, the grin still curling the corners of his mouth.

'Listen, little English girl—whatever your name is—you've made several major tactical errors in the past few minutes, and Fahad and I could have had our evil way with you a couple of times each already if we'd wanted to. That's what you're afraid of, isn't it?'

Suzie, the proverbial beetroot colour by now, couldn't bring herself to look at him. She was acutely conscious of Fahad, just behind him, struggling not to laugh.

'I know things aren't always what they seem, and your mother told you never to trust strange men—especially Arabs——' there was a snort from Fahad '—but you'd better off with us for the moment. We'll escort you to the entrance, and we might be persuaded to find you a lift back to Amman if your bus has gone. You can even have a lift to the entrance, if you like.' The grey-green eyes looked at her speculatively. 'Now, which of us do you trust least, I wonder?'

Suzie, too transparent, glanced nervoulsy from one to the other. It provoked another guffaw from Fahad, although Ahmed preserved a relatively straight face.

Fahad urged his mare towards her. 'It's all right, really,' he said. 'Ahmed believes he is the reincarnation of your English Sir Galahad. Even your mother would trust him! What is your name?'

'Suzie.' Off guard as she was, the answer came too easily.

She glanced quickly up at Ahmed. This time he didn't even smile.

'See what I mean? Your mother, trusting me apart, should never have let you out alone. She's not on the bus, is she?'

'Of course not!' she retorted, stung by this attitude. Untravelled she might be, but she wasn't exactly a naïve teenager, even if she had made one or two unwise decisions in the course of the day.

'Pity.' He sounded disparaging. 'She might have had the tourist police out after you by now and saved us the trouble of having to protect you from yourself. Firstly——' he was clearly assessing her now, and made no attempt to hide it '—you're a very pretty girl, blue-eyed Suzie. Secondly, the way you're dressed is interpreted in this country as an open invitation to any able Arab male who sets eyes on you—as I've mentioned before. And thirdly, you don't seem to know how to look after yourself.' He leaned towards her and reached down his hand. 'Come on. If you've never been on a horse before, now's the time to try it out. Guaranteed one hundred per cent safe ride—and I promise I won't even try a little quiet rape. Scouts' honour!'

She glanced quickly from Ahmed to his companion, and back again. The whole situation was getting far beyond her control. She didn't want to be involved with either of them but, for no good reason she could think of, she was inclined to trust them—then wondered if she wasn't making a terrible mistake.

Ahmed sighed, with obvious patience, but didn't withdraw his hand. 'Suzie, this is an unrepeatable offer. It's not every sixteen-year-old that gets the opportunity to ride through Petra with a couple of doubtful Arabs——'

'You speak for yourself, my friend!' It was Fahad.

'I was.'

Suzie, irritated by his patronising attitude, and on the point of denying the age he had just attributed to her, caught his eye.

'Don't tell me,' he said. 'You're all of twenty-five.' He held her gaze for a few seconds and then suddenly, inexplicably, most of her fears disappeared and she found herself half smiling at him. She rather liked Ahmed, doubtful Arab or not.

At least he had a sense of humour.

He grinned back at her, his teeth white and even, and the disconcerting grey-green eyes full of friendly amusement.

'Well, Arab friend—I think I win this one?' It was obvious he was referring to her decision to trust him rather than Fahad.

He took hold of her arm and told her to put her foot on his in the stirrup, and, before she was fully aware of his intentions, with one powerful tug he had swung her up in front of him. Both her legs hung one side of the horse's neck, and she could feel the short hair of its coat pricking her bare skin. She was precariously balanced on the edge of the saddle and powerful shoulders of the horse. She was afraid she would slip off once the animal began to walk, but was too tensely aware of the man in the saddle behind her to sit further back.

He chuckled, almost in her ear, and she could feel his Arab headcloth brush against her hair as he slid one arm round her waist and pulled her against him.

'Come on, Suzie. I told you I wasn't after your honour, didn't I? You're going to fall if you sit like that. Shift round sideways a little bit more and hold on to me. This horse would never win the Cheltenham Gold Cup, but if he shies at something you'll be sitting back in the dirt again. You didn't hurt yourself before, did you?'

'No.' Her reply was very low as she adjusted her position. The only way she could hold on to him, apart from putting her arms round his neck, was to slide one arm round his back and put a hand on his waist, in the way he had taken hold of her. She was too nervous to hold him very firmly, and she was acutely aware of all the contours of his body as she sat against him. Her head was against his shoulder.

'Comfortable?'

'Yes, thank you.'

'Not the conventional first riding lesson, I'll grant you, but at least you can admire the scenery.' He was trying to put her at her ease, talking to her almost as though she were a child! Half irritated, half reassured, she gave a quiet smile, and his companion laughed.

'For a man who is posing as saintly Sir Galahad, you certainly have an unexpected way with women, Nat. Perhaps you would like to change horses, Suzie? You would like to try mine?'

Nat? But wasn't his name . . .? Suzie surreptitiously studied the face of the man behind her. The headcloth shaded a little too much for a clear view, and leaning back as far as she dared in the circle of his arm it was difficult to see more than the straight nose and firm jawline, the tanned skin and dark eyelashes . . . dark, but not black. And the tan was very golden, almost Mediterranean, and the eyes were . . . How could she have been so stupid? No wonder he had teased her!

He was leaning slightly away from her so that he could watch her expression. And grinning. He must have caught the exact moment of realisation as it dawned in her eyes. He answered for her, 'No, thank you, Fahad,' making fun of her English politeness. 'She prefers to be with me, don't you, Suzie? Especially as she's just discovered something, and is wondering how to ask me. Gee up, Neddy!'

The horse moved smoothly into a walk, but Suzie involuntarily caught at the rider behind her as she felt the sudden change. He chuckled and gave her a squeeze. 'Don't worry. The jumps aren't till later.'

No one spoke for a while. Suzie adjusted to the movement of the horse, listening to its hoofs clopping quietly over the sun-white dust of the track, beating an irregular counter-rhythm to the mare behind. She kept her eyes studiously on the walls of rock that surrounded them, unwilling to draw upon herself further teasing. The vertical planes of pinkish-grey rose to several hundred feet in places, pillared and decorated. The rock-cut façades gave the impression of a strange deserted city, shadowed at intervals by the irregular dark entrances of caves, some inhabited by Arabs and their long-eared goats.

'Go on, Suzie, say it—I can't stand the suspense!' said a voice in her ear, and she flinched at the unexpected closeness. Mercifully, he didn't draw attention to her reaction, but demanded, 'Well?'

Despite herself, she looked up to catch his eye, and then grinned. 'All right, if I have to . . . You're not an Arab.'

He leaned back a little, an expression of mock amazement on his face. 'Good heavens! However did you guess? Do you mean I wasn't one hundred per cent convincing?'

She laughed, the nervous tension in her suddenly easing. 'It wasn't until your friend called you Nat that I even began to put two and two together.'

'I know.' He flipped the loose end of the reins backwards so that they flicked her wrist. 'I saw the little wheels grinding round behind your eyes.'

She didn't quite know how to answer that without being rude, so she asked, 'You're English?'

'I'm afraid so. But Fahad is the real thing. Aren't you, Fahad?' He twisted round in the saddle to address the man behind him, causing Suzie to clutch him again nervously as his change of position altered hers. She couldn't see him, but she could hear the Arab chuckle.

'Genuine twenty-two carat,' he said. 'But I don't know how you managed to take her in, Nat. Your impresonation of a sheikh is terrible.'

'Don't embarrass me before strangers,' Nat replied plaintively. 'Suzie's big blue eyes are already like saucers.' Then he twisted forwards again to concentrate on guiding the horse past a jumble of stones to the side of the track. He held the reins lightly in his right hand. His fingers were long and strong, and back of his hand lined with sinews and the shadowing of viens under the tan. The hair on his arms was bleached a light gold; she had been stupid not to notice such a giveaway before.

Turning a bend in the track, they were at the entrance of the Siq, to their right the so-called 'treasury' flanked by its high pink columns cut into the rock, and to their left the narrow entrance of the famous hidden way into the city—a mere passageway beween towering walls.

'Do you want to get down and walk, or are you happy to stay on the horse?' Nat asked.

'Why? Aren't you allowed to ride throught the Siq?'

He shrugged, and she felt the movement against her own body. 'It's fine, unless the horse gets nervous and decides to bolt. It's a bit narrow for trick riding.' He drew the rein gently towards him as he spoke, and the horse stopped obediently. 'Now, let me have a privileged view of one of those lovely long slim legs of your while you swing it over his neck. He's not used to the damsel-in-distress side-saddle style.'

The manoeuvre wasn't achieved with quite the ease his instruction had suggested. She wasn't quite sure how it happened, except that it had something to do with Nat switching the reins unexpectedly from one hand to the other, but she found herself leaning right back against him to give herself enough room to disentangle her foot from the reins and get her leg across the horse. She was afraid he might suspect her of doing it deliberately, the whole thing seemed so clumsy, and she blushed furiously. Then suddenly he was on the ground, and she was sitting precariously astride the horse.

'But I can't ride him!' she protested, curling her fingers desperately round the edge of the saddle.

Nat grinned up at her, the headcloth shading most of his face. 'You won't have to. I'll lead him. You just sit there and hang on. You won't need these—move your knee.'

Suzie watched while he did something with the leathers that brought the stirrup up to the saddle, and then crossed round the horse's head to do the same on the other side. Inadvertently, his knuckles brushed against the inside of her thigh as he slipped the iron upwards. He didn't appear to notice, but Suzie, shrinking back hastily, was acutely conscious of the contact.

Fahad, with a comment in Arabic, rode on ahead and was already out of sight by the time they rode down the Siq. At first Suzi was so apprehensive about the horse, she hardly dared to lift her eyes from its ears, but it plodded quietly on with Nat at its head, and after a while she began to look about her with more enthusiasm.

On her approach to the city, she had been worried about keeping up with her tourist group. They were all strangers to her, and she had spoken to none of them, but she had kept her eye at first on a couple conspicuous for their coloured clothes, and a man in an unflattering Christoper Robin hat. Later, lingering too long in one of the stone chambers and taking a different route back to the path again, she had lost sight of them and all her earlier fear of losing the group had returned.

Now, trusting Nat to manage the horse, she enjoyed the

extraordinary experience of being carried along that historic channel that had protected a long-vanished civilisation for centuries from the surprise attack of its enemies. She watched the changing dark reds and purples in the vast walls of the natural formation towering above their heads. A few green plants sprung from the crevices where they were shaded from the hot summer sunshine.

Finally they emerged as the Siq opened out to a wide track with boulders on either side. There was no sign of Fahad ahead of them, and Nat stopped the horse and looked up at her. 'Well?' he asked. 'Enjoy it?'

A kind of dreamy exhilaration had come over her, driving out all her earlier apprehensions, and she glanced down with shining eyes. 'It was fantastic! I didn't notice it the first time, I was so busy trying to keep up with the group.'

He made a sound to the horse, and gave it a gentle tug to start it walking again before he continued, 'What exactly happened to the group to make you so late for your bus?'

She repressed a shudder, remembering only too clearly the chase through the rocks and what happened before it. 'It wasn't the group—it was my fault. They all split up, and some of them were keen to climb up to something they called the monastery . . .'

'I know it. It was once used as a Christian church, but it's quite a way further on.'

'I was sort of following a few people, and then I must have taken a wrong turning and when I looked round for them they'd gone. I spent ages looking for them.' She paused for a moment, reluctant to go on with the story. She knew it would make her sound like a prize idiot, and in normal circumstances she'd never have dreamed of going off alone in some rock valley with a complete stranger. 'I wandered round on my own for a while until I met a couple of tourists who had nothing to do with the group. They were talking to an Arab who was going to show them some Roman legionaries' tombs up in the back of the rocks, and they asked me if I wanted to go with them . . . It was all right for a while, then they decided to go back, and the guide wanted to show me some more. He'd been OK. Till then.' The hesitation in her voice became more marked.

'I can guess the rest,' Nat said. 'It's an occupational hazard for all tourist females in these parts.' He sounded almost cheerful. 'But you did ask for it, didn't you?'

Unexpectedly, she found herself dangerously near to tears. Her encounter with Fahad and Nat had presented her with immediate problems, real or imagined, and coping with new difficulties had distanced her from the danger and very real fear she had experienced just before. She generally had too calm and practical an approach to life to allow what was safely past to disturb her unduly, but in this case just talking about it brought it all back vividly.

As though he hadn't noticed her silence, Nat went on, 'You're a bit dirty as tourist females go, and you've got a nasty scratch you don't seem to have noticed, but I'd guess apart from that you're pretty much OK—am I right?'

He glanced up when she didn't reply, and she nodded, not trusting herself to speak. Yes, she was OK, if you called it OK to have bruises all over your back where a lust-crazed maniac with terrifying strength had just flung you again a rock—and a memory that seemed as though it would forever warp your view of normal relations between men and women when you couldn't forget the way he had thrust himself against you, and the feel of the stubble on his chin grazing your face as he tried to kiss you, and the way he tried to get his hands under your clothes and pawed you . . .

'How do you come to be sightseeing all on your own in Jordan?'

If he hadn't sounded so cheerful, and kind, and interested, she wouldn't have cried. But she remembered how isolated she had felt once Katrina had gone, and how lonely she was going to be for the next week, and when she put up her hand to hide the fact that her eyes had filled with tears, she started to sob so hopelessly, she knew she wasn't going to be able to stop.

And then, without quite knowing how it happened, she found herself being gently pulled off the horse and slipping into the arms of a total stranger who let her cry against his shoulder.

CHAPTER TWO

SUZIE sniffed, and wiped her eyes with the back of her hand. The trouble was, once you started to cry, it was difficult to stop. The stranger whose name was Nat held her gently from him and said, looking down at her, 'You really shouldn't be let out on your own, should you? How old are you?'

'Twenty-one.' Old enough to know better, she thought miserably. 'I'm s-sorry. I didn't mean to do that.' It wasn't easy to speak coherently after such a collapse, but the man holding her seemed to be able to interpret accurately

'There's no need to apologise. Do you want to talk about it?' She shook her head, her eyes still brimming with tears. He brushed a thumb lightly across her cheek.

'I suppose crying is one way of washing your face,' he remarked, and then his tone suddenly became more serious. 'You are all right, aren't you? Sometimes it is better to talk, even if you don't think so at the time. It's a good way of forestalling nasty dreams.' His grip on her arms shifted, and she flinched. He glanced down quickly, opening his hands. 'Sorry—did I hurt you? You've got a fine bruise coming up there.'

'It was when—when he . . .' she faltered, remembering how she'd tried to twist out of the man's grasp.

 How did you get away?'

'I'm not sure . . . He must have lost his balance when I tried to get free. He caught the camera strap and it broke. Then I just ran.'

'It sounds as though you've lost the camera for good. He'll probably have kept it as a consolation prize.'

She shuddered. 'I don't mind. At least I did get away.'

He smiled at her, a kind, charming smile that reached his eyes. 'That's a very positive attitude to take. Now we'd

19

better get a move on before Fahad comes galloping back to
rescue you from my predatory clutches. I call this creature
Neddy. Do you want another ride?'

He was talking to her in a manner calculated to reassure, but
he had an air of confidence about him that was reassuring in
itself. She couldn't tell how old he was; the Arab head-dress
hid too much of his face. He could have been about thirty.

She gave a half-successful smile, and looked at the horse.
'No, thanks. You make him sound like something off a
fairground.'

Nat chuckled, and gathered up the reins in his hand. 'I don't
know his real name. Something Arabic, I guess. I rode him for
the first time yesterday. He belongs to a friend of Fahad.'

She walked beside him as he led the horse. It wasn't far back
to the entrance now. There was a small hotel there, with a
restaurant and guard post.

'What do you do in Jordan?' she asked, after a short
silence.

He glanced at her, and adjusted the head cloth, pulling it
back to reveal more of his face. She noticed that he had
slight hollows under his cheekbones which emphasised the
fine lines of his face, and the strong jaw.

'I'm a computer engineer.'

'Have you been working out here long?'

There was a slight hesitation before he answered. 'No.
I'm a sort of technical trouble-shooter, if you could call it
that. I work for an electronics company that sells big
systems to foreign clients, and when something goes wrong
with their innards, they send out a computer engineer to
sort it out. We only have a couple of installations in this
country, which is why we haven't got anyone out here on a
more permanent basis. Normally our Middle East guy
would deal with it, but he's got a lot on his hands in Saudi
at the moment.'

'Are you on holiday now?'

'You could put it like that. On the other hand, I might be
on the first flight home tomorrow. I have to keep in touch
with base, and it depends what turns up.'

'Being a computer engineer sounds like quite a glamorous

job,' she remarked thoughtfully.

To her surprise, he burst out laughing, overcome by a very genuine amusement. 'Tell that to the average engineer and he'll probably spit in your face with fury! In the computer world it's considered pretty menial, despite the fact that without the technical back-up the smart software guys would get nowhere. And it's comparatively badly paid.'

'Do *you* like it?' She hoped she wouldn't sound too inquisitive.

He paused deliberately before answering, and, still very much amused by some private joke, and said, 'I wouldn't be here if I didn't.'

'Despite the fact that you don't get paid a lot?'

'Despite the fact that I'm paid comparative peanuts for a job like this. That's part of the challenge. I like meeting people, and I like having to sort out some almost impossible and some-times ludicrous situations—anything from a malfunctioning Arab, to rats gnawing through the power supplies.' She laughed, and he glanced down at her. 'That's better. You look almost human now. We'll be at the café in a minute and I'll buy you a drink. They mightn't stretch to anything more invigorating than Coke or lemonade, I'm afraid—though half the supplies of that have probably gone to the Petra supermarket.'

'Where's that?' she asked in surprise.

He grinned at her. 'Didn't you see it? It's a cave run by an Arab with a donkey, and stocks everything from metal bracelets to plastic cigarette lighters. Want to go back for another look?'

She gave an irrepressible little shiver. 'No, thanks. Arabs in caves are not my scene at the moment.'

Fahad was waiting at the café when they arrived. He raised a hand in greeting to Nat, and smiled at Suzie.

'Your bus has gone. It left twenty minutes ago. They waited for a short time, but the guide said it was impossible to stay any longer. There will be another tourist bus later.'

'How much later?' Nat was hitching the grey to a nearby tree, cowboy style. The surrounding buildings included a guard post, and the café was part of the old rock-built

Custom House, further inside which was an expensive-looking restaurant.

Fahad shrugged. 'Tonight? Tomorrow?'

Suzie looked helplessly from one to the other. 'Does that mean there won't be one?'

'It means,' Nat said, 'that you're going to have a pretty long wait. How do you feel about spending the night here?'

'Do you think there might be any tourists who would give me a lift back to Amman?' Suzie asked, with no real hope in her voice.

'It's not impossible,' Nat replied vaguely. 'Fahad, do you think we can take a female as dirty as this one, with hair like a bird's nest, into that smart Jordanian version of an exclusive restaurant?'

Fahad grinned, his dark Arab face all glittering eyes and white teeth. 'Perhaps. If she doesn't sit on the furniture.'

Nat gave her a little push towards the entrance to the restaurant, which was also the foyer of the hotel. 'Go on. Go and get tidied up. Which do you prefer, Coke or lemonade?'

'Coke, please, but——'

'Go *on*.'

It was easier to give in than to get involved in further discussions at this stage. Not particularly decisive or adventurous by nature, Suzie found that the events of the past few hours had sapped any spirit of independence she had had.

There was a smartly dressed Arab in well-fitting shirt and light trousers in the entrance hall. He appeared to be a member of the staff and she half expected him to order her out, but he gave her a smile and gestured towards a door displaying the obvious symbol for a ladies' washroom.

Surveying herself in the mirror, Suzie was rather taken aback by her appearance. 'Bird's nest' in the circumstances had been a polite description. Her long, straight, dark brown hair had originally been wound into a coil and pinned on top of her head. As various parts of it had collapsed during the day, she had gone on pushing pins in haphazardly until the overall effect resembled a matted bundle of old wool, with wisps and trails sticking out round her face and neck. It was full of dust, and her face and arms were streaked with dirt.

Crying hadn't done much to enhance the general effect.

She fished out a comb she kept in the discreetly designed money-belt she was wearing, and studied her face in the mirror. Her eyes, normally a deep brilliant blue, were her most striking feature, but now their clear whites were suspiciously tinged with pink, and her dark eyelashes spiked from crying.

She surveyed the streaks of dirt on her skin critically, and then decided to wash before she attempted to do anything with the mess of hair. Then she brushed the superficial dust off her skirt, but the improvement was minimal; there seemed to be reddish dirt marks on the bodice as well. She took all the pins out of her hair and bent over to comb it, pulling out the worst of the tangles as she worked through the thick mass now hanging down in front of her. She could leave it loose but it was too hot, and she flicked her head back to gather it into a plait which she pinned up behind her head. Unsophisticated, but practical.

She emerged finally to find Fahad seated at table outside the café. There were three cans of Coke in front of him, their sides running with condensation. He reached for a glass as he saw her and poured the contents of a can into it.

'Drink this,' he smiled. 'You'll feel better.'

She was beginning to lose her nervousness of the hawk-nosed Arab and smiled back, the blue of her eyes suddenly sparkling. She saw Fahad's own eyes widen for a second in acknowledgement.

'You look very different! Now I shall have to protect from Nat.'

'Where is Nat?' She glanced round as she sat down opposite the Arab.

'He had gone to talk to some tourists. He is trying to find you a lift.'

'He's very kind,' she said appreciatively. There was a short pause, and then she asked, 'Have you been friends long?'

'I know him through our work. We met only a few days ago—I have business with his company.'

She watched him pouring out a second glass of Coke. 'What do you do?'

'My boss is one of the owners of the business that has

installed his computers. I am a lawyer.'

'You speak wonderful English.' She smiled, and then added quickly, 'I hope you don't think that's rather patronising.'

The white teeth flashed in another smile. 'Thank you for the compliment! But I ought to. I was at school in England for four years, and I went to law school in the States for a while.'

She watched idly a tourist approaching from the guard post. He was just over medium height, his light brown hair a little too long, and bleached superficially by the sun. His walk was powerfully athletic, and he was slim-hipped and broad-shouldered. She wondered if he was an American. He wore jeans and a shirt like——

'Nat!' she exclaimed, startled. He was closer now, and she could distinguish the features she had studied at such close range only half an hour earlier. What an idiot she was not to recognise him!

'Why the surprise?' he asked, stopping to check the horse standing patiently under the tree.

She looked confused. 'You seem so different without that Arab headgear.'

His eyes surveyed her coolly. 'You look so different without all that dirt.' He took the chair next to her and sat down, pouring himself the remaining Coke. 'We're not having much luck with the tourists at the moment. There seems to be a shortage. There's an American couple who have hired a car, but they're not going to Amman. Still, there are other solutions to the problem.'

Suzie sipped her drink thoughtfully. She could only think of one, unless some more tourists appeared. 'There is that other tourist bus.'

Fahad shrugged dismissively. 'That could be next week.'

'Can you afford to stay at the hotel here?' Nat asked.

She knew it was out of the question. There was no point even discussing it. 'I can only afford to stay where I am in Amman. I came with a friend originally, and we had planned on splitting everything two ways. Travelling on your own is much more expensive.'

'This friend of yours, where is he now?'

'She.' Suzie sighed. 'You don't really want to hear about it.

It's a long story.'

Nat grinned. 'Nonsense. Fahad and I have nothing better to do. And it give us an excuse to look at you.'

She wasn't quite sure how to take his last remark, but before she could reply Fahad asked, 'She's run off with a handsome Arab who told her he was a sheikh?'

'Not quite like that,' she replied, deliberately avoiding Nat's gaze. 'Katrina's hobby is millionaires.'

Nat choked suddenly. 'Always in the plural, or will just one do?'

Suzie had very strong views about Katrina's interest in money, but she wasn't prepared to discuss them, and now she regretted the way she had phrased her reply. After all, Katrina wasn't there to defend herself, and Suzie wasn't prepared to criticise her to strangers.

'Bob's her boyfriend,' she said defensively.

'An Arab sheikh and he calls himself Bob? Your friend is even more innocent than you, Suzie!'

Suzie caught an exchange of glance between the two men. It was obvious they were both deriving a certain amount of amusement from her. She decided to fight back.

'Bob's an American—you were the one who said he was a sheikh!'

But Nat wasn't going to be put off. 'So your friend Katrina has abandoned you in favour of an American millionaire?'

'Not exactly. There was a possibility that Bob might turn up, only neither of us really thought he would when we booked the holiday.' In fact, she reflected dismally, very little so far had gone according to the original plans. Day one of the long-discussed holiday, they had arrived. Day two, they had gone sightseeing in Amman and almost literally bumped into Bob, hotfoot in pursuit of Katrina. Day three, Katrina had left. Then Suzie was on her own, wondering how on earth she was going to get through the rest of the time alone, when everything was going to cost considerably more than she had budgeted for. The trip to Petra had been her one bid to see something of what had originally brought her to Jordan, before her money ran out.

'How well do you know Katrina?' It was Nat again.

'She's a sort of old school acquaintance—she's a few years older than me, and she was looking for a flatmate at about the time I went to London to work. We share the flat now.'

Fahad asked, 'What do you do in London?'

'I'm a secretary—well, a rather low-grade secretary. I do a lot of temping.'

'And is Katrina a temp, too?' Nat queried.

Suzie shrugged. 'No. She's much more high-powered. She works as a personal assistant at the Institute of Directors. But I don't suppose that'll continue now she's met Bob.'

She hadn't been able to keep the faint edge out of her voice as she made her final comment, and Nat caught it. 'Do I detect a note of disapproval there, or were you keen on Bob, too?'

'No, I wasn't!' she replied with a vehemence that surprised her. She was still a little upset with Katrina for having so blithely left her, but it was much more than that. Katrina's blatant pursuit of money, her constant harping on the topic of rich men, and her instant assessment of the men she met in terms of their bank balances, assets, investments and financial reputations repelled her. She had romantic ideas of her own, totally opposed to Katrina's mercenary notions, but they stemmed from a past she wasn't prepared to discuss. She was used to Katrina's teasing, but she didn't want her own beliefs ripped apart by strangers for their amusement.

She was deliberately evasive in answer to Nat's next question. 'Are you not in favour of marrying millionaires in any circumstances, or is it just that you object to your friend's predatory instincts?'

'Katrina and I get on very well mostly. It's just that we have different ideas when it comes to things like that.'

Nat tipped back in his chair, his long fingers touching the table-top. The appraising look he was giving her was disconcerting. She couldn't tell what he was thinking.

'So Katrina's going to marry a millionaire. What are your plans for the future?' he asked, after a pause.

That was easy. She didn't have to give him the answer he had been looking for. 'To get back to Amman,' she said with a grin.

One corner of his mouth curled into a smile, but the grey-green eyes continued to assess her.

'Then we're going to have to arranged it, aren't we?' He let the chair fall back suddenly into place. 'Drink up, Arab friend. We're about to do some more prospecting.'

A couple of minutes later, he and Fahad had left Suzie to finish her drink in solitude. 'Stay here till we get back,' he had instructed, 'and don't speak to any strange men—especially Fahad.'

She had smiled at him, looking him full in the eyes. There was something in his expression she couldn't now help responding to—a mixture of kindness and humour that encouraged her to trust him—and there was something genuinely reassuring about his manner. It was almost fraternal.

On reflection, she found herself wishing just a little that Nat could see her in a light somewhat different from that of an inept and inexperienced younger sister. She knew very well that after her experience in the rocks she would never have trusted him if he had shown any sexual interest in her, but she wasn't indifferent to his good looks.

It occurred to her that if she were Katrina she might be making the most of the situation. But no—Katrina would never be interested in Nat: she was too obsessed with money. By his own admission, Nat was a comparatively penniless computer engineer. She was sure that 'penniless' was an exaggeration; he must be paid something in addition to all the expenses or whatever it was you got on that sort of job, but he wasn't in Katrina's league. She would have thought he was handsome, maybe even a bit romantic if he'd rescued her from rape among the rocks, but not worth wasting any serious time on.'

She wondered how old he was—middle twenties, perhaps; not more than thirty. Maybe he had a sister her own age. It would be interesting to know if he had any family.

She thought suddenly of her own family: her half-sister, nine years old, temperamental and infuriatingly curious about every detail of Suzie's life; her stepmother, placid and friendly, totally involved in the life of the small Cambridgeshire village they had lived in since her father's divorce from her own mother; and her father, a quiet, dependable solicitor, undemonstrative of his affections but prepared to give his wife and daughters the moon if they asked for it.

The safe home environment they had created provided the solid background to Suzie's world, and their support gave her the courage to try a new life in London, knowing that she was not committed to it irrevocably, and that she could leave it to return to more familiar ground if she chose. They would be horrified if they could have an inkling of her present predicament, and angry with Katrina for leaving her.

What she had told Nat was true. She and Katrina had both attended the same local private school—a small and very unacademic establishment near Suzie's village. Katrina had been four years ahead of Suzie, but their parents had known each other. After Suzi had finished her secretarial course, it had been decided that she could move into Katrina's flat in London. Suzie had been scarcely eighteen at the time, and her stepmother had expressed doubts about the suitability of the twenty-two-year-old Katrina as a stable and reliable friend in the unknown world of the city. She had described her in old-fashioned terms as 'flighty', which meant the sort of girl to get herself heedlessly into all sorts of trouble—'trouble' being the two unspoken horrors of pregnancy and drugs.

Suzie quickly learned, however, that Katrina, despite her careless manner, was sensible and hard-headed when it came to her own life. She knew what she wanted and was determined to get it. She admired the way the older girl could size up a situation and make the most of what came her way; Suzie herself lacked the necessary drive and ambition to pursue clear goals, and was far too diffident to assert herself in the way Katrina did.

If Suzie's stepmother had known how she now spent most of her London evenings, she would have given up worrying about Katrina's influence. While the latter passed her time with an ever-changing string of young men, always tempted by someone apparently richer or more glamorous than the last, Suzie stayed in, watching television or sewing, both of which she enjoyed, and went home most weekends. There had been a time when she had gone out with Katrina's friends occasionally, until she had met Gerald.

Unlike Katrina, she had never been interested in young men

who spoke chiefly about their career prospects or tried to impress her with their cars or flats, and at first it had seemed that Gerald Sharman was not one of the ambitious and often ruthless young men she too fequently encountered in Katrina's company. She had been barely nineteen at the time, and her only previous romantic experience had been while she was still at school. It had never developed into anything more than a few experimental kisses at a film, or at the local disco, and had cooled off once Suzie had left to go to secretarial college. They had kept up a correspondence, and she still regarded the quiet, studious and unassuming Duncan as a friend.

Gerald had been a complete contrast. Inexperienced as she was, it was inevitable that she should lose her heart to the first good-looking man who showed a flattering interest in her. She was impressed by his confidence, and dazzled by his considerable charm. He was tall, fair-haired, well-dressed and—it seemed—refreshingly unconcerned about money and personal success. He took her out to discos, and to dinner, and to parties with friends, and had given a very good impression of being in love with her. In the romantic whirl of that summer her feet had scarcely touched the ground.

But all the while there was an inner cautiousness in Suzie, and a reluctance to commit herself fully, especially in a world of money and glamour, of which she already had a deep-seated mistrust. It had kept her from entering into a full-blown affair with him, and all along she had known that it wasn't marriage he was after. She had hoped for it, but she hadn't been blind to the fact that he had avoided all mention of it.

Later, when she could view the whole thing more dispassionately, she could see that Gerald's real interest had been in the rich and glamorous daughter of a very successful company chairman. He had even been seeing her while he had been dating Suzie.

She knew now, though it hurt to admit it, that he had found her an amusing contrast for a while, and perhaps a bit of a challenge, and she often wondered whether, if she had agreed to go to bed with him, she would really have been able to keep his interest longer. The end would have been inevitable. She had no money, and no powerful connections in the business world, and power and money were underneath what he really wanted. Love, it seemed, was for him just an amusing game.

The bitterness of her involvement with Gerald, and prolonged contract with Katrina, had caused her to adopt attitudes almost exaggeratedly opposed to those of her flatmate on the subject of marriage. Where Katrina blatantly sought wealth, Suzie would shun it, her own deeply buried mistrust of those who relied on money to create a superficial glamour now reinforced by her experience.

Her thoughts brought her back to Nat—self-confessed badly paid computer engineer. He looked so different without the Arab head-dress, she could scarcely believe he was the same person when she had seen him approaching the restaurant earlier. At first she had regarded him as a threat, then as a potential escape route from circumstances she could no longer cope with. Then he had become, very literally, a shoulder to cry on, and finally a sort of humorous Sir Galahad, as Fahad had called him. She was glad she hadn't met Fahad alone; his 'predatory Arab' good looks would have proved such a barrier between them; he would never have gained her trust the way Nat had done.

Perhaps she was being naïve, she told herself, and it was just because Nat was an Englishman with an educated English voice, and therefore sounded respectable, that she had such total confidence in him. A tactful and humorous way of dealing with things had also had gone a long way towards persuading her. But there had been more to it than that. Just once or twice the look in his eyes had hinted at a kind of quiet power; she wouldn't like to find herself crossing him.

Then she thought of the way he had laughed at her sillier reactions, and joked about her all too obvious suspicion of himself and Fahad, and her lips curved in a quiet smile— partly at herself for being so hysterically silly. She was beginning to wonder why on earth she had made such a fuss about the Arab in the rocks. After all, she had got away.

'That's a very enigmatic little smile, Suzie. You practising for the next Mona Lisa look-alike competition?'

She glanced up quickly from her unfinished drink to see Nat approaching the table. There was no sign of Fahad. 'What's the matter with the Coke?' he asked. 'Do you suspect my Arab friend of drugging it?'

Her smile widened a little. 'No. I was watching him closely all the time he was pouring it into the glass.'

Nat pulled out a chair and sat down, watching her. 'Ah, but they have ways of injecting things into the cans directly.' He leaned towards her and narrowed his eyes, lowering his voice conspiratorially. 'You can't be too careful.'

She was amused. Was this all part of his Big Brother Nat act again? Or just his sense of humour? She didn't mind—it was adults indulging in the kind of game she played to amuse her little sister. She leaned towards him, and said in a stage whisper, 'I think you ought to know. I switched glasses with you!'

He grinned at her. 'Drink the rest of the stuff, for heaven's sake. Waste not, want not. Especially at that price.'

Her eyes widened in mock amazement. 'Do they really pay you that badly?'

'I have Scottish ancestry.'

'So have I—and from one Scot to another, stop mangling that empty can—you might be able to get some money back on it!'

'OK, Flora McScrooge,' he said, amused. 'But now, here's something serious. About our little problem—want to hear the solution?' She nodded, and he continued, 'Fahad has someone to see here, and he's got to make sure the horses get back to his friend. Now, don't argue and don't interrupt. We were originally going to stay here until tomorrow, but frankly the delights of riding round the rocks of Petra have palled a little after today's adventure. My chances of rescuing another beautiful maiden in distress are pretty slim. Distress, yes; maiden, doubtful—I hope I'm not embarrassing you—but beautiful, no. It'd be some over-endowed American matron who had lost her contact lenses in one of the tombs.'

'A real Sir Galahad wouldn't make such distinctions!' Suzie said, and then spoilt the mock reproof by laughing.

Nat grinned. 'Ssh! I told you not to interrupt. I'm driving you back to Amman tonight. We'll have to make a start soon or we won't be back until very late. You're staying in a hotel?'

'Yes, but——'

'No *buts*. And you remember where it is?'

'Yes. But——'

He gave an exaggerated sigh. 'You're not very obedient, are you?' I'm going to deliver you back to your own doorstep, and after that it's up to you to fight off the hotel porters, doormen, receptionists and managers. OK?'

'But what about Fahad?'

'He's fine. He's coming back with a friend tomorrow. He has innumerable friends, all of whom seem to owe him favours.' He got up from the table. 'Do you think you'll be ready to leave in the next five minutes? I'm just going to get the keys of the jeep from Fahad.'

Suzie looked at him consideringly for a few moments. Then, 'Speaking of favours—what favour does he owe you?' she asked, with a mischievous sparkle in her eye.

For a second he looked at her with an expression she couldn't interpret, and then he said, 'You've got a more suspicious mind than I thought. But as a serious answer to your question, he doesn't. He's just a very nice man.'

Yes, she thought, he probably was—but his willingness to co-operate could also have had a lot to do with Nat's quiet air of authority. It wasn't difficult to see who was the chief, and who the Indian—or should it have been sheikh and tribesman?

The drive back to Amman was a long one, and it was dark long before they reached the city. At first she had looked about her with interest; they were still in the rock desert regions that were strange to her, and the barrenness of the landscape fascinated her. Once or twice in the distance they saw bedouin herding their goats, and once a herd of camels, tawny and angular, almost indistinguishable from the desert which surrounded them.

Nat was informative about the area, and seemed to have spent some time exploring it.

'I thought you said you came here to work on computers,' Suzie commented.

He shrugged dismissively. 'I've been here before.'

When she asked him for details of his job, he lectured her with a certain amount of amusement on the basic principles of a working computer. She thought she understood it at the time, but she found later that she had retained very little of it, the only image remaining in her mind that of Nat's hands on the steering wheel of the jeep, and of his profile beside her. His hair grew a little too long over the collar of the blue shirt he wore, and she could see a hint of stubble beginning to grow on his chin, and the hollows in his face under the high cheekbones. She had noted where the slightly winged eyebrows had dipped towards his nose in a frown of concentration as an oncoming driver swung out into his path to overtake, and the way he bit his lip once when a lorry narrowly avoided another vehicle in head-on collision some way ahead of them. She expected him to swear as her father would have done, but he merely grinned at her, his eyes amused, and looked back to the road.

He woke her when they arrived in Amman. There was still plenty of traffic, but the hectic, undisciplined circus track of the daytime had died down, and he didn't need her to guide him to the district in which the hotel was was situated.

He parked in front of the hotel, and got out to open the door for her. She climbed out reluctantly, and he guided her into the foyer, his hand just touching the small of her back. There was a hint of intimacy in the contact which made her realise suddenly how relaxed she had grown in his company. She thought with a stab of dismay that it was probably the first and last time they would ever meet. She couldn't really ask to see him again, and it seemed a bit obvious now to ask the name of the computer company he worked for.

He spoke to the man at the desk in Arabic, and handed her the key of her room.

'Sleep well,' was all he said, and turned to go.

She turned his arm, struggling to find the right words to thank him. Her eyes were enormous with fatigue, and her words came out with awkward formality.

'Nat—I don't know how to thank you . . . You've been so kind. Thank you so much for everything you've done . . .'

He put a finger briefly against her lips. 'Any time, honey. And now, go to bed.'

He pinched her cheek before striding out through the glass door of the hotel. She found herself staring at the reflection of the foyer lights in them.

He had vanished. There was no reason they should ever meet again.

CHAPTER THREE

ALL Suzie wanted to do was to shut herself up for the remaining six days until her flight. She wouldn't go outside the hotel door to shop, walk or even eat. She wouldn't talk to the hotel staff. She had enough money to pay her hotel bill and her fare back to the airport, and if she lived on hotel breakfasts between now and Saturday she would survive the experience. Once she was home, never, *never* would she go abroad again. Anywhere.

The events of the previous day had persuaded her that not only was Jordan a country fraught with dangers for the unwary female tourist, but that she, Suzie McClaren, was of all people least fit to deal with them.

That effectively meant that she was confined to her hotel bedroom for the next one hundred and forty-four hours, at a rough estimate. She didn't quite know how she was going to get through the twenty-four hours of every day, and it was impossible to sleep away all of them. When Katrina had left her, she had been determined to see Petra—originally the whole point of their holiday—and had thought that an organised excursion would be the only feasible way of getting there, despite expense. She had then planned to spend the rest of the time exploring the capital on foot and eating cheap snacks to make up for the extravagance. But all that had been before her encounter with the Arab.

Her hotel bedroom was very small. It did have a private shower, but that was about its only advantage. The one she had shared with Katrina had been better, but she hadn't been able to afford to keep it on alone. Here, there was very little room between the dressing-table and the end of the bed, and between the bed, which was against one wall, and the other wall.

Now, sitting in bed with her knees drawn up to her chin

under the sheet, she could see herself reflected in the mirror that hung above the dressing-table in the bright, hot sunlight of late morning. She had woken up too late for breakfast, worn out by a very late night and the strain of the day before. It meant, of course, that she wasn't going to eat for the next twenty-four hours, but she told herself to think of it as slimming. She could drink water to take the edge off her hunger.

It was ten minutes before she could summon up the resolution to get out of bed, but once under the shower she was revived by the cool water, and stood for some time letting it ruin down her hair and back.

Finally she turned off the taps and groped for her towel, only to discover she had left it in the bedroom. Her footprints left wet patches across the tiled floor, and as there was only one towel she didn't know whether to dry her body or her hair with it first—the long dark strands were dripping down her back to make more pools on the floor. Still, it didn't really matter; she had all day—and all night.

She put on her underwear, and then a loose shirt. There was no point getting dressed, but she didn't want to wander round with nothing on in case one of the hotel staff came in to clean the room. She was sitting on the end of the bed combing her hair when there was a tap at the door. There was no telephone in the room, and she wondered nervously if it was the management coming to investigate her non-appearance. Then she told herself they would hardly notice, or care even if they did. The room was hers to occupy as long as she paid the bill.

The tap was repeated. 'Mees McClaren?' The voice, male, could be one of the hotel staff.

'Yes?' she answered hesitantly.

'Mees McClaren, there is a visitor for you downstairs.'

Suzie wondered if it was some ploy to get her to open the door—maybe the man wasn't one of the staff, and even if he was it was no guarantee he would behave himself. Ater yesterday, anything could happen. 'I'm not expecting anyone. I don't have any visitors.' Her voice didn't sound as firm as she would like.

'He says it is important! He is an Englishman.'

If the last statement was intended to make her feel more secure, it had the opposite effect. No Englishman she knew could be here in Amman. It must be a trick.

'I don't want to see anyone just now,' she said in what she hoped was a final and dismissive tone. 'I'm not dressed yet.' That was probably a mistake, but at least whoever it was couldn't expect her to open the door.

'But Mees McClaren——'

'I don't want to see him. Tell him to go away!' More positive that time.

The pleas were not repeated, and Suzie was left, comb in hand, breathing rather fast and wondering suddenly if it couldn't have been Nat. But Nat had said nothing about seeing her again, and he didn't seem sure whether he would still be in Amman or not.

A couple of minutes later there was another knock, more peremptory and purposeful this time, and unmistakably Nat's voice, saying, 'Come on, Suzie. Put your clothes on and open the door.'

'Just a minute——' It was no use keeping him out. She saw him as the sort of person who would go to the hotel manager for a duplicate key—and get it. She dragged her jeans off the dressing-table chair and hauled them on. There was no time to find anything else. Then she opened the door.

One shoulder against the doorframe, arms crossed, he was casually propped against the doorpost waiting for her. She had remembered the sun-blond hair and the tan, but she had forgotten the direct glance of those grey-green eyes. They surveyed the room instantly, and then met hers with cool amusement. Suzie was uncomfortably conscious of the unmade bed and strewn clothes behind her. There were still wet footprints and pools on the floor.

'Oversleep?' he asked politely.

Suzie blushed. 'Something like that.'

'Can I come in?'

She hesitated. 'Well, yes. I suppose so.'

'You mean I'm not doing your reputation any good with the hotel management, and you'll have them all queueing up tonight if word gets round?'

It was a sensitive subject, and Suzie wasn't ready to be teased.

'Don't say that,' she replied quickly. 'You might think it's funny, but I don't.'

'That's what I've come to talk, to you about.' He glanced at the bed. 'May I?' Without waiting for a reply, he pushed aside a tumbled heap of clothes and blankets, and sat down gingerly, taking her hand to pull her down beside him as he did so. He was watching the expression on her face as she resisted.

'Now don't look nervous again. Sit on the floor, if you like—though there's not much of it. Even the cockroaches probably go in single file.'

She couldn't repress an involuntary shudder, but she didn't say anything. He let go of her hand.

'It's not the world's best hotel, is it?'

'It's all right,' she said defensively.

'How much money have you got?' he asked abruptly.

She tried to sound offhand. 'Enough to pay the hotel bill when I leave.'

'Is that all?'

'No. I can get a taxi to the airport—or a bus.'

'And what about sightseeing?'

He wasn't going to be put off, and she avoided his eyes. 'I'm not keen on sightseeing any more.'

'Oh?'

This time she caught the grey-green eyes directly. 'I did listen to what you said, you know . . . about English females wandering round on their own half-dressed.'

'And what's your solution—stay in your hotel room until your flight, or buy a suit of armour in the *souk*?'

Suzie's blush would have told him his first guess had been right, even if he hadn't known—which he obviously had. He was far too good at verbal fencing for her, and she gave away something every time she opened her mouth. She didn't know how to reply; he had a way of cutting the ground from under her feet.

'Stop standing there like a schoolgirl being interrogated by the headmistress. You remind me of my niece—except that she's now got no respect for my authority at all, if she ever had any. Apparently I do a very bad impersonation of the Head.' He had a very disarming grin. He reached for her hand again. 'Sit down?'

Without a word, she sat beside him on the bed, leaving a respectable distance between them. He didn't move, and he didn't let go of her hand. His clasp was firm and warm. There was nothing threatening about it, but Suzie was acutely conscious of his touch.

'That's better.' He was still watching her. 'How long will it take you to pack your things?'

'But——' She looked at him in astonishment. His lips twitched into a smile at her reaction, but the expression in his eyes was serious.

'You have two choices,' he said firmly, before she could add anything else. 'Either you spend your time here doing nothing for a week and having a nervous fit every time someone knocks at the door, or you spend your week in Jordan keeping company with an idle and lonely old computer engineer. He'll otherwise have to while away the hours alone in a large flat a friend has lent him. Will you come? It doesn't seem to me that there should be much of a difficulty over the decision.'

'But Nat, I couldn't!'

'Why not? One poverty-stricken tourist isn't going to have much fun alone, but two might think of something to do.' Then he added quickly, 'Before you leap to any conclusions about my having any evil designs on you, I want to make it clear that I haven't got any designs at all of any kind—except that I thought we might explore a bit of the desert. You seemed to like the look of it yesterday. Every seen inside a bedouin tent?'

She shook her head, still doubtful. She could, if she let herself, feel very excited at the prospect of what he was offering her, but it seemed such a risky decision to take.

'A friend of mine has one,' he went on. 'We might get invited to tea.'

She was surprised into laughter. Somehow the idea of an obscure bedouin offering tea and sandwiches at four o'clock seemed absurd.

'I mean it!' he protested. 'They put cardamom in it and brew it over an old iron ring on the ground. If you don't die of something nasty from the unwashed glasses, you'll enjoy it. The particular tent I was thinking of is near an old fort used by Lawrence of Arabia. It's in a spectacular valley.'

There was a sudden silence between them. Nat had let go of her hand, and she sat on the edge of the bed staring at the floor. The offer was a very tempting one, but never in her wildest dreams had she imagined herself going off with a complete stranger to stay with him in a flat she hadn't even seen. At least the hotel was safe. Nothing could happen to her there, and she would be stupid to take such an unnecessary risk. On the other hand, the prospect of six days shut up in her room with nothing to do but count the passing minutes like sheep was awful. Almost anything would be better than that.

And then there was Nat. What exactly could happen to her if she decided to trust him? Rape? Murder? Somehow neither of those seemed very likely, and she was far from being an ideal kidnap victim! Besides, she liked Nat, and she was beginning to find him very attractive. If she really could trust him, then there was no difficulty about the decision—it was a straight choice between six very miserable days alone, and six days doing some of the things she would like to be doing but had dismissed as impossible.

Abruptly, Nat got up from the bed. 'Before my prolonged visit here confirms their very worst suspicions of English girls in the minds of the management, I'm going to make your decisions for you. I know what you're thinking and I know what you think you should say.' He stood looking down at her while she stared at the floor. 'Give me your money, and I'll pay the bill while you pack. I'll wait for you down in the foyer, but don't take too long, or I might be tempted to abscond with the loot.'

'I don't——'

'If you're going to trust me, Suzie, there can't be any half measures. It's all or nothing.' He took her chin between finger and thumb, and firmly tilted her face so that she was forced to meet his eyes. 'If my appalling niece got herself into this situation, I'd do like to think that some chivalrous English gentleman like kind old Uncle Nat would get her out of it. But Ali's not quite so wet behind the ears as you appear to be—and that's not a joke about washing your hair. You can choose your room in the flat, and you can lock yourself into it all day if you want to. But I'd much rather you came exploring with me. I may not have any money but I've got a lot of friends, and Fahad has extended the loan of the jeep—I spoke to him on the phone this morning. So what about those bedouins?'

He was treating her like some half-grown teenager again, but she supposed in a way she had asked for it. She couldn't have made a very positive impression so far, and if it meant she could trust him, and accept his invitation—even if he was going to treat her as his surrogate niece—so much the better. Then, for the first time in her life, Suzie took a calculated risk. Her blood almost ran cold at the thought of what might happen if she was wrong about Nat, but without giving herself time to change her mind she reached for her bag and extracted her wallet. She looked up at him before she put it into his hands. 'If you say one word about how stupid I'm being letting you take this, I'll never speak to you again!'

The winged eyebrows shot up, and Nat gave his customary disarming grin. 'With all these riches, do you think I'll be around to listen?' He flicked her on the cheek with one finger. 'How long are you going to take with all this mess? I'm not waiting more than half an hour.'

She shrugged doubtfully. 'The packing won't take long, but my hair won't be dry.'

His eyes rested for a moment on the towel that swathed her head.

'I shouldn't think wet hair is going to make one jot of difference to the reputation you have certainly established for yourself by now with the reception.'

'You mean the reputation *you* have established for me!' she countered with an unexpected flash of spirit. Nat might be taking over her life, but she wasn't going to let him think she was utterly meek and mild.

His eyes told her that he acknowledged her reply, but he only said, 'Half an hour—no more!' And he was already shutting the door behind him.

Suzie worked in a litter of garments, bottles and plastic bags for the best part of fifteen minutes, and then decided to take time off to do something with her hair. Despite the initial chaos, which was uncharacteristic of her, she had managed to pack quite neatly, and had no difficulty in zipping up her large bag once she had thrown away most of the clutter of tourist handouts she had collected during her one day in Katrina's company.

Her hair was uncompromisingly damp, and she hadn't brought a hair dryer with her; the easy solution was to make a single plait and pin it up the back of her head. It didn't take her long, and she made the best use of the remaining time applying light make-up to her eyes and lips. The dark mascara and touch of shadow enhanced the already deep blue of her eyes and made them look even larger. She hoped the lipstick would add a hint of sophistication—without it she did look very young.

She surveyed herself critically in the mirror. She wasn't sure she wanted Nat seeing her as his niece's alter ego. He was treating her as someone much younger than she really was, and although it had been initially reassuring, she was beginning to wish he would see her less as an inexperienced teenager to be protected from her own inadequacy, and more as a companion.

She was satisfied with her appearance. Her jeans, conveying the casual student image, were at least well pressed and very well fitting. They showed off her long legs and neat hips, and the loose striped shirt she had put on earlier looked quite smart. She added what jewellery she possessed—a slim good chain round her neck and a couple of heavy Arab bangles that she had bought in the bazaar on her first day with Katrina. Her hair suited her up, and drew attention to the delicacy of her features and long slim neck, but Suzie was without vanity. Not particularly objective about her appearance, she erred very much on the side of underestimation.

There was a knock at the door, and the voice, once again, of the hotel menial. He sounded slighly aggrieved.

'Mees McClaren? The English gentleman has say I fetch your cases. OK? He *tell* me to!' he added plaintively.

Suzie opened the door, doing her best to appear cool and serious. 'Thank you. It's just one bag.'

He came into the room with evident curiosity, and glanced instantly at the rumpled bed; he didn't have the nerve to smirk at her and Suzie was determined not to give an inch.

She met his eyes coldly. 'That will be all, thank you. I'll be down in a minute.' She waited until he had left the room before she gave a sigh of relief, and then had a half-guilty glance in the mirror to see if she was blushing. She was.

She waited until the colour had slowly faded from her cheeks before she gave the room a final check. It would be too embarrassing to ask Nat to come back and fetch something—a toothbrush, or a shoe left under the bed.

When she stepped out of the lift, Nat was waiting for her, her bag slung casually over one shoulder. He raised his eyebrows briefly at the sight of her, and there was a suspicious twitch in the corner of his mouth. 'Looking like that, you've just signed and sealed your testimonial from this establishment. You're supposed to be my young and innocent niece, not my concubine.'

'Did you tell them that?'

'What—that you're *not* my concubine? Would they have believed me? You convey these things by subtle impressions, transmitted with delicacy and tact—sorry, have I lost you there?

His relaxed, bantering tone gave Suzie confidence. She grinned at him. 'Sometimes you make me want to hit you.'

'That sounds very like Ali—much more reassuring. Come on.' He put a casual hand on the back of her neck and steered her towards the entrance.

'Have you parted with all my hard-earned money?' she asked, merely to distract herself from the easy familiarity of his touch.

'Certainly not. I have a certain financial acumen, though you may doubt it. I even managed to get them to reduce the price of the room.'

As Nat drove fast and skilfully through the tangle of traffic, Suzie reflected on her inadequacies. It would never have occurred to her to haggle over the price of the room. Going off with Nat might prove to be the most stupid thing she had done in her life—on the other hand, if he proved to be as nice as he seemed, it could be the biggest stroke of luck. She tried to study Nat in careful sideways glances, until she caught his eyes on her once, and saw the amused look in them. He had known perfectly well what she was doing. There was no point in any pretences—she gave a grin, and turned her attention to their surroundings.

Most of the roads were wide and newly constructed, with impressive avenues and roundabout systems, but Nat seemed to know his way though the back streets that finally took them into a respectable residential area, with tree-lined roads, evidently catering for the professionals and businessmen who thought little of tourist-haunted, 'picturesque' Arab quarters. Many of the flats had balconies, some of which trailed an exotic collection of plant life.

The flat, which turned out to have been lent by a friend of Fahad's, was on the top floor of an expensive block of apartments, and had a roof garden. 'He says we've got to look after the plants,' Nat told her, as he showed her through the rooms. It was a relief to see that, far from lying about the situation, he had been understating the size of the flat—there were three large bedrooms to choose from, in addition to the master bedroom which Nat was already using. He left her to make her own choice while he made a couple of phone calls in the sitting-room—a large, light room with enormous windows and a white marble floor scattered with rich rugs. The furnishings were in the traditional browns, creams and blacks so favoured by Arabs, and the lamps, vases and ornaments looked intimidatingly expensive.

Suzie chose the smallest of the three bedrooms offered to her. Even so, it was four times the size of the one she had occupied in the hotel. It had the advantage of being next to the bathroom, which she suspected, with some relief, she wasn't expected to share with Nat. There were none of his things in it, which seemed to indicate that he had his own.

The windows of her room were curtained in the finest white open-weave linen, that allowed the light to enter and wouldn't have excluded the air if she had wanted to open the window. However, with such efficient air-conditioning she would have been opening the windows to warm the room up, not cool it down. The floor was once again smooth marble, lined with streaks of beige and grey, and the basic furnishing colours of pale lemon, cream and gold again created an impression of taste and wealth. She found herself wondering what Fahad's friend did for a living. Nat was certainly very fortunate to have such contacts through his work.

She hung up her clothes in the wall-to-wall wardrobe. It amused her to see how incongruous they looked hanging in the vast empty spaces. She had two respectable dresses and a couple of shirts and skirts, but the offending sundress lay igominiously at the bottom of her bag. She wasn't even going to bother to unpack it.

Once she had tidied away her things, she wasn't quite sure what to do. She was reluctant to disturb Nat—not wanting him to think her a nuisance—and lay down on the edge of her bed, idly looking at the rug spread out beside it. The dyes, mainly reds and dark blues, were very slightly varied, and the geometric patterns were not always even. Needlework and home economics were the only things she'd ever been any good at at school, and it interested her to know how such a rug had been made.

'Suzie?'

'I'm in here!'

Nat was in the doorway in an instant, and she sat up quickly. 'What are you doing?'

'I was just looking at the patterns on the rug. I've finished unpacking.'

'Fine.' He walked round the edge of the bed and stood looking down at the rug. 'That's from Baluchistan. In fact, it's quite a nice one.'

Puzzled, she asked, 'What do you mean—you like it?'

He squatted down on his heels and ran a bony, long-fingered hand over the surface. 'I mean it's a good one—the sort of thing a lot of people would like to have.'

'How do you know where it comes from?'

'It's the designs they use and the colours of the dyes.' He pointed out a couple of geometric shapes. 'They're all hand-made on big looms, and the colours they use are extracted from vegetables. Are you interested in this sort of thing?'

'You mean rugs?' She shook her head. 'I don't really know. It's the first time I've really seen anything like this. How did you learn about them?'

'I happened to acquire a couple myself, and that gave me an interest.'

'Are they expensive?'

He rubbed a finger across the bridge of his nose, and then looked at her speculatively. 'It depends on what you call expensive,' he said. 'To the likes of penniless computer engineers and typists, yes, they are. Why—were you thinking of flogging it if we run out of money?'

She looked indignant. 'No! Of course not! Would you?'

He sighed, and a blissful expression stole across his face. 'Suzie, you're so wonderfully teasable.'

Half annoyed, half amused, she gave a reluctant grin but wouldn't meet his eye. He had every excuse for treating her like his niece.

'You're lovely when you blush like that. Has anyone ever told you?'

Even more embarrassed, she looked at him in confusion, feeling herself turning a deeper crimson with every second.

There was a pause. And then, somewhere in the midst of her acute self-consciousness, she became aware of how close he was. She was alone with him in this vast flat, and he was in her bedroom, inches from the bed on which she was half sprawled, and he was suddenly looking at her in a way she couldn't interpret. But it didn't look like teasing any longer.

In that instant, something happened to Suzie. For no reason she could identify, she could never again look at the man in front of her in quite the same way. Before that inexplicable moment, she had been seeing an amused, and amusing, stranger, who was possibly quite kind, probably in search of some entertainment one way or another—she didn't want to think in any great detail about 'another'—and certainly very unpredictable. And afterwards . . . well, she wasn't quite sure what she saw, but she found herself studying the way his hair, a light brown partly bleached by the sun, had a tendency to flop over his forehead. He had the faint lines of creases between his brows, and fine lines each side of his mouth where his face creased into a smile, although he wasn't smiling now.

He was probably the most good-looking man she had ever met. She wondered, stupidly, why she hadn't seen it before; the fright she'd had at Petra, and the fear and shock she'd suffered afterwards were her only excuse. She must have been blind! He was every girl's dream of a knight in armour—well, almost. He had been wrapped up in that awful Arab head-dress the first time she had seen him. And it was difficult to see anyone with such a sense of humour who insisted on treating you as a delinquent teenager in any very convincingly romantic light.

But unless she was going to spend the rest of her time with him agonising over whether or not he was what he seemed, she'd better accept the fact that she'd been extraordinarily luckly, and that Katrina, far from abandoning her to an unkind fate, had done her a favour.

Nat was looking across at her, his grey eyes equally thoughtful. Then suddenly he broke the spell that seemed to have been holding them both and, getting up from the floor, bent towards her. For one second she thought he was going to kiss her, but he only pinched her cheek and turned towards the door.

He missed the renewed flood of colour in her face. If he had known what she had imagined just then, what would he have thought of her? After all the fuss she had made over the Arab, and all the unnecessary suspicions she had had of him and Fahad—and of him especially!

There had been a tiny prick of disappointment as well as a considerable feeling of relief in that moment when his fingers had touched her cheek. She had half wanted him to do something very different, but the relief had been because she knew she would have been filled with panic if he had. She knew she wouldn't have been able to cope with it—it would have seemed like a threat.

Nat was actually speaking, she realised, but his words were prosaic enough to restore some of her former composure.

'You like hamburgers?'

She nodded dumbly, and then realised he was already out of the room. She got off the bed and followed him, examining herself in the mirror as she went. The flush was already fading, but her eyes seemed unnaturally bright.

'Yes. Why?'

'Because between us I think we can just about afford to eat lunch from the local American hamburger bar, which also does good take-aways. Can you cash the rest of your traveller's cheques tomorrow?'

She looked puzzled. 'Yes. Why?'

'Because, my dear child, we may have a palace to live in and a vehicle to drive, but we do need to eat—and so does the jeep.'

She followed him into the kitchen.

'Look.' He fished into the pocket of his jeans, and then into the pockets of his leather jacket, which was draped across the back of a chair. He held up a fistful of notes and coins, and then dropped them on to the table. 'This is my contribution to our enterprise—probably a little less than yours—and this . . .' he reached again into the inside pocket of the jacket to draw out her wallet ' . . . is yours.'

Cashing all the traveller's cheques suddenly seemed like a terrible risk. What if Nat *wasn't* honest? 'But if I give you all of it,' she protested uncertainly, 'how am I going to pay for a taxi to the airport?'

He tossed the wallet on to the table with a sigh; this time he didn't sound amused. 'Suzie, I promise you you'll catch your plane.' Then, after a slight hesitation, he went on, 'I'm not sure if I could guess what was going through that nervous little mind of yours a couple of minutes ago in the bedroom, but whatever it was, you've got to decide to trust me. If you can't people, life isn't worth living, believe me. I see enough skulduggery and backstabbing in the business world to last anyone a lifetime.' His expression hardened for a moment, and suddenly she felt intimidated by him. 'I know I've been warning you against predatory Arabs, but if you can't tell the difference between lust-crazed rapists and ordinary, decent engineers, then there's no hope for you.

'Now, are you going to trust me, yes or no? Because if you're not, then neither of us is going to be in for a very pleasant week, and you might as well go back to the hotel.'

Her reply, when she could get it out, wasn't much more than a whisper. 'Yes.'

'Look at me and say that.'

She forced herself to raise her eyes to meet his, and tried to sound more positive, but it wasn't a very convincing attempt, despite the fact she meant it. 'Yes.'

'Good girl.' He drew the tip of his forefinger down her nose, and turned her by the shoulders abruptly towards the door.

'First we're going to find those take-away hamburgers, and after that I think we'll plan a little trip into the desert.'

CHAPTER FOUR

THEY ate their hamburgers in the street, trying to catch the cucumber relish as it oozed through the gaps between the buns. Suzie, though initially hungry, couldn't finish hers. Nat ate it.

'Do you want to go back for some chips?' she asked him. 'You still look food-minded.'

He glanced speculatively at the sky, and then at her. 'Nope,' he said at last. 'There's no R in the month.'

Suzie, trying to following his reasoning, frowned in concentration until he grinned.

'Give up,' he said. 'There's little logic to a gnat's brain.'

More accustomed to his teasing now, she grinned back. 'At least I understand the puns! My sister Judy's keen on them—she's nine and impossibly lively. She's got some terrible jokes about whales.'

'Most people have,' he said dampeningly. 'Shall I tell you one on the way to the museum?'

'Are we going to the museum?'

He took her by the shoulders and swung her round to face in the opposite direction, towards the flat they had left an hour before. 'First we'll go and have a look at what the Arab scene is supposed to be, and then we'll go and sample the real thing. There's an ethnic museum near the old theatre. Have you seen that yet?'

They were walking back towards the flat. Nat was evidently in no hurry. He seemed to take everything at a casual pace, and Suzie was very content to fall in with whatever plans he might have. She was now convinced that she was very bad at making decisions on her own.

'The theatre? Yes, Katrina and I went to have a look at it the second day we were here. It's Roman, isn't it?'

He nodded. 'Mm. I'm surprised your friend Katrina is

interested in culture—or did she identify it as a likely stamping ground for tourist millionaires?'

Suzie felt obliged to defend her absent friend. 'She was very keen to come to Jordan. She'd read about Petra, and she really wanted to see it. She was the one who made me want to come on this trip.'

'And how long exactly did she devote to the cultural aspects?'

'What do you mean?'

'Let's put it another way. How long is your holiday supposed to be?'

'Ten days.'

'Poor Suzie!' He slung an arm casually round her shoulders, and gave her ear a pinch. 'Do you think she's going to get to Petra?'

'I don't know. Bob was going to take her to Aqaba, and then they thought they might go into Israel.'

'Israel's a bit out of our range, I'm afraid—they calculate the hotel prices by the hour there when inflation is high. But we could go to Aqaba.'

She turned to him, her eyes shining. 'Wasn't that where Lawrence of Arabia went?'

He laughed. 'Yes, but there's not much "Lawrence of Arabia" about it now, I'm afraid. Too many oil tankers. But we could go swimming and look for coral and exciting fish. We could even go out in a glass-bottomed boat. Have you ever done that?'

She shook her head. 'I can't believe all this! It's not really happening to me—Suzie—who gets up for work at seven every day and sits down looking at typewriter keys until it's time to go home again. The furthest I've ever been without my family was Paris, and the only exotic fish I've seen were in the London Zoo. But it sounds very expensive. Are you sure we can afford it?'

Nat's easy pace slowed to a halt, and he turned her to face him, his hands resting lightly on her shoulders. The grey-green eyes had a smile in them. 'Do you know, that's the first time you've said "we"? Could this mean you're no longer thinking of me as a potential thief and rapist? Or am I jumping to absurd conclusions?'

'Nat!' she protested. 'You know I never thought of you like
that!' Her blush gave her away. Nat was genuinely amused,
but at least he wasn't offended, Suzie thought with relief. It
wasn't a very flattering image.

'You know very well that you did!' he accused. 'You had me
identified as a potential rapist from the first moment you set
eyes on me, and poor old Fahad as infinitely worse. It was only
because I spoke better English than he did that you
condescended to sit on my horse—and don't try to deny it.'

'All right—I won't. But I think I had some excuse—you
should have seen yourself in that bandit's headgear.'

He grinned. 'So you're advising me not to audition for the lead
in the next "Lawrence" remake? But, in answer to your question,
I don't think money is going to pose too much of a problem.
These things can usually be arranged somehow. It might be a
good idea to make a few telephone calls to Fahad. He's bound to
have a friend of a cousin of a brother—or similar.'

When they got back to the flat, Suzie watered the plants on
Nat's instructions while he made the promised telephone calls,
and then they took the jeep into the centre of Amman to the
museum. It proved small but full of interest for Suzie, and she
emerged from the exhibitions in a dream, impressed by Nat's
informative commentaries as much as by what she had seen.

'How did you learn all that?' she asked, with obvious
admiration. 'You're better than a guide-book! And when did
you learn Arabic?'

'Oh, I just picked it up.' The expression on his face was one
of carefully contrived modesty, and made her laugh.

'I might have guessed you wouldn't give me a sensible
answer—as if anyone could "pick up" a language like that! But
honestly, Nat, all this is so romantic—it's just like something
out of the Arabian Nights! I can't believe it's real, and I'm
here, seeing it.'

Nat looked down at her, an unreadable expression on his
face, and for a second he didn't say anything. When he spoke,
he sounded unexpectedly serious. 'I hope the reality won't
disappoint you. Don't expect too much.'

'I won't—I don't,' she promised. 'But when you've scarcely

been out of England before, *everything's* wonderful.'

'Even nasty Arabs in the rocks at Petra?'

Her smile vanished. 'Well, maybe not that. I meant being here——' She was going to add 'with you' but something stopped her. She broke off lamely instead, and turned away in the direction of the jeep.

'Suzi?'

She looked round. He hadn't moved.

'I'm sorry. I didn't think. I shouldn't have reminded you of that.' He hesitated an instant, and then appeared to come to a quick decision. 'Come and see the bazaar. That'll be a kill or cure remedy.'

'What do you mean?'

Unexpectedly, he took her hand. 'I mean you'll be groped, pinched, molested, propositioned and all but assaulted within the first few minutes. And if I'm offered a good enough price I'll sell you. But that apart, having a moderately tall tourist male with you should work to your advantage. It should help to give back some of that confidence you lost in the Petra episode. I don't like to see your eyes look scared. You've got the most beautiful smile and I want to see it there all the time. The bazaar's a very lively place—you might even enjoy it.'

Nat's quick assessment of the *souk* proved fairly accurate, and once Suzie had got used to doging potential gropers and pinchers, and treading hard on sandalled feet of those who weren't quick enough to get away after achieving a brief triumph, she began to find herself very entertained. She stayed close to Nat's side as they pushed between the crowded and colourful stalls. There were few women, she noticed, and those were veiled in black and avoided direct glances from anyone. She herself drew the eyes of every man she passed, and if she hadn't had Nat with her she would have felt threatened. There was no mistaking the looks she was being given.

She bargained for a silver bracelet with Nat's help, and he himself was stopped twice and addressed in Arabic. A short conversation followed each time. After the second incident, he laughed and put an arm around Suzie, pulling her against him.

'Know what that was about?' he asked, looking down at her with a grin. She shook her head. 'It wasn't a bad offer—but I don't think I'll sell you yet! Had enough of this?'

'Just let's go on a little further, please. We've just got to the spice sellers.'

'And this is the girl who was scared to set foot outside her hotel!' he teased.

'Ow!'

'What's the matter?'

She pulled an expressive face. 'I've just had my bottom pinched again.'

He was grinning. 'How do you know it wasn't me?'

'Nat!' She stared at him in horror. 'It wasn't, was it?'

'Why all the outrage? You were pretty blasé about it a minute ago.'

'Yes, but that's because I thought it was an Arab.'

Nat began to laugh, and and it was some time before he could trust himself to speak. He had infectious laugh, and Suzie noticed several Arabs looking at them.

'So it's all right for any old Arab to pinch your bottom, but it isn't all right for me, is that it?'

Suzie redded. 'You know that isn't what I mean. Nat, we're attracting attention.'

He was still chucking. 'That's nothing unusual. What *did* you mean—that it is all right for me, but not in an Arab market? Where would you prefer exactly? Back at the flat?'

She couldn't meet his eyes. A personal element had suddenly entered the conversation, and she wasn't prepared to cope with it.

'It's just that I didn't expect it to be you, that's all. It wasn't, was it?'

He still had his arm round her, and without warning she found herself being held close. 'No.' He smiled. 'But this is.'

Before she could protest he slid one hand quickly up her thigh and gave her an unmistakable pinch, and then, as she gave a little gasp of surprise, kissed her on the mouth. It was no more than the briefest contact, and, she thought afterwards, probably no more than he'd given his niece, but it left her staring up at him, wide-eyed.

The curious crowd that had gathered laughed, and there was much comment in Arabic.

'That's what you get for underestimating me!' Nat teased, and then gave an incomprehensible reply to one of the commentators. It caused further laughter.

Suzie, torn between embarrassment and curiosity, asked tentatively, 'What did you say to him?'

'It's unrepeatable,' said Nat shortly. 'We were going to look at the spice sellers, if you remember?' After that, things became calmer for a while.

Later, Nat decided to find a small restaurant in the back streets, pointing out that it was cheaper and easier than taking food back to the flat to cook. 'That is assuming, of course, that you *can* cook?'

He was watching her out of the corner of his eye, but this time she knew she was being teased.

'If you listen to my sister, it's all newt's eye stew and barbecued toad's legs.'

'And is it?' He looked perfectly serious.

'Of course,' she said nonchalantly. 'There's no fooling a nine-year-old. But you can choose whether you get them French, Italian or Chinese style. I'll even teach you if you want to learn—you never know when it might come in useful. Unless you think a man's place isn't in the kitchen?'

'Who said anything about my having to learn? I just thought a bit of practice on your part might enhance your market value when I finally decide to sell you. Hell broth apart, are you a good cook?'

'It was one of the few things I was any good at in school.'

'One of these days you're going to have to make good that boast, but not tonight. I think we'll try this one.'

They were standing outside a small restaurant, very basic in appearance with its plain painted wooden tables and battered chairs. Any form of tablecloth was obviously considered unnecessary, and the lighting was very dim.

'Ignore the interested glances,' Nat instructed her as they went in. 'They've probably never seen a tourist female in here before.' Suzie became uncomfortably aware that the clientele was entirely male, and that every pair of eyes in the room, except Nat's, was fixed on her. Her experience in the market had given her a certain amount of courage, but she felt as though she were running the gauntlet between the tables.

They ate kebabs, and hummus, a dip made of chick peas and olive oil, served with coriander leaves and oil and large oven-warm slices of pitta bread.

'Eat up,' Nat encouraged. 'We might starve tomorrow in the desert.'

'We really are going to find the bedouin?' she asked incredulously. 'I thought you were just joking.'

He smiled at her, and waved a chunk of lamb in the air. 'Of course. I thought we'd go down to an old fort that Lawrence of Arabia used. There are some bedouin tents there, and in one of them, rumour has it, is the famous friend of a friend of a friend. There's also a desert police station, and some pools up in the rocks.'

Somehow, Suzie was having difficulty persuading herself that it was all quite real. While the prospects of tomorrow seemed like some romantic dream, she still couldn't believe in the reality of the day she had just lived. Even the sight of Nat scarcely a couple of feet away from her on the opposite side of the dimly lit restaurant table didn't help. Only yesterday he had been a complete stranger, and now he was—well, it was hard to define exactly.

On the drive back to the flat, she couldn't help wondering what would happen when they arrived. So far, Nat had been careful to treat her, as he said himself, as he would treat his niece, but she wondered about what had provoked the kiss in the market. He liked teasing her, that was obvious, and he was amused by the ease with which he could shock her. So in many ways he couldn't have chosen a safer place to tease her in that way, since the circumstances couldn't be interpreted as either conducive to romance, or favourable to any predatory designs.

She had no fear of him now, but she was still a little apprehensive. She had wanted him to kiss her earlier that day in the bedroom, and had been aware of a tiny pang of disappointment because he hadn't. After the kiss in the market, she had found herself wishing—only to dismiss the thought guiltily—that it had lasted a bit longer, and been less of a kiss for a surrogate niece, and more of something quite different. Then she wondered what she would do if he really made a serious pass at her. After all, her strongest reaction this morning to the fact that he hadn't had been one of relief.

As it was, she need not have given the situation a moment's thought. Nat pushed her gently through the front door of the flat in the direction of her bedroom. 'Go to bed,' he instructed. 'And sleep well. We'll probably be spending tomorrow night in the desert, and you mightn't find it very comfortable.'

She smiled at him. 'Goodnight, Nat. And thank you—for everything.'

She woke up suddenly, not quite sure at first where she was. The way the light fell on the ceiling and walls was unfamiliar, and she wasn't sure of the time. She lay staring at the window for a few moments, and then reached for her watch: half-past seven. She could hear no sounds in the flat, and wondered whether she should get up. Perhaps Nat was up already. She didn't want to keep him waiting.

She had a quick shower, and put on a pair of yellow cotton trousers and a loose white shirt. It was still comparatively cool, although she knew it would get very hot later. While she combed her hair and twisted it up in a plait, she listened for sounds of Nat. There was nothing.

Eventually she decided to go in search of him. The sitting-room was deserted, although he had left a couple of maps spread out on the table and there was a coffee-cup beside them with the cold residue still left in the bottom. It obviously hadn't been made that morning. She took the cup into the kitchen and washed up. Perhaps he had gone out.

'Nat?'

There was no answer. She decided to try his bedroom, and tapped tentatively on the door. 'Nat?' Are you awake?' No reply. She turned the handle and pushed the door open.

She was almost into the room when she saw him. He was lying in bed. He turned over suddenly, stretching, as she said in confusion, 'Oh, I'm sorry. I thought you must have got up.'

She found herself staring at him, at the dusting of light gold hair on his chest, and the darker hair under his arms, and the muscles of his broad, naked shoulders. He was evenly tanned and his hair was slightly tousled. The sheet was pulled down his waist and he didn't seem to be wearing anything.

He smiled, a lazy, good-natured smile that lit his eyes. 'Good morning. Late nights seem to be catching up with me. You look horribly bright and energetic.'

She smiled back and hoped she wasn't blushing. She'd never seen a naked man in bed before, except in films.'

'Do you want some coffee?' she asked quickly. Perhaps he would have got up by the time she had made it.

He yawned and stretched again, his muscles cracking with the tension in his extended arms. 'That sounds like a good idea. Black with no sugar. There's lots of milk in the fridge, though, if you want some.'

She smiled, and retreated hastily.

It didn't take long to boil the kettle and find the jar of instant coffee. She thought she would give him time to get up, and delayed while she sipped from her own mug. It was too hot, but any more milk would have made it too weak. Then she heard Nat's voice. 'Suzie, woman, what the hell are you doing with that stuff—still picking the freeze-dried granules off the bushes?'

She carried both mugs to his bedroom and went in. 'Sorry. I thought you were getting up for it.'

He was still lying in bed, half propped up on a confusion of pillows, his hands behind his head. He grinned at her.

'When I can have room service? You must be joking.'

She put down his mug carefully on the onyx-topped bed-side-table. It was a pale green, flawed with white and a faint thread of brown, and had a gilt surround and spindly gilt legs, and supported an expensive-looking lamp made from a Chinese vase.

'Do you think putting hot things on this table is going to ruin it?' she asked doubtfully.

'Don't worry. It isn't going to be there long enough.' And then, 'Don't go——' as she made a move from the bed. 'Stay and finish your coffee here, and I'll tell you what the plans are.

She sat down on the edge of the bed, aware that he was watching her.

'Don't look so nervous—I'm not about to impersonate grandmother wolf!' he teased.

She met his eyes, which were fully of lazy amusement, and decided to fight back. 'I'm thinking of the table-top,' she said tartly. 'How are you going to explain it if it suddenly starts to melt, or crumble to dust or something?'

He laughed. 'All good solid Harrods merchandise, this. Ever wondered where it all went? Now you know.'

She took a sip from her coffee. 'That explains the gold taps in the bathroom.'

His eyes narrowed a fraction, and he looked at her consideringly. 'You don't sound as though you approve.'

She wished she could think of something to say that would sound ambiguous. She couldn't help feeling that they were the sort of thing Katrina would have liked, simply because the bathroom décor had obviously cost a lot of money, but they didn't appeal to her. On the other hand, if Nat liked that sort of thing, she didn't want to sound rude.

'Katrina would love it,' she said at last, hoping she had hit on an answer that wouldn't betray her own views too clearly. To his dismay, Nat burst out laughing.

'Which means you don't, I suppose!'

'I didn't say that!'

'You didn't need to. It's written all over your face. Lots of people would be impressed. Why aren't you?'

'I just think some people have more money than sense,' she said crossly. 'There are a lot of poor people in this country—we saw dozen of beggers in the streets yesterday. The money that paid for the bathroom could probably have fed them all for weeks.'

'You've got a puritanical streak in you, Suzie. Don't you enjoy luxury?'

Of course she did, in a way. But it wasn't quite the point, and she certainly wasn't going to admit it. 'I just don't see why I should admire something because it cost a lot of money!' she protested.

'I entirely agree with you. But be careful that in despising Katrina's views you don't go to the other extreme. Do you really think that the owner of this flat would have distributed his filthy millions efficiently among the poor if he had decided, just for a change, he didn't want an extravagant bathroom?'

'No, of course, I don't. But. I'd have thought more highly of him, if he hadn't wanted to spend it the way he did.'

'I don't think we're in a position to knock him, do you?' Nat queried. 'He is, after all, lending us this flat for nothing.'

'I wasn't trying to criticise him exactly,' she replied defensively. 'He's obviously very generous to his friends, and I appreciate it.'

'Then what were you trying to criticise? Money? Or people who have it?'

'Well, it was only that I . . . you asked me for an opinion——'

'And now I'm asking you why you formed that opinion. After all, it's not every girl who'd fail to be impressed.'

'Do *you* like it?' she challenged, cornered. Nat was too good at these verbal exchanges.

'Like you, I can think of better ways of spending the money,' he said. 'But I'm interested to know if it's money itself you disapprove of, or is every millionaire by definition a baddie?'

'I think money has a way of destroying people, that's all.' She picked up the watch that was lying on the bedside-table, wondering how to change the subject. She was thinking of her own mother, and the way she had one day walked out on a husband, and a six-year-old daughter, for a man who could offer her luxury but surely never as much love. Her feelings were still too deeply buried for her to be able to discuss them dispassionately, and there was no way she was going to let Nat dissect them. Nor was she going to tell him about Gerald. She glanced down at the watch in her hand. It was gold, and something about its plainness and restraint made it look very expensive. There was a Swiss name on the face. She turned it over. 'Is this yours?'

Nat was looking at her with that expression she couldn't quite interpret. 'Yes.'

'I haven't seen you wearing it,' she commented. The letters N.L. were engraved on the back. 'What do the initials stand for?'

'Nathan Laird. It happens to be my name. And since we seem to have reached the time for introductions, what's yours, apart from Suzie?'

'Suzanna McClaren,' she said, and grinned at him. It was ridiculous to be telling him her name when she was sitting on his bed after spending a night in his flat. 'But didn't you find that out when you paid the bill in the hotel?'

He grinned back at her. 'Just checking. You could have given the hotel a false name, after all!'

'I could still be giving one.'

He looked at her with amusement. 'Possible, but not probable from what I've seen of you. You seem to be singularly low in basic cunning—which is allied to a sense of self-preservation.'

The subject seemed to have shifted into dangerous waters again.

'I like the name Nathan,' she said quickly, in an effort to put him off. 'It's better than Nat.'

His lips twitched. 'I prefer Ahmed, but my family didn't think of it in time.'

'Have you got a big family?'

'My father's dead, and my mother lives with my eldest brother. He's married and has three children—one of whom is my niece, Ali. I have another younger brother who is also married.'

At that moment, Suzie realised that she had taken it for granted that Nat didn't have a wife. He wore no ring, but that was no reliable guide. Although she didn't stop to analyse her reasons, or to examine the way she knew she would feel if he was married, it seemed very important to know.

He offered no further information, and she said awkwardly, 'Are you . . . do you have any children?'

She wasn't going to meet his eye—sometimes the knowledge that he found her so amusing was a little hard to take—but to her relief he didn't actually laugh.

'It's not impossible,' he said slowly. 'But I'd be very upset to think that their mothers hadn't seen fit to tell me about them.' So he was letting her know he'd had affairs, some of them probably casual, but it didn't answer her unspoken question. She tried again.

'Have you . . . ever been married?'

'No,' he said. 'Have you?'

She couldn't repress a smile. She knew very well he thought her naïve and inexperienced. 'You know I haven't!'

'No,' he said seriously. 'I don't know that, although I'd guessed it. It's dangerous to jump to conclusions about people. One day please remember I said that, and chalk it up in my favour.'

Her eyes were puzzled. 'I'm not quite sure what you mean.'

He took a gulp of coffee and choked. 'Ugh. I'd forgotten it was so hot. Well, Suzanna McClaren, now that the formal introductions are over, you'd better go and pack. We won't be coming back here until the night before your flight. We're spending tonight probably in the desert, and a couple of nights in Aqaba.'

'Are we going to sleep in the desert?' she asked in amazement.

'We certainly are—what are you waiting for? Hang around here much longer and I'm going to outrage your maidenly modesty by leaping out of bed.'

She didn't wait to be told a second time.

The drive out to Lawrence of Arabia's fort took them several hours. The sun was already blazing hot, but once they got out of the fumes and confused traffic of Amman itself the open sides of the jeep created their own cooling system. The Jordanian landscape was very barren, but Suzie looked at everything with interest. It still held the quality of a dream for her. Occasionally they would pass settlements of low mud-walled houses that grouped themselves round wells or springs, and were distinguishable from a distance by their palm trees, the only trees in the wide barrenness of browns and duns.

The spring-water courses left wide, boulder-strewn channels in places, sometimes beside the road, and Nat explained how the force of the rains could carve canyons, or *wadis*, where the flood water had swirled down to find sea level. 'I know it sounds ridiculous,' he commented, 'but people have actually drowned in the desert. When there's a rainstorm, there's nowhere for the water to go, and the land's too dry and hard to absorb much of it. It's crazy when you think of the number of people and animals that must have died of thirst. What do you think of it so far?'

Suzie gazed out of the jeep, fascinated. There was no hint that any drop of water had ever fallen on that scorching landscape, and now a shimmering heat haze hung over it, distorting the distance in planes of heat.

'I think it's beautiful,' she said. 'But it's also very frightening.'

He nodded. 'There's something about deserts. It's difficult to explain exactly, but it's something to do with the fact that they reduce man to his most basic. For people like us, it provides the sort of challenge most of us have forgotten about, or possibly never experienced. Some of those old bedouin have next to nothing in our terms, but they have more dignity in one little finger than a lot of our boardroom tycoons with all their country houses and Rolls-Royces. If you can live with dignity in the desert, then you have a lot going for you.'

'I suppose that was what I was trying to say this morning: that you don't need money to make an impression.' Then she added after a pause, 'But I suppose what the bedouin would like is enough money to have gold taps and country houses and drive Rolls-Royces, too.'

'Don't sound so downcast about it! There's nothing romantic about poverty—a lot of disease and suffering you see in the poorer countries of the world just doesn't have to happen in richer societies. And it's a strange paradox that it's money that allows spoilt westerners like us the luxury of playing at being nomads. It ought to make us ashamed, but it doesn't make it any the less valuable experience. Did you stop to think when you booked your flight here that it was money you didn't actually need that you were spending on a holiday you didn't actually need to take in this way? Isn't that a luxury?'

Suzie felt strangely vulnerable again. It was as though she was under attack once more, despite the fact that Nat's voice never sounded anything but quietly good-humoured. She hesitated, not knowing how to reply; it wasn't exactly a personal attack, but she couldn't help wondering if he disapproved of her. What he had just said was quite true—what she was doing now would be accounted a luxury beyond the wildest dreams of many of the beggars she had seen in the streets. She *did* feel ashamed.

'Do you think I'm spoilt?' she asked at last, and then regretted her impulse, nervous of the reply she was going to get.

Nat glanced across at her, and then took her hand, holding it on his knee. 'Darling Suzie, you're one of the least spoilt girls I've ever met. I didn't think they made creatures like you any more.'

He held her hand loosely in his for a little longer. Suzie felt as though the contact was burning all the way up her arm. He had called her 'darling'—she knew it was only a casual term of endearment and had no significance for him, but it made her suddenly feel warm inside. She would have liked him to put his arms round her.

He gave her fingers a squeeze, and then released her hand to take the steering wheel again. The conversation after that turned to Nat's work, which fascinated her, and he entertained her with tales of installations that had gone wrong, and stories of the people he'd met. He had obviously travelled widely, though not always in connection with his work, it seemed, but he was as interested in the challenges of his job as he was in the places he had visited.

'I like a challenge,' he commented. 'When things are too easy, it's tempting to sit back and take it all for granted. That's why this job is never dull. You might know the answers in theory, but every situation's different and it isn't until you've got to put it all into practice that you find you're alive.'

Lawrence's fort was situated in one of the *wadis*—a wide, flat-floored canyon flanked by towering rocks. Nat told her that some of the bedouin had virtually settled there. The Lawrence connection and the spectacular appearance of the *wadis* brought in tourists, to whom they could sell refreshments and local Arab handicrafts. There was very little to see except the place itself.

The evening she spent with Nat in the desert, Suzie would remember for the rest of her life. It was as though everything she'd heard about, or seen in films, had suddenly become real for her. In such a small settlement it wasn't long before Nat, speaking Arabic, had discovered his contact through Fahad, and both he and Suzie were invited to drink tea in one of the long, low bedouin tents. Woven from goats' hair in natural colours of brown and grey, they consisted of little more than striped awnings, with loosely attached back and sides. One side was completely open, and the tent she saw was partitioned in two inside: one are for the men and visitors, the other strictly for the women.

Long-eared goats eyed the visitors curiously, bleating and jostling each other. There were several very dirty small children who tumbled about among the goats, and a couple of slim, quick-eyed boys, who had obviously picked up their 'Allo-ow-are-you?' from the tourists.

Suzie was invited to sit on a long, uncovered mattress, its ticking undisguised, and as she sat down with Nat beside her he said in her ear, 'I've told them you're my niece. Act accordingly!'

She gave him a calculating smile. 'All right, *Uncle* Nat.' Her reply was loud enough for her host to hear. Nat flicked herr cheek with one finger, and turned back to the Arab.

Fahad's friend was a tall, lean man with a fine, hawklike face and greying beard. He wore a long white robe and the traditional checked headcloth with black band. He called some- one from the other side of the tent, and a girl, about ten years old, appeared, a coloured veil draped round her head and shoulders, but showing all of her face. Nat, translating, introduced her as Hamid's daughter, and she gave a friendly smile to both Suzie and Nat, before squatting down in the corner or the tent to light some sticks with a couple of matches. Despite the shade within the tent, the light was so strong that the flames were almost invisible as they licked round the tinder-dry sticks. The patch of ash and scorched stones indicated that this was the bedouin equivalent of a fireplace, and the small tripod surmounted by an iron ring was their cooker.

The tea was boiled in a battered compromise between a kettle and a teapot, and served in small glasses which had been rinsed in a tin pan of doubtful-looking water. Suzie remembered Nat's remarks about unhygienic glasses, and saw him watching her out of the corner of his eye, but she didn't bat an eyelid when she was handed one by the smiling girl, and smiled her own thanks in return. The tea was sweet, with an elusive flavour that she would never have identified as spice if Nat hadn't told her. She liked it, and accepted a second glass at the insistence of the girl, although she didn't know whether or not it was polite to do so. She had heard that Arabs were noted for their hospitality, and that they also had strict codes of manners. She hoped that Nat would warn her if she was about to make some terrible mistake, but although she caught his eye from time to time he said nothing.

After a while, he turned to her to translate for the girl. 'She asks if you would like to meet her grandmother?' he said, after there had been a long exchange between the girl and her father. Suzie eagerly agreed, and Nat translated again.

'You're on your own now. I won't be invited into the other part of the tent. It's for women only.'

Curiosity got the better of Suzie's momentary apprehension, and when Nat gave her an encouraging smile she got up to follow the girl.

The women's section was very similar in appearance, except that it was stacked with an assortment of boxes—some cardboard, some wooden crates—and there was even an old Singer sewing machine on a mattress.

The girl's grandmother had her veil over her face as Suzie appeared round the partition, but dropped it when she saw that she was alone. She was an elderly woman, with wrinkled, tanned skin and the dark blue-black circles of tattoos on her cheeks. She was dressed in black and wore heavy bracelets on her arms. She motioned Suzie to sit beside her, and said something to the girl, who disappeared round the partition again to come back carrying two more glasses of tea.

The conversation, such as it was, was carried on entirely in sign language, with one or two words in incomprehensible Arabic from her hostesses, and one or two words in English from Suzie. They showed her how to bake bread on a flat convex iron pan over a fire, and gave her some to taste. It was flat and stretchy, and rather gritty, but tasted quite good. She was also shown the machine, but understood, after some demonstration, that it was broken. She examined the garments they produced for her—most of them unwashed but finely stitched—without paying much attention, her mind on an idea that had just occurred to her. After admiring the exhibits, she made a sign to indicate 'wait' and went round to the other side of the tent.

'Nat, do you know anything about the insides of sewing machines?

Nat looked at her carefully. 'No. Why?'

'You don't think you could mend one?'

He groaned. 'Don't tell me, I can guess the rest——' And he turned to Hamid. There was a short exchange in Arabic, and Hamid left the tent, to reappear with his daughter and the sewing machine.

'It's a bit like an old one I used to have,' Suzie explained. 'My sister's got it now and it keeps breaking down, so I think I know what might be wrong with this one. But I could mend it. If I'm wrong, it won't make such difference to it, but at least we could try.'

'You mean, *I* could try,' said Nat ominously, and turned the machine on its side.

Suzie was amazed afterwards at how something which had started off as just a good idea turned into a major event in the life of the community, and long after that she was to find how significant a part it had played in her own life.

After explaining carefully to Nat how she thought the sewing machine worked, and Nat peering into its insides in an attempt to verify her accounts, he decided he needed several tools Hamid couldn't provide. One of the small boys hovering by the tent was despatched to a friend, and the search for a screwdriver and a pair of pliers eventually involved most of the other tents. A crowd of men and boys collected to watch Nat. He grinned at them all, and greeted them cheerfully, only to mutter privately to Suzie, 'They'll probably chop off my ears if I can't get this thing right. Now see what you've let me in for! I hope you know what you're talking about, and I'd be happier if someone hadn't had a go at this before me. Whoever it was hasn't made the problem any simpler.'

Suzie glanced at him anxiously, wondering if his easy manner hid a genuine irritation, but his face gave nothing away. She watched his long-fingered hands on the tools, and the way a slight frown of concentration appeared on his face, drawing two fine lines between his brows as he tried to correct the fault in the mechanism. He was quick at making deductions from her inept and un-technical description of what went on inside the machine, and with the help of the borrowed tools, a couple of pieces of wire and some engine oil, he finally managed to effect some temporary repairs.

He asked Suzie to test it, and after further consultations with Nat as interpreter, some thread and a bobbin were produced from behind the partition. Suzie threaded the machine.

'I've got to have something to try it out on,' she said doubtfully. If she had been wearing a skirt, she could have run it round part of the hem. 'I suppose I could test it on the end of my shirt.'

Nat looked up quickly from his final check on the machine. 'For heaven's sake don't pull that out!' he said. 'They'll think you're going to undress.'

Suzie gave him a speculative look. Something had already occurred to her, but she wasn't quite sure if she had the nerve to do it. It would, after all, be one way of testing how far Nat's tolerance really went. Her eyes began to sparkle.

'Roll down your shirt sleeves, *Uncle* Nat,' she demanded.

Nat gave a half-smile but didn't catch her eye, and dutifully rolled down the sleeves of his striped cotton shirt. 'You sure you need both?' he asked doubtfully.

'Absolutely. I can't just try it out on one.'

She would be sewing through four thicknessess of material, but she could see that the machine had been used to sew coarse fabrics, and there was no possibility of fine adjustment. She hesitated a moment while she wondered if she really had the nerve to make a fool of him, and then, with uncharacterisitc daring, took both cuffs and clamped them under the metal foot. He must have guessed what she was going to do by now, and she caught his eye as she knelt on the ground in front of him with the machine between them. The circle of Arabs laughed.

She couldn't interpret Nat's expression—she wasn't sure he'd ever show open anger, but in a way that was more frightening. Still, he had said nothing, and taking courage from that she ran a neat seam down the overlap between the two cuffs, broke off the thread, and set him free—effectively handcuffed.

From their immediate reaction, it was clear that the Arabs were enjoying the joke, and there was a lot of comment. Hamid was smiling, and his little daughter, with squeals of delight, ran round the tent to tell her grandmother.

Between Nat and Suzie there was silence. He was looking at her strangely, with a smile on his face, but there was that look behind his eyes she couldn't identify. Her heart began to beat faster, and she could feel the colour heightening in her cheeks. She wondered if he was indeed angry and whether she had just done something very stupid—she had, after all, made him look a complete fool. She didn't know how to break the silence that seemed to be lengthening interminably between them.

'As nieces go,' he said at last, his eyes still holding hers, 'I think I prefer Ali—for a variety of reasons.'

'That was revenge for yesterday,' she said quickly. 'You pinch my bottom in front of a whole market of Arabs—I sew your cuffs together in front of a bedouin encampment.'

'OK. That just about makes us quits. Now you'd better undo them, because we've been invited to a feast, and eating with both hands is distinctly bad manners. You're only allowed to use your right.' He paused, and then the corner of his mouth twitched into a half-smile. 'Do you think you could behave yourself for a while, or will I have to send you to sit in the jeep?'

Relieved, Suzie smiled at him, and while Hamid restored the machine to his mother, she and his daughter turned their attention to unpicking the seam it had sewn so effectively. The stitches were small and tight, and the two of them, Hamid's daughter with a tendency to giggle helplessly, applied themselves with a hairpin and the screwdriver to releasing Nat.

There was a continual exchange between Nat and his audience, now far too well entertained to think of leaving, and Suzie glanced up once or twice at the laughter. She and Nat were very close; he was seated cross-legged in front of her on a mattress, while she sat on the ground, the Arab girl, one grubby arm round her neck, rendering unhelpful assistance whenever the giggles subsided.

'If you want to know what they find so amusing,' Nat offered after a while, 'I told them I was going to beat you when I got you home, and I offered to sell you chastened and repentant to the highest bidder.'

'And did you get any offers?'

'No,' he said glumly. They think you're too naughty.'

'That's because I was badly brought up by you, *Uncle* Nat,' she returned sweetly.

She heard his infectious laugh again as she glanced down at his hands, lying passive between her own, but she was aware of a pang of disappointment that had something to do with the way in which Nat had reacted to the silly trick she had played on him. She hadn't wanted to see his anger, but, despite her inexperience in his eyes, she wasn't in reality the incompetent teenager he liked to imagine—there was a whole world of experience between herself and the schoolgirl Ali.

It was, of course, her own fault; she was regretted now the fact that he had so firmly identified her with his niece . . . She couldn't help thinking about what it would be like to be held by those strong hands with their angular bones, and caressed by them in a way that had nothing to do with relationships between a man and his brother's child.

CHAPTER FIVE

SUZIE lay on the ground looking at the stars for a long time. Nat, similarly rolled in a sleeping-bag, was less than a foot away from her. She was very conscious of his closeness; it was unfamiliar and pleasantly disturbing.

He must be asleep; she could hear his even breathing and he hadn't said anything for a long time. They had been watching the sky together for a while. She couldn't believe the brightness of the constellations, nor the thickly scattered stars that occupied every minute particle of space.

Nat had given her the option of sleeping in the jeep, but she preferred to stretch out on the ground, despite apprehensions of scorpions and snakes. The jeep would have been cramped, and cut off her view of the sky, but more important, Nat himself had made it clear he was going to sleep outside.

'The sky at night is one of the reasons we spoilt tourists come into the desert—that and the "back to nature" challenge I was talking about this morning.'

'But what about the creepy crawlies?'

He had laughed. 'Your chances of being attacked by anything bigger than an ant are pretty slim. After all, the bedouin sleep on those terrible old mattresses and they don't seem to worry.'

The desert temperature dropped at night, but he had packed sleeping-bags and rugs in the jeep. He had parked at some distance from the tents, partly concealed by a jutting outcrop of rock, which curved away back to form a small, protective crescent. He had been unusually silent on their walk back, and had said little before they lay down to watch the stars, merely telling her not to undress.

'Sleep in your clothes; it's much more practical, and if they look like a wreck tomorrow, it doesn't matter. You're not trying to impress anybody. We'll wash them when we get to

Aqaba.'

It was strange that he was so reluctant to talk, he was usually
so full of easy humour and conversation, but he had made
monosyllabic replies to many of her remarks, and she had
quickly taken the hint, and given up any attempt to chat.
Perhaps his mind had been taken up with the images that now
filled hers.

For her, the feast had begun when Hamid's little daughter
had dragged her back into the woman's section and much
excited chatter had gone on between her and her grandmother.
Suzie had been greeted by the latter with a warm smile, and a
gesture towards the machine, evidently an attempt to convey
thanks. She had been seated beside her and offered yet more
tea, and a kind of nutty sweet, very sugary and difficult to
identify. They had been joined in a few minutes by Hamid's
wife, and her younger sister, a beautiful woman of about
Suzie's age, wearing heavy gold ear-rings, and carefully veiling
herself on approach to the tent.

Between them, after much discussion and laughter, they had
produced a dress of dark blue cloth with wide sleeves, like a
caftan, and embroidered with red and gold at the neck and
wrists. Examined critically the garment looked cheap and
tawdry, but in the context of the desert, among the goats and
veiled women and dark tents, it had a certain exotic splendour.

They dressed Suzie like a doll, unpinning her hair, and
slipping the dress over her clothes. Gold ear-rings were hung
in her ears, and more bangles added to her own. Then her hair
and shoulders were draped in a fine black veil. She had no idea
what she looked like, and let them dress her largely to please
them, smiling a delight she only half felt—she was
embarrassed and too nervous about what might follow to enjoy
it. They seemed to admire their handiwork, and the small girl
was excited and affectionate.

The feast itself started before nightfall; the women had been
cooking all day. A huge cauldron had been brought out to stew
the goat which had been killed that morning, and another in
which to cook the heaps of saffron rice that were later piled up
on brass trays and served to the guests.

The woman's function was to serve the men, or to stay

secluded until it was their turn to eat. Suzie wished she could be with Nat—whatever she did was more fun with him. But she sat smiling, watching their dark, Kohl-rimmed eyes flash with humour, and the expressive gestures of their hands. There was no way they could include her in the conversation.

There was a glowing fire where the men sat, beyond the partition, and a screen of woven stuff divided the women's group very effectively from the talk and laughter of the men. She didn't want to be with them, but she wanted Nat, and now that she had been with the women for what seemed like hours she was wondering how she could return to him without offending them.

Suddenly a small boy appeared round the partition. He addressed Hamid's wife, and from his manner to her she guessed that he was her son.

He then approached Suzie. 'Come!' he said peremptorily. It was obvious from his manner that he had already learned that men were to be obeyed. She smiled at him, but looked doubtfully at the women. They were laughing, and Hamid's wife gestured towards the partition. It was evident that, although they had indulged her by dressing her up and inviting her into their domain, they regarded her as something very different from themselves. She could go among the men where they could not, but she was not sure whether they approved of her greater freedom.

Hesitantly, she stood up and allowed the boy to pull her by the arm, but at the entrance to the men's area she hung back in embarrassment. What on earth would they think of her—what would Nat think of her dressed up like this?

'Come!' said her little companion again. 'It's OK!' It was definitely not 'OK' from Suzie's point of view, but she was pulled into the firelight before she could make any further protest.

The men were sitting in a haphazard circle, their faces out-lined by the glow of the charcoal and wood embers. At first there was not one she could identify, and all eyes seemed to be turned on her. She felt ready to sink into the ground. There was a lot of comment, some good-natured laughter, and then Hamid was at her elbow, smiling and gesturing her forward. It wasn't until she found herself being shown to a rug on which to sit that she realised she would be beside Nat. The feeling of panic that had come over her made her blind to everything but those dozens of watching eyes.

He was sitting on the ground, cross-legged, looking across at her. At first he wasn't smiling and she stared wide-eyed at him, her heart beating nervously, wondering if he was going to disapprove. Or worse—tell her she had committed some dreadful social blunder. Then he grinned.

'You look scared to death,' he said. 'For heaven's sake, smile, and come and sit down. You're supposed to be enjoying this.'

She swallowed quickly. 'I am, honestly. It's just that I didn't quite know what to expect.'

He stretched out a hand to her. 'Well, I'm not going to sell you yet. Come over here.'

She walked across to him with Hamid, wondering what sort of a ridiculous Arab she made in her long, dark robe with its flashy ornamentation, her dark veil and gold ear-rings. Her long hair spilled over her shoulders and hung below the draped veil. At least she wasn't a blonde.

She took Nat's hand and sat down carefully beside him. She was offered food by the man sitting on the other side of her, and by the boy who now had appointed himself her protector and personal servant.

'He's basking in the reflected glory,' Nat commented in her ear. 'He sees how much attention you're attracting and knows the best way of getting some for himself.' She smiled, but kept her eyes lowered.

'Try some of the rice,' Nat encouraged, 'but don't forget to eat it with your right hand—I won't explain why just now. You blush too easily.'

She didn't catch his eye, and wondered how well he could see the colour rising in her face by firelight.

Unaccustomed to eating one-handed, she found it strange to be scooping up the rice and meat in her fingers, and putting it straight into her mouth, but the bread was easier to manage and she wasn't hungry. She ate merely for politeness' sake, while Nat translated for her some of the conversation round them, especially when it concerned herself.

'They want to know how old you are. They're also keen to know if a marriage has been arranged for you yet. What shall I tell them?'

Suzie's eyes sparkled with the same amusement she had seen in Nat's. 'Tell them I've had three husbands, and I've got into the habit of choosing my own!'

There were further exchanges, and then, while the conversation was being conducted by one of their neighbours, Nat said in her ear, 'They think you should marry soon, otherwise—to put it poetically—your beauty will fade like a flower in the desert. And to put it crudely, which is nearer to the way it was reported to me, your market value will drop considerably. Oh, and they like your blue eyes.'

'But they can't see what colour my eyes are by firelight!'

'True. But I was able to enlighten them when the subject was discussed, and Hamid verified it. I happen to like your blue eyes, too——'

He sounded quite matter-of-fact, but she couldn't immediately think of a reply, and turned to him, to find him looking at her. He was smiling, but the expression in his eyes was unexpectedly serious.

Just then, Hamid's son presented himself to Nat and addressed him briefly.

'Farouk and his friends want to show you their game,' Nat translated, 'and will I allow you to go and watch.'

Suzie looked up at the boy, and smiled at him, stretching out her hand to him. He grasped it firmly and began to pull her to her feet, wide, friendly grin in his face.

'Well, *Uncle* Nat,' she said provocatively, 'am I allowed?'

'I'm giving up nieces as a spiritual exercise,' he said looking up at her. 'Behave yourself—and don't get carried away, by a camel or anything else.'

Despite the mock warning, in a sense Suzie did get carried away; once she had left the light, and the watchful faces round the fire, she became completely relaxed. She was well used to entertaining her young half-sister and her friends with games, and had no difficulty in communicating with the ragged assortment of bedouin children, despite the barrier of language. They were merely showing off to her at first, playing a game of catching each other, but Suzie became involved when she stooped to pick up one of the smaller girls who had fallen and hurt herself.

In an attempt to distract the child from her bruises, imagined or real it was impossible to tell in the dark, she decided to teach them a simplified version of hopscotch, marking out the squares with sticks. The game proved such a spectacular success that the boys joined in with rather too much enthusiasm, and she decided to appeal to Nat, who had been watching her across the fire.

'For heaven's sake, explain to them that they're supposed to take it in turns!' she begged. 'It's like a stampede!'

He grinned at her. 'You don't need a translator. You're getting on fine—they've made up their own rules.'

A couple of the older girls, seeing her talking to Nat, approached him with a certain amount of unnecessary giggling, and there was a brief conversation in Arabic.

'The girls want you to play with them now,' Nat told her. 'It seems you're favouring the boys.'

As a result, she found herself playing with an impromptu ball of rags in the dark beyond the fire, and ran and chased with them until, tired by their energy, she made her way back to Nat. Several of them clung to her hands and skirts, trying to draw her back into their play—she needed no interpreter this time to understand the wheedling note in their voices: she'd heard it too often from Judy. She smiled at them and shook her head, and finally they allowed her to take her place beside Nat again.

They had left soon after that, Suzie to return briefly to the women and give back her borrowed finery. She thanked them as best she could in English, hoping that they would understand her intentions if not her words. They watched her, smiling and strangely distant, and she was most pleased by the little girl's obvious disappointment that she was leaving. She hung on her arm and chattered incomprehensibly, until Hamid appeared to take her back to Nat.

Now, lying gazing up at the myriad stars, she was astonished at herself. A week ago she would never have had the nerve to dress up as she had today, and appear before a host of strange men. Certainly, the adventure in the market had helped her gain some confidence, but above all it was Nat by his very presence who gave her the ability to enjoy what would otherwise have been something of an ordeal. She saw her experiences instead in the light of a wonderful, Arabian Nights adventure, with Nat himself hovering somewhere on the borders or reality and romance.

The light was grey when she woke, and the air surprisingly cold. She felt slightly chilled and cramped from lying on the ground, and started to sit up to see if Nat was awake. He was sitting a couple of feet from her on the edge of the rug, half turned away from her, his hands loosely linked round his knees. He was staring thoughtfully at the rocks, and she could see that he was frowning from the line of his eyebrow visible in profile. He had a dark jersey on, and his collar stuck up untidily, half hidden by the way his straight, floppy hair curled at the ends over it.

He didn't appear to have heard her move, and she watched him for a few seconds; for a man who had been a stranger to her forty-eight hours earlier, he had become surprisingly familiar. She had an almost overwhelming impulse to turn down the ridiculous collar, and smooth that straight, silky hair, a warm brown, bleached superficially by the sun.

'Nat?' she said at last, and he turned quickly and smiled, his eyes an intense grey-green.

'Sleep well?' he asked.

She pulled a face. 'It's not so much the sleeping, as the waking up,' she complained. 'All my bones have stuck together.'

'Well, you have a delicious breakfast of old bread and lukewarm coffee to get up for. This is what staying in the desert's all about. And to think I said you weren't spoilt!'

'I'm not really complaining,' she said earnestly. 'I'm enjoying it every bit, Nat, honestly. Please don't think I was serious!' She was afraid she might sound critical or ungrateful.

Nat stared at her in silence, and there was a curious pause. It was as though the whole exchange between them had suddenly switched into another gear. Inexplicably, he looked different, too—seconds ago he had been the smiling friend who treated her like his niece for his own amusement, and now he was almost a stranger—a man whose expression had become suddenly remote, even a little hard, the other Nat, perhaps, that she hadn't wanted to see. She bit her lip nervously, and stared at him, wondering what she had said to offend him.

Then, without warning, he leaned forward and touched her cheek with the side of one finger, and brushed a thumb gently across her lips. 'Don't do that,' he said. Even his voice sounded strange. Her lips parted in astonishment, and he got up abruptly. 'Suzie, you're impossible.' His tone was harsh.

He had already turned his back on her and was walking towards the jeep. She stared after him, her heart beginning to thump in her chest. How had she made him angry? One minute he had been talking to her as normal, and the next a sort of gulf seemed to have opened between them.

She felt insecure and alone all of a sudden, something she hadn't felt since Nat had walked into her life—or rather ridden, on that Arab horse, wearing that absurd Arab headgear. But now he looked nothing like a good-natured, teasing friend who, in ways she hadn't fully examined yet, had become so important to her. He looked older and tougher and less indulgent; shut off from her in a curious way. But then, she didn't know very much about him—most of the questions had been on his side, and he was too good at finding out things about her.

Before she had had time for further reflection, he had turned back with a thermos flask in his hands, and a loaf of bread wrapped in a piece of paper. The expression she had thought she had seen on his face had gone, and the old Nat was back again. She wondered if it would be wise to ask him what had been in his mind just then, but before she could speak he said, 'You've got five minutes to finish this, and then we're climbing the rocks. There are some pools up there somewhere. Hamid was telling me last night.'

She had almost plucked up courage to question him, but now that could wait. 'What exactly do you mean by climbing?' she asked hastily.

He watched her while she wriggled out of her sleeping-bag. 'Don't worry, I'm not talking about mountaineering. I doubt if you'll find it much of a challenge.'

She accepted the mug of coffee he held out to her, and straightened her clothes and pinned her hair while she drank it. Then Nat handed her the whole loaf. 'Pull off a chunk,' he told her. 'True desert style. At least the coffee's still hot.' He took a sip from her own mug. 'There's no sugar in this. I forgot. Do you mind?'

Secretly wondering if the ominous mood of a moment ago had really vanished, she said, 'It's a bit late now—I've finished it. But I don't take sugar anyway.'

'Neither do I. That's another thing we have in common.'

'What is?'

'We don't take sugar. We like deserts. We like dressing up—and don't tell me you didn't like appearing as a bedouin lady because I won't believe it. Oh, and we like hamburgers.' The corner of his mouth had twitched into the familiar half-smile. 'Don't frown. It'll give you wrinkles, and you're too beautiful to spoil.'

He was teasing her again, and she knew how to handle that. She pulled a face at him, and bit off an enormous piece of bread. At least he couldn't expect her to say anything for a while.

Once they had finished, Nat was anxious to explore the rocks before the sun got up too high. 'It's very hot up there by late morning, and I want to be out of there before then. We've still got to get to Aqaba, and that's a couple of hours' drive away at least.'

Although the cliff of rock looked daunting at first, Suzie found that it was quite easy to climb. The vertical ascents were no more than six or seven feet at a time, and there were plenty of hand and foot holds. In places, there was even the vestige of a track. She followed Nat, but didn't attempt to keep up with his pace. He liked to climb fast and efficiently, and then sit and wait for her to follow him, once he had made sure she would be all right on her own. Once, where the levels of pink-grey rock evened out for a while, he took her hand, and they went on in silence, she virtually walking on his heels.

It wasn't hard to guess they had reached a pool when, instead of the smooth, dry contours of the rock, and the patches of dusty gravel where the stones had crumbled, they found plants growing from the crevices, and a fringe of comparatively lush greenery. The pool was not deep, but it was shaded by a rocky overhang and covered an area of several square yards.

'There must be a natural spring somewhere,' Nat commented. 'Rainwater would never have lasted like this, even shaded from the sun.'

'Is it clean?'

He grinned at her. 'Do you mean have any goats been in it lately?'

'Well, sort of.'

'I'm not sure I'd drink it, but you can wash in it, if you like. Why not take your clothes off and get in?'

She knew that her 'No, thank you' sounded prim, and wasn't surprised when he laughed. 'I'll wait until I get to Aqaba.'

She knelt down to wash her face and hide the blush she was sure was going to appear. The water was pleasantly cold on her face and neck, and running down her arms.

Then she watched Nat as he knelt a couple of yards away. He had taken off his jersey and slung it round his neck while climbing, and now his shirt was open to the waist. He got a great deal wetter than she, and flicked some water in her direction, splashing her down the front of her own shirt. She retaliated, and a childish battle developed briefly, Nat coming off worse because he minded less about getting drenched.

Afterwards they lay along the sides of the pool on the damp rocks to recover their breath. The former relaxed atmosphere seemed to have been restored between them, and Susie decided that it was her turn to ask questions. Nat was lying with his eyes shut, his lashes still spiked with water.

'Nat,' she said slowly, 'you know you said you had a look at my passport when you were in the hotel? Don't you think it's only fair that I have a look at yours?' She knew it would make him laugh.

'What terrible fact about me is it you want to know?' he chuckled. 'My passport's in the jeep, but I can tell you what it says. Eyes: grey. Height: five ten. Distinguishing marks: none. Visas: innumerable, and likewise entry and exit stamps. What else?'

'How old are you?'

'Thirty-one.'

'And you're not married?'

'No. That's the second time you've asked me. Why? Do you think I ought to have settled down by my advanced age? I suppose to someone your age I must seem ancient.'

There was just a hint of something in his voice that reminded her of their curious exchange earlier, and she spoke quickly to avoid any further awkwardness building between them. 'Of course you don't. But I suppose most men marry in their twenties. Why didn't you? Were you having too good a time being a computer engineer and travelling round the world?' Then she thought she had been tactless—it might be a sensitive subject. 'Don't answer if you don't want to. It's not very polite to question you like this.'

'Surely it shouldn't be a question of politeness between us by now? But anyway, you've more or less answered the qustion yourself. I was a bit too busy with my work to think about having time for a wife. It doesn't seem fair to expect someone to sit at home waiting for a call from the office every night to say that I'll be late again, or that I'm flying off to Timbuctoo in a couple of hours.'

'But won't your job always be like that?'

'It doesn't have to.'

'Does that mean it's changed? If you couldn't stay at home enough then, why can you now? Isn't it the same job?'

''n a sense, yes. But now perhaps I could afford to spend more time digging the garden, and cooking the Sunday joint.'

'Do you earn more money? Is that why?'

'In a sense, yes,' he said again. His eyes opened, and rested on her for a moment. 'Got any more questions saved up?'

She looked away quickly. 'I'm sorry. I didn't mean . . .'

'Well, don't ask me to reveal all my fascinating secrets this morning, that's all! Let's save some of them for when we run out of conversation, shall we?' He was grinning at her again, and propping himself up on one elbow. 'It's time to go. The sun's already warmed up quite a bit.'

They took their time about the descent, largely because

although Suzie had found it quite easy to climb up, getting down the longer vertical sections proved more difficult. Twice Nat waited for her, telling her where to put her feet as she scrambled down backwards, and then they came to a section she couldn't remember having climbed at all—there seemed to be no footholds. Nat had swung himself easily over the edge, and, taller and stronger than Suzie, had had no difficulty in letting himself down the face to drop on to his feet.

Suzie stood above him, looking down doubtfully.

'I'm not too sure about this.'

'Jump. I'll catch you.'

The suggestion appeared impossibly dangerous, even though it was probably only a matter of seven or eight feet. 'I can't,' she protested. 'I'd knock you over.'

'That doesn't say much for your confidence in me. What do you think I am—an eight-stone weakling?'

She gave a half-smile. 'You're not exactly Tarzan, either. It—it just doesn't seem like a good idea.' Far more unnerving to her than the prospect of his dropping her was the thought of being held in his arms, but she hoped he wouldn't guess that. He had no sexual interest in her, and she was afraid she might betray some of her awakening feelings for him.

Finally she compromised, sitting on the ledge with her legs dangling over the edge, and then letting herself slowly down like someone gingerly entering a swimming bath, until she could bend her wrists and arms no further and was forced to let herself drop, or fall. Nat was waiting for her, and caught her as she stumbled with the impact and fell forward. There was no avoiding him. She found herself being held against him, her cheek against the damp front of his shirt.

For what seemed like a full minute, but could only have been a couple of seconds, they stood without moving, Suzie startled into feelings she could hardly define by the contact of Nat's body against hers, and the feel of his arms round her and his hands on her back. Nothing in all that heady, unreal romance with Gerald had prepared her for anything like this. In comparison, Gerald had been just a dream lover. She was shocked now to discover that he had never been much more to her than an intensely romantic fantasy. His physical presence had scarcely been more real to her than the image she perpetually carried in her mind, and the pleasure she had taken in his kisses and caresses merely a continuation of that world of her romantic imagination. In real terms, she had been completely unawakened.

Now this man only had to hold her in his arms, and it was as though an electric current had passed right through her. She was aware of his almost overpowering masculine presence, and her whole body was tingling, almost agonisingly awake, while somewhere deep inside she seemed to be melting, even her bones turning to jelly. One moment she had been dropping off a rock face, wondering if she could avoid Nat catching her, and the next . . .

She could hardly breathe and didn't dare to move. It was as though something momentous would happen if she did, and she wasn't sure she could cope with it or understand it. Nat had made her adventurous—had enabled her to deal with circumstances and people that would have daunted her only a few days ago—but now he couldn't help her, since he himself was partly the cause of her fear. No, it wasn't fear exactly—it was something to do with a powerful alien force that threatened to engulf her, and she was frightened of the consequences. It was of the tension between them, not Nat himself, that she was nervous. Any expression of it would seem like an irrevocable step in their relationship, and there would be no going back. Once again, she was afraid of losing herself on a new, wholly unknown road.

'Suzie?' Nat's voice was very low, just above her head, and she could feel the side of his face against her hair.

She gave a little gasp and tried to push herself off his chest. 'That wasn't exactly the easiest way of getting down,' she said foolishly. Anything to break the tension.

His arms relaxed and he let her go.

He was half-way down the next level before she had time to react. It struck her afterwards that she had never seen him move so fast. Perhaps it meant he was relieved that he didn't have to do anything one way or the other? Perhaps, she thought, with a little shiver, he wouldn't have wanted it at all, and so for his own reasons was just as anxious to avoid it as she had been.

They returned to the jeep in a silence that Suzie found strange. There was no hostility in it, yet it seemed that, for all her fears of what might have happened between them, in reality something had indeed taken place; just by refusing to accept whatever physical expression of it that might have occurred—assuming of course that Nat had wanted it, too—she hadn't succeeded in keeping things exactly as they had been. As they drove towards Aqaba along the desert roads, she was wholly preoccupied by the man sitting beside her, and the nature of her feelings.

She couldn't flatter herself that he would share any of them. He showed a certain friendly liking for her, and while teasing her unmercifully he was also protective towards her when it mattered. It was just the way a genuinely kind and generous person would react to someone younger and more vulnerable than himself—especially when he looked on her in the same light as his niece.

Initially, the fact that he saw her as another Ali had helped to gain her trust, but it was posing problems. He was older than she had at first thought, and that widened the gap between them. There was no way a thirty-one-year-old man was going to see a particularly inexperienced young woman ten years his junior as a likely object of his romantic interest, she told herself firmly.

But if there was one thing Suzie was now sure of, it was that she wanted Nat, at some unspecified date in the future, to feel about her exactly the way she did about him. Whatever she had imagined she had felt about Gerald bore no relation to what she had now experienced with Nat, after only three short days.

The drive to Aqaba took a couple of hours, as Nat had said, and most of the way she stared blindly out of the window, the desert an endless expanse of brown and grey before her. Nat was only inches away, and when he touched her once or twice, casually, reaching across her to shut her door properly, or taking the map from her hand, the contact was so distracting it drove all thoughts from her head but the awareness of his body's nearness. After that endless moment in the rocks, so quickly passed in reality, it was as though every nerve had come alive in his presence. It was ridiculous when she thought of the way she had been suspicious of him at the beginning. She didn't know what was happening to her.

She began to daydream about lying in his arms, and about saying all sorts of silly, affectionate things to him—the sort of things she could never have said to Gerald. He had been far too slick and polished, and she had been a little in awe of his sophistication.

She was in awe of Nat too, sometimes, but that was when she was reminded that he could represent an alien world to her—the competent, intimidating world of men who took planes half-way across the planet as though it was all in a day's work, and who could probably direct you round the back streets of Singapore from memory; who talked among themselves about company business and who understood the complex electronic workings of computers. It was a demanding, adventurous world remote from hers, but she had discovered nothing about Nat which linked him to the power and money pursuits of Gerald and his friends, and she felt instinctively that if—by some miracle—he ever came to love her, there would be nothing, however foolish or intimate, that she wouldn't be able to say to him.

It was with a sense of shock she realised not only had her thoughts about Nat moved on a whole stage further since the incident that morning, but, if he ever really wanted her, there was no way she would be able to resist him, even if she knew it was no more than a passing interest with him. Because, without knowing how it had happened, she was falling hopelessly in love with him. And this discovery imposed a new awkwardness, as though they had newly become strangers again because she could no longer see him in the same way any more.

Aqaba was much smaller than Suzie had imagined, and the most attractive streets were those near the big hotels. Advertised as the 'French Riviera' of Jordan, the town was both a fashionable tourist resort and a commercial port. Its glamorous billing exaggerated its appeal, but the newer streets were wide and there were plenty of modern buildings. The palm trees beside the roads and hotels gave the resort its tropical air. Its real interest for foreign tourists lay in its under-water forests of white coral, and the variety of semi-tropical fish to be found among them, but the attractions of the beach were a little spoilt by the vast bulks of the oil tankers, looming some way offshore like dark monsters.

'You can't have everything,' Nat had warned her. 'Oil is the major industry of the Middle East, after all, and the Red Sea is just a giant shipping lane. Things have changed a bit since Lawrence rode his camel round here.'

The hotel in which they were staying was one of the largest and smartest. Nat had explained casually that he knew the hotel manager's brother, and that they were being lent a room.

'Another one of your favours?' Suzie asked, her heart suddenly beating unexpectedly fast as she wondered if she dared comment on the word 'room'. Would it mean that she was expected to share a bed with Nat? The thought filled her with such a confusion of emotions she couldn't face the idea of his teasing, and decided not to say anything.

Nat himself didn't seem to think it was worth commenting on, which might indicate that the use of the term was casual, and the nature of the relationship between them would automatically dictate that they were given not one room, but two, however small. He explained instead the Arab idea of hospitality, and the manner in which business contacts had a way of becoming friends.

'They'd expect the same kind of hospitality if they came to England.'

'You mean free hotel rooms?' she asked, taken aback.

'Not quite on that scale. I've only got a flat, but I'd have them to stay there.'

Suzie smiled. 'It looks as though you're going to have a constant stream of visitors when you get back.'

'I like visitors—and they'd be welcome to use the flat when I wasn't there. Arabs like staying in London, and I reckon in many ways it'd be a fair exchange. I expect Fahad will be over before too long. If I'm away, you'll have to look after him.' He had glanced at her sideways as they pulled up in front of the hotel. 'Don't worry—he wouldn't make any advances to you!'

Suzie gave a half-smile, and turned to open the door of the

jeep to avoid his too observant eyes. That wasn't what she had been thinking; it was the first time that Nat had referred to any continuation of their relationship beyond the present casual companionship that had, up to now, been all that he was after. It must mean that he liked her enough to go on seeing her. Or perhaps it meant no more than the fact that she might be the only person who knew Fahad in London apart from Nat himself. She had benefited from his hospitality in Jordan, and it would be fitting if she were to make some sort of return.

It was some time before they were shown to their accommodation in the hotel. Their arrival entailed a surprising series of introductions, and even drinks with the manager in his splendid 'office', which suggested to Suzie that most of his work must be done while sitting on beautifully upholstered cream leather sofas with cigars. He was a tall, grey-haired man with a well-clipped moustache and fine dark eyes, attractive in appearance although tending a little to overweight. His manner towards Suzie was courteous and friendly, and towards Nat full of welcoming hospitality, and something else which puzzled her. If Nat had been the older, more obviously powerful man, she would have called it respect. But it didn't make any sense in the present context, and she dismissed it, wondering if she wasn't more tired than she had thought—fatigue must be warping her judgement.

The conversation was chiefly conducted in Arabic, with occasional general remarks in English for Suzie's benefit. She was offered whatever she wanted to drink, but opted for lemonade, no matter how unsophisticated it sounded: she and Nat had eaten nothing since their breakfast in the desert, and she was afraid alcohol would go straight to her head.

She was glad that the incomprehensible Arabic meant that she wasn't expected to join in the conversation. She would have liked to have been able to wash and comb her hair before finding herself having to exercise social graces in such opulent surroundings. It didn't seem to have crossed Nat's mind that the clothes he had spent the night in were in any way unsuitable for drinks with the manager of one of an international chain of hotels.

Finally, to her relief, both men got up, and Nat smiled at

her. 'Suzie's thinking we both look as though we'd spent the
best part of a week living rough, and we're not properly
dressed for the occasion. We'd better get cleaned up before we
sample the delights of the hotel.'

Disconcertingly, he had read her mind again, and Suzie
opened her mouth to protest, but the manager didn't bat an
eyelid.

'You are very welcome, Suzie. You look beautiful just as you
are. Nat is a very lucky man. I hope you will both enjoy your
stay.'

She couldn't remember afterwards how she got out of the
room, or what she said, the manager's words had thrown her
into such confusion. What on earth had Nat been telling him?
And what was Nat expecting? Had he been waiting all along
for this? A feeling of panic engulfed her and, unable to form
any definite decision, she followed him mechanically.

Their bags had already been taken up, and it seemed that
they were being given accommodation on the manager's
private floor. One of the under-managers, distinguished from
the rest of the hotel staff by a smart, light-coloured suit and tie,
showed them up to the private floor, using a special pass key in
the lift. Suzie hadn't known such things existed, but she
scarcely gave it a thought. She knew that Nat was watching
her, although he said nothing. She was wondering what on
earth she'd do if the thing she half wanted and half feared
turned out to be true.

The hotel official left them with a polite smile at the door to
their room. It was unnumbered, and he opened it for them.
'Welcome to our hotel. Please ask for anything you want. Just
call reception.'

Nat caught her eye, but she looked away quickly, trying to
hide her inner turmoil. When he turned to thank the other
man, she walked into the room, praying for an appearance of
composure.

They had been given not a room, but what was evidently a
suite of rooms, furnished in a style to make the flat in Amman
seem like a poor man's dwelling. The cool freshness of the air-
conditioning meant that the rich carpeting of the main sitting-
room was not inappropriate, and it was strewn with silky

oriental rugs that were only too obviously insurable for vast sums of money. All the furniture consisted of European antiques, and the pale silk-covered walls displayed a variety of paintings, all of them original. There was a private balcony, festooned with greenery, and a set of chairs and sunloungers with a colourful umbrella. One door, which was open, led to a tiny kitchen, equipped with a fridge and sets of glasses and jugs, and there were large, panelled double doors on the opposite wall. But, before she had a chance to discover for herself what was behind them, Nat had crossed the room to open one, and look inside.

He leant back against the doorframe, and, arms crossed, surveyed Suzie with obvious amusement. 'What are you looking so nervous about'

'Nothing,' she said, the lie all too clearly written on her face.

'It wouldn't have anything to do with what the manager said, by any chance? If so, I can assure you it was merely a general compliment to you, and had nothing at all to do with me—apart from the fact that I seem to be the person who's spending most of his time in your company at present. So just in case you thought I'd been making the most of your ignorance of Arabic, and laying evil plots to trap you, I assure you I haven't.'

'I didn't . . .'

'Yes, you did. If you want to change rooms, I'm sure it can be arranged, but I'd say, for want of any other information, they'd reached an elegant compromise.'

Her mouth felt dry. He must have opened the door to the bedrooms—or was it *room*? She wasn't sure what she really wanted to find.

'What do you mean?' she asked, a frown beginning to draw the finely arched brows together.

'It means that you get to choose which bed to sleep in,' he said, and held the door open for her.

Afterwards, she could never decide which of her immediate responses was the more overwhelming—relief, or disappointment.

CHAPTER SIX

THE ONLY room that didn't surpass its equivalent in the flat in Amman, Suzie decided, was the bathroom. She lay back in the bath, which was no more than a conventional shape and size, in a cloud of bubbles and exotic essences, and closed her eyes. It was a remarkable contrast to that early-morning splash in the rock pool.

She knew Nat was not in the apartment. He had another mysterious contact on the hotel staff to see, and it seemed sensible for him to use the bathroom first and then to leave her to the luxury of a long, uninterrupted soak while he made his social call. He had taken a quick shower and changed into light, well-cut trousers and a surprisingly expensive-looking shirt of fine striped cotton. Suzie, because it was the sort of thing Katrina was constantly noticing, suspected that his Italian leather shoes were far from cheap. She wondered if she oughtn't to adjust her ideas of what a computer engineer earned.

She had been lounging in a chair in the sitting-room when he had emerged from the bedroom, and her face had obviously registered surprise at his appearance. His hair, newly washed, flopped over his forehead, the fine, sun-bleached, superficial layer making him look fairer and more tanned. Seeing her look, he grinned.

'This is known as "impress the potential clients" gear—very much in the interests of the company. The bathroom is all yours. Don't drown while I'm away. I won't be long.'

'Nat——' she said tentatively.

He was already half-way to the door. 'What?'

'Why do you have to go round impressing clients when you're on holiday? The company expects quite a lot of you, doesn't it?'

'Not really. Devotion to the interests of the company is in a

88

sense devotion to my own interests—I'll explain it to you another time. And if by chance I get held up, there's a bottle of champagne in the fridge, compliments of the management. But don't drink it all or I'll have something to say about it when I get back.'

Before she could think of a reply, he was gone.

Now, as she lay in the bath, her eyes full of the image of a tallish, sun-fair man with strong shoulders and slim hips, she remembered the way he had looked at her when he had opened the bedroom door less than an hour before. At first she had thought he was just amused, but now she considered it the grey-green eyes had seemed to hold a question. But she wasn't sure if she was ready to think about that yet. If anyone had suggested to her three days ago that she would be sleeping in the same room as a man who was at that time still a stranger to her, and offering not one word of protest, her reaction would probably have been one of horrified disbelief. But if they had told her that after sixty-odd hours almost exclusively in his company she would be missing him after an absence of less than sixty minutes, she would have thought them completely crazy!

She got out of the bath eventually, with great reluctance, and wrapped herself in a towel that felt as soft as velvet, and found another for her hair. It was a marked contrast to her hotel in Amman, where one towel had to do for everything. Luxury certainly had its appeal.

She didn't want Nat to come back and find her half-naked, and quickly picked up the clothes nearest to hand, dressing hastily. She had a skirt and top in a synthetic silk fabric that, while looking exactly like the real thing, had the advantage of being uncrushable. It was a dark, discreet blue, and looked expensive, which was satisfying as she had made it herself. She slipped on a pair of white high-heeled sandals, and then examined her appearance in the huge gilt-framed bedroom mirror. She hoped she might now be able to do something to counteract the impression she must have made in a pair of grubby trousers and a shirt that had survived the day in the desert. She also couldn't help a secret hope that the change of image might have some effect on Nat.

She was out on the terrace combing still very wet hair when she heard him return.

'Suzie, where are you? It's very definitely champagne time—if you haven't finished the bottle already.'

She got up off the lounger on which she had been perched, and looked up to see Nat already in the doorway.

'Do you want——' He broke off suddenly, looking at her oddly. 'It isn't just "making an impression time" for engineers, I see. I was asking you if you'd like some champagne, but perhaps a hairdryer would be more appropriate?'

Suzie had actually imagined that she had felt her heart turn over at the sight of him. She had been keyed up by his absence, nervous at first in case he came back before she was dressed, and then strung between a longing to see him and a foolish apprehension that must have something to do with the fact that she had accepted with such outward coolness their sharing a bedroom. Now she stood staring at him, just as he had discovered her, comb in hand and wet hair trailing over one shoulder, already dampening the front of her silky top. Her eyes, reflecting the colour of her clothes, were a deep, intense blue, and her cheeks were flushed from the desert sun. Her lips were slightly parted. Then she smiled.

Nat seemed to have been holding his breath—and then he remembered to breathe out very suddenly. Suzie told herself firmly that he had probably had an unexpectedly tricky meeting with his business contact, but she couldn't entirely stifle a tiny voice inside her that told her that he might be reacting to her. He came towards her, and put his hands lightly either side of her waist. She dropped her eyes. There was something in his scrutiny she found too disconcerting to meet. Then he flicked the strands of hair back from her top, looking at the darker patches the damp had made across her shoulder and breast. She had to stop herself from reacting to his touch.

'From someone who slept in her clothes and washed this morning in a rock pool, you don't look too bad,' he said at last. 'But there's a hairdryer in the bathroom if you look for it. Drying your hair on your dress is going a bit too native for this sort of hotel.' He moved away from her, heading back to the sitting-room. 'Go on,' she heard him say, 'no champagne until you've finished.'

It wasn't until she had dried most of her hair that she emerged again from the bedroom, the glossy brown strands hanging straight almost to her waist. Nat was lounging casually on the sofa, reading a newspaper, and the neck of a bottle, wrapped in a napkin, protruded from an ice-bucket on the table beside him; there were too long-stemmed slim glases on a tray.

'I hope you don't like champagne,' he remarked without glancing up, 'because that means all the more for me.'

Suzie laughed, and sat down on one of the elegant chairs. 'Then I'm sorry to disappoint you. I like it a lot!'

He groaned. 'For a girl who prefers the simple things in life, that's a very bad start. Where did you acquire the taste for it?'

'I haven't acquired a taste for it—I'm still practising! I don't suppose I've had more than half a dozen glasses of it in my life.'

Nat had kept his eyes on the paper, scanning the columns of newsprint, and now he glanced up.

There was another silence, and despite her light-hearted reply Suzie felt her nervousness beginning to return. She had been aware of a sort of tension in him ever since the bedouin feast; he had taken just as much trouble with her, and been just as nice to her, but perhaps he was beginning to regret the fact that he had involved himself in this way with her. In comparison with many of the women he must meet, he would surely find her very dull. She was ignorant and unsophisticated. In making the comparison between her and his niece, it was evident that he found her childish.

She smoothed the silky fabric of her skirt, and wondered what she could say to break the silence. Then he said, 'Do you know that you're very beautiful?'

only half admitted to herself, there had been somewhere the wistful hope that he might make a favourable comment on her appearance, other than his rather enigmatic first greeting. She was unsure that what she had on was really suitable, and needed his approval. She would have been very willing to change again. Now she kept her eyes fixed, unseeing, on her skirt. She couldn't look up. Desperately, she reminded herself that he often said nice things to her, but it didn't mean he expected her to believe them. She hoped that nothing of that surge of joy she had suddenly experienced showed in her face.

She heard the paper rustle as he put it down on the table, and then he said, 'Blushing doesn't make any difference—you can't hide behind it. You're very lovely, Suzie—and added to that is the further attraction that you obviously have no idea how beautiful you are. So, before I do something I might regret, try the champagne, and then let me know your ideas about the rest of the evening. We've got a lot of possibilities—getting drunk is only one of them!'

His return to the familiar tone of light-hearted banter gave her the courage to look him in the face, and she caught the one-sided twist to his lips. He was laughing at her again.

A tiny fleeting pang told her that she was disappointed—it was as though in some way he had retreated from her. Or perhaps she had been the one doing the backing out? She wondered what he meant exactly by 'something I might regret', but his tone indicated that they were to return to the known patterns. She smiled, and dropped her gaze again to take a sip of champagne. It was very dry, the bubbles no more than a fine stream or two of minute sparkles rising in the glass.

'Well?' he demanded. 'Does it meet with approval or are you going to spit it out?'

'You mean this is only an experimental bottle for wine-tasting? Then I think we ought to get in a very large supply—I think I might even take to this for breakfast.'

Nat was amused. 'You've decided on drunkenness for your preferred option for the evening. Now you're going to have to make another decision. Do you want to have dinner sent up here, or would you prefer to eat downstairs? It won't make any difference to the food, but it might to the service.'

'How do you mean?'

'They'll send it all up here on a trolley with a waiter just for ourselves. We can keep him hovering around watching every mouthful, or we can send him away.'

Eating alone with Nat in such intimate and luxurious

surroundings had its awkward aspects, but it appealed to her more than the hotel dining-room.

'Let's eat up here,' she said slowly, 'but we'll send the waiter away.'

They took their champagne out on to the balcony. It was cool now and the sun had gone down in a haze, achieving no more than a pale gold before it disappeared for good. Stars were already dimly visible.

'I know what you're thinking,' Nat said suddenly.

'What?' she asked, wondering if he would guess how she had been assessing how drunk she felt—or worse, how underneath all the time her blood was singing because of his nearness to her.

'You're sorry you're not back in your room in Amman. You'd be lying there comfortably now, counting the flies on the ceiling and wondering how many days, hours and minutes it was until your flight.'

He was teasing again, but her answering smile was vague. She put her glass down carefully on the small balcony table, her heart beating with increasing rapidity. She knew where she was with Nat's teasing: it was safe, and she could tease back. But she also knew now that for her it was a sort of cowardice; things she would have found it easy to say only days ago—to thank him for his care of her, for the trouble he took to entertain her—had taken on a new significance. She couldn't any longer utter those words without an awareness of the feelings that were behind them. And yet now was the perfect opportunity. She didn't want him to think she was taking it all for granted.

'I was thinking that . . . in a way,' she said at last. She forced herself to meet his eyes. 'Only I was thinking about it the other way round.' He was smiling, but the grey-green eyes held a question she had seen in them before. 'I . . . I was thinking that I was here, having the time of my life . . .' She hesitated, and then said simply, 'Thank you, Nat. I hope I'm not too boring as a companion.'

He put his glass down on the table next to hers, and took a step towards her, moving with almost deliberate slowness. There was scarcely any distance between them. He was looking down at her, studying the lines of her face. Then both hands were on her face and his thumbs brushed across her cheeks. She had no doubt, at last, what he was going to do, or that this time she really wanted it. It was what she had been longing for, and afraid of. Half fearful, her eyes looked into his, and then he bent his head and his lips brushed the side of her mouth in the gentlest of caresses. His hands slid into her hair, and she turned her head a little so that he could take full possession of her mouth, but his lips touched hers again in the lightest of kisses and then her cheek. She just stood there, almost afraid to move, and scarcely conscious of her involuntary response as her lips parted slightly in invitation.

It was over almost before it had begun, and Nat had drawn back from her a little and was looking down at her again; her lips were still parted, and her eyes clouded by the unfamiliar sensations he had evoked in her. He smiled at her, the laughter lines etched more deeply in the tanned skin. The grey-green of his eyes was lit with a warm light.

'I never could keep my hands off a beautiful woman,' he said.

Suzie continued to gaze up at him, almost uncomprehending. The strange weakness that had overcome her body seemed to have invaded her mind as well. She was incapable of coherent thought. His hands still rested lightly each side of her neck, and every pore of her skin seemed alive under his fingers.

'Does that mean—does that mean you've had many beautiful women?' she faltered, and then could have bitten her tongue for the naïveté of the question.

But as he looked at her his eyes changed, and the laughter disappeared. There was no teasing when he eventually spoke.

'I'm sorry. That was a cheap line. Don't look so embarrassed. You had every right to ask.'

She couldn't meet his eyes now. 'I'm sorry—I——'

'No,' he interrupted quickly. 'Don't be. I was going to answer you. If you're talking about lovers, yes, I've had a few—I suppose it's a fairly modest number for a man in my line of business. I don't know. National averages in such matters are hardly a consideration.' He hesitated then for so long, she wondered if she should say something, but then he went on, 'This mightn't make much sense to you yet, Suzie—I'll explain more about my job some time—but I get to meet a lot of very attractive women, who make it clear that they are . . . well, available. But there have been very few, in the words of that cheap joke just now, that I *haven't* been able to keep my hands off.' The smile in his voice encouraged her to look up again. 'As you see, I haven't yet been able to take my hands off you—but then I've never met anyone quite like you before. And I can't yet believe my luck . . .'

'Nat!' She could scarcely say his name; he had almost literally taken her breath away.

The half-squeaky whisper made him laugh, and he pinched her cheek in a familiar gesture that broke whatever spell it was that had been weaving itself between them.

'It's your turn to pour out the champagne. I'll go and see what I can do about summoning that waiter. Trust me not to poison you?'

She nodded, wordlessly. She needed time to think about what had just happened between them, and what he had said.

But she had no time to think during supper. She could never remember afterwards how many dishes they were given, and Nat dismissed the waiter almost as soon as he had brought them in on a trolley covered with a white damask cloth. There was a second bottle of champagne, but neither of them drank much of it. Nat made sure she tried all the dishes, and she thought it was a pity that she wasn't hungry—the champagne had dulled her appetite and she merely picked at the food to taste it. There were plates of rice cooked with nuts, pine kernels and different spices, meat prepared in sauces and yoghurt, various vegetable dishes and different kinds of salads. She felt guilty that so much of it was being wasted.

Nat kept her entertained with engineering anecdotes, and teased her occasionally until the old ease had been re-established between them. Then he said, 'We've been invited to have coffee with the manager.' He was watching her. 'You don't have to do anything except sit there looking beautiful.'

'That's very nice of him—he must be tremendously impressed with you!' She managed to sound enthusiastic, although it wasn't exactly her idea of the perfect ending to the evening. She wasn't used to making conversation with sophisticated businessmen, but she didn't want to make her reluctance obvious; Nat must be getting bored with her childish reactions by now. Instead she smiled at him, and didn't find an excuse to look away when she knew he could read her and he tried to hold her gaze.

Nat's look was thoughtful and a little speculative as he leant back in his chair, pushed slightly away from the table. His thumb idly traced the line of his jaw; he seemed to be making his mind up about something.

'My niece is devoted to discos,' he said at last. 'There's one in the hotel tonight. Want to go?'

It was a pity he had mentioned Ali again—it was telling her firmly that he was trying to amuse her in the same way, but she tried not to let the thought show.

'I'd love to!' she replied eagerly. 'After or before the manager?'

He laughed and got up. 'Definitely after. I think we ought to turn up looking presentable this time, don't you?'

One of the hotel staff came to escort them along the corridor to another suite of rooms on their private floor, where Suzie was greeted with a warm handshake by the manager.

'Miss McClaren! Aqaba seems to agree with you—you look wonderful. I hope you found everything to your liking?'

Suzie smiled warmly. 'Yes, thank you—it's like paradise after rock pools and camping breakfast!'

The conversation continued, easy and relaxed, and Suzie's questions produced a great deal more information about the desert, and Jordon in general, from both the manager and Nat.

They spent about an hour over coffee, but she was surprised to find that it passed very quickly. She was impressed by the consideration the manager showed towards herself, and the interest he had in Nat. She remembered her earlier impression of the manager's attitude, and revised her conclusion: there *was* a certain deference in the way he spoke to him. Nat seemed to have an extraordinary talent for earning respect, as well as friendship.

It was after ten when Nat got up to leave. He had hinted

Secrets of Love

Dare you unlock these pages of sensual Temptation?

Discover your own **FREE** *Gift...*

Dare you experience TEMPTATION ?

Naked love...powerful, provocative, sensual...

That is the theme of Mills & Boon's Temptation series – when the chemistry between a man and a woman is so overwhelming that they cannot resist the touch...the kiss...the embrace that sets light to the senses. And when love is ignited, every aspect of their lives changes...

Told with the candour, the honesty and realism – and the tenderness – of some of our most appreciated authors, the Temptation Experience could be for *you*.

And now you can sample FOUR FREE TEMPTATION NOVELS in your own home. Yours to keep even if you never buy a single novel!

We will also reserve a subscription for you, so that you can continue to receive four brand-new Temptation titles every month. PLUS free membership of Mills & Boon Reader Service – the privilege that brings you all the exciting benefits detailed overleaf.

It's an astonishing no-risk offer – with 2 Free Gifts!

Don't resist a moment longer – Fill in your claim card NOW!

Not just a token...
a real gift for you

This 2-part glass oyster dish is **FREE** together with a surprise mystery gift for every reader who decides to sample the Temptation Experience.

Exquisitely modelled to add a pretty touch to your sitting room, hall or bedroom – these two dishes fit together elegantly like a genuine oyster shell. Both gifts come absolutely FREE if you fill in the claim card and post it off today for your four free Temptation novels.

Yes Please send me, free and without obligation, four Temptation novels, together with my free glass dishes and mystery gift – and reserve a Reader Service subscription for me. If I decide to subscribe I shall receive four new books every month for just £5.00 – post and packing free. If I decide not to subscribe I shall write to you within 10 days. The free books and gifts are mine to keep in any case.

I understand that I may cancel or suspend my subscription at any time simply by writing to you. I am over 18 years of age.

PLEASE WRITE IN BLOCK CAPITALS   2A9T

Name_____

Address_____

_____

_____ Postcode_____

Signature _____

Are you already a Reader Service subscriber? YES ☐   NO ☐
If you are, you can still receive Temptation in addition to your existing subscription.

Yes Please send me my FOUR FREE TEMPTATION NOVELS as soon as possible, without any charges for post and packing.

Yes I would also like to receive a 2-part glass oyster dish and a surprise mystery gift.

Yes Please reserve a Reader Service subscription for me so that I can enjoy all these benefits with no obligation to purchase a minimum number of books

- free newsletter packed with author news, free competitions, previews and special book offers

- free postage and packing

- the latest titles reserved for me and delivered direct to my door

Remember, your Free Gifts and your Four Free Temptation novels are yours to keep *without obligation!*

Reader Service
FREEPOST
PO Box 236
Croydon
SURREY
CR9 9EL.

earlier that he was Suzie were going on to the disco, and the conversation had then turned to pop music and various related topics for Suzie's benefit. Earlier, when the conversation had turned on matters of business or international affairs, she had offered opinions when asked, but had tried to make sure that she drew out the two men to talk, asking questions likely to provoke interesting responses so that she could sit and listen, rather than trying to join in.

She had caught Nat's eye on her once or twice. He had given her a reassuring smile, but the look in his eyes had been thoughtful. By the time they left, she felt almost drained—she had never been required to make quite such a conscious effort before.

'I'd like to point out that you can let your hair down now,' Nat said to her in the lift, 'but as you already have, very literally, it seems unnecessary.'

She turned to him, her eyes beginning to sparkle with the sense of an ordeal over. 'Does that mean you could see "the wheels grinding round behind my eyes" in an effort to keep up with the conversation?'

He laughed, and put his hands on her arms to draw her towards him. She took a step and found herself standing only inches from him, her whole body suddenly taut once again with anticipation.

'*I* could see them, but I'm sure the manager couldn't. He's obviously totally charmed by their mysterious depths. I was expecting another offer for you any minute. You did very well.' He leant back against the side of the lift, surveying her quite coolly. 'You surprise me all the time.' His fingers slipped down her arms to take her hands in his own.

She wasn't sure what would have happened next if the lift hadn't stopped for them to get out. He waited for her to pass, and she felt his hand on her elbow, guiding her towards the steps that led down to the disco.

Since the days when Gerald used to take her out, she had been to an assortment of discos with Katrina and her friends. It was usually when Katrina needed a fourth to make up a party. Suzie had sometimes enjoyed the evening very much. Too often, however, Katrina's prospective boyfriends had

boring companions who either couldn't dance and insisted on
doing so, or who preferred to sit with a line of drinks in front
of them, shouting an occasional banal remark in Suzie's ear
over the noise from the amplifiers. Of the two, she preferred to
dance. It was something she was good at, and if she made sure
to choose only the lively ones she could keep her left-footed,
rhythm-insensitive companion at a distance for most of the
night.

Dancing with Nat, she thought ruefully, the opposite was
the problem. He was as good a dancer as she, but unless he
was playing the same trick as she had employed in the past
deliberately to keep a distance between them, then he must
genuinely like only the energetic records.

They sat down at one of the tables several times for a rest,
and Nat ordered drinks. She kept very firmly to orange juice;
she had never had so much alcohol in one night before.

As it grew later, the number of slower records increased.
They had both been dancing with rather less energy, and Suzie
had sat down gratefully for a brief rest, lying back for an
instant with her eyes shut, Nat's arm flung casually along the
back of the sofa behind her, when the disc changed and Nat
said suddenly, 'I like this one. Come and prop yourself up on
me if you're tired, and we'll go afterwards if you want to.'

She opened her eyes and smiled. 'I'm not that tired!' she
retorted, but she let him pull her to her feet.

He led her into a space among the slowly moving couples,
most of them thoroughly wrapped round each other, and drew
her gently into his arms. He held her loosely at first, obviously
aware of the sudden tension in her. Her whole body was
reacting to the light contact with his, and she was afraid to let
herself relax in case he could read too clearly the sensations
that almost overwhelmed her.

After a minute she felt his arms tighten, and he drew her
close against him. 'What are you frightened of?' he murmured,
his face against her hair. She resisted for a second longer, and
then allowed herself to yield to the persuasion of his body, her
limbs moulding themselves against his so that they moved
together. In her high heels, she found that there was not so
much difference between their heights, and they were perfectly

matched as dancers. After a while, he put his hands over hers, resting on his shoulders, and looked at her. She could see the glimmer of his eyes in the near darkness, and in the intermittent flashing of the disco lights saw the white of his teeth as he smiled. Then he caught her elbows, and made her put her arms round his neck while he pulled her even more intimately against him, his arms round her back and waist, and his thigh almost between her legs.

She was oblivious to everything but the sensation of his body against hers, his movements dictating her responses. She had never danced so intimately with a man before, alive to every inch of him, and at the same time almost overwhelmed by indefinable longings. Even with Gerald, although she had found him attractive and exciting, she had never danced quite like this.

The passage of time meant nothing to her, and one after another record passed in the same way, until they changed the tempo again, and Nat said in her ear, 'Don't go to sleep,' and slowly disengaged her clinging arms.

They danced once more, this time apart once again, the music impossibly lively. Suzie was quickly shaken out of her trance, and when the disc changed they left. They almost lay against the walls on opposite sides of the lift, before Nat fitted the key into the controls.

He was looking at her, and Suzie felt obliged to say something; the intimacy of their long dance hadn't been entirely dispelled by the brief session at the end, and she wasn't sure how to continue. Nat was giving her no cues. To break the silence, she smiled and said rather formally, 'Thank you. That was wonderful—I've never had such a good time at a disco before.'

He gave her a considering look. 'Neither have I.'

At least that made a favourable comparison with his niece for once, she told herself.

He made no movement towards her when they arrived at the apartment, but switched on a lamp in the sitting-room and said, 'Do you want the bathroom first?'

She shook her head; there was a certain awkwardness, despite his casual tone. It was difficult to forget that only minutes ago she had been in his arms, her body moving so intimately against the contours of his that they might almost have been making love.

'No,' she said abruptly. 'You're quicker than me.'

Without further discussion, he opened the bedroom door and went in.

Suzie passed the time pinning her hair up to avoid tangles when she slept, but she didn't dare get undressed in case he came out of the bathroom before she had herself decently covered. She went into the bedroom and found her kimono, but before she could delve to the bottom of her bag to find the T-shirt she normally wore in bed, Nat emerged from the bathroom, dressed in a towelling robe.

'It's all yours,' he said.

Without meeting his eye, she waited for him to pass the end of her bed, which was nearest the bathroom, busying herself with taking off her shoes, and then went in still fully dressed. She knew she was inviting some teasing remark, but he made no comment, and she shut the door and resisted the temptation to lock it. She was sure he wouldn't come in, but he would certainly laugh at her for virtually barricading herself.

She had a quick shower and cleaned her teeth, and then regretted that she had made things difficult by leaving the T-shirt unpacked. She couldn't put it on in front of him, and it would mean a very obvious withdrawal again. The alternative was to sleep in the silk kimono. She hadn't done it before, and it would mean doing the same thing the next night unless she was going to invite comment, but it really didn't matter.

She found a pair of clean lacy briefs—quickly retrieved washing from the hotel in Amman—in her sponge-bag, and slipped them on under the kimono. Its double-sided reversible silk in cream and apricot was not transparent, but its fineness clung to her body and would have revealed the fact that she was naked. She crossed the top over carefully, but couldn't find the sash. Then she opened the door of the bathroom, switching off the light behind her.

Nat was lying in bed, the sheet up to his waist, its whiteness, and the whiteness of the pillow at his back, emphasising the tan of his naked body in the subdued lighting of the bedroom.

'That's nice,' he commented.

'I made it,' she said as dismissively as she could. The awkwardness she had thought she had lost in his company was beginning to creep back. She wondered if he would think she was boasting, since he had paid her a compliment, but she had only said it as something to say. She had embroidered a Japanese pattern on the back of the silk. It had taken her a long time, but it hadn't mattered—there had often been little else to do during her evenings in the London flat.

Nat looked at her speculatively. Then he apparently took the hint that any more comments on her appearance at this stage might be unwelcome. 'You know, Suzie, you rather underestimate your talents. Why did you end up doing a secretarial course? Why didn't you go to art school or something?'

She shrugged, grateful for the moment that the conversation hadn't taken a more intimate turn. 'I wasn't good enough. You have to have a lot of flair. And anyway, it never occurred to me.'

'You could still make money out of it.'

She shook her head. 'No, I couldn't. It takes too long to finish something like this, and I couldn't sell it for enough.'

He was silent for a moment, and then he said, 'I'd guess there's a glimmering of a business brain somewhere in there.'

She laughed nervously, but they were on more familiar ground now. She could manage the teasing. 'You are silly, Nat. I was never the least good at maths.'

'I wasn't talking about maths. All right then, what about becoming a photographic model?'

'*Me?*' she almost squeaked. 'You're joking! Anyway, I'm not tall enough.'

'Yes, you are. And you've got the right sort of figure—from what I've seen of it. You're beautiful, and rather unusual. What other qualifications do you need?'

Suzie was blushing to the roots of her hair. It wasn't that she believed a word of her potential as a model, but Nat had sounded so matter of fact when he said he thought her beautiful, and everything had taken a dangerous step away from safe teasing.

'I'll introduce you to a friend of mine when we get back to London, if you like. He's a photographer, and he's worked on and off for *Vogue*.' He paused, and then shrugged. 'It may come to nothing, but you never know.'

Suzie found her voice at last. 'You seem to have friends everywhere, but I don't want to be a model. I wouldn't fit in to that sort of life.'

There was another silence, and then he asked, 'What *do* you want to do? Spend the rest of your life typing letters in a different office every week, and every evening in your flat wondering what Katrina's up to?'

She tried to sound casual in her reply, but the fact that she believed in her answer did nothing to fade the blush on her face. 'Get married, and have children.'

'And who are you going to marry? Someone romantically poor just to spite your friend Katrina, and then starve in a two-bedroomed flat for the rest of your life, with two kids and heaps of washing?'

'I'd rather starve in a two-bedroom flat with someone who's nice than live in a palace with some of the people Katrina goes out with!' she flashed at him unexpectedly. It hurt to have her ideals attacked—by anyone.

'They're not all bad, surely?'

'No, of course not. It's just that underneath they all tend to assume that money can do everything. And it can't.'

There was slight hesitation before he spoke, then Nat said slowly, 'What exactly are your objections to money, Suzie?' He was watching her.

'It's not the money-itself,' she denied hotly, as though he was trying to make a fool of her. 'Money is only so many bits of metal, or paper. It's what it does to people. It changes them, and makes them think they're important just because they've got a lot of it, and that they can buy people as well as things . . . They end up possessed by their possessions, and they don't know any longer what the real things in life are all about.'

Nat took a deep breath, and then let it out slowly. 'That's as good as a sermon,' he said quietly. 'And now, calm down, and tell me where you got all these ideas from in the first place. What makes you so anti rich men?'

Suzie swallowed hard, and sat down on the end of her bed, clutching the kimono round her. She had deliberately avoided telling him once before, but it didn't seem honest to evade it again.

'Are you—are you sure you want to hear?'

'Of course.' He sounded kind, and interested.

She stared at the floor. The silence grew harder and harder to break. She didn't know where to start. Although the pain of her mother's divorce had long healed, it had left its mark, and she had never been asked to give a coherent account of it before.

She began hesitantly, 'You never asked me anything about my family . . . even though I know something about yours.'

'I know you've got a little sister called Judy. She likes puns.'

'She's my half-sister. My stepmother, Louise, married my father when I was eight. She's a lovely person—very warm and kind and concerned about people—but I think to begin with my father was really still in love with my mother, despite everything.' She paused, 'I think he felt at the time he had to marry again for my sake . . . Of course, he was very fond of her, but it wasn't until Judy was born that we felt like a family.'

There was another silence, and then Nat asked, 'Where's your real mother?'

'I don't know any more. At first, when I was very young, she used to write a lot and send expensive presents. But she's separated now from the man she left my father for.'

'They were divorced?'

She nodded. 'My father's a solicitor, but he wan't always as comfortably off as he is now, and when they first married they couldn't afford very much. My mother was very attractive and vivacious and used to having a lot of fun—then she had me in the first year of marriage, and I suppose she got bored with looking after a house and a small child all day.

'My father told me a long time afterwards that she met David at a friend's house. He was rich and influential, and gave her a lot of the things my father couldn't. He even gave her lots of presents—jewellery and things—which she didn't show my father until one day when she just walked out. I suppose there were rows before that, but I never knew anything about them. It seemed to me that one minute she was there and then the next—just gone.'

She was aware of Nat watching her, even though her own eyes were on the hairpin she was fiddling with in her lap; it was easier to talk that way.

'And what happened after that?'

'My father agreed to a divorce. He'd tried, unsuccessfully, to make her come back, but he could see she was unhappy with him—and with the life they were leading as much as anything. Maybe he thought David really could make her happier. David used to send me presents, too. An attempt to buy my affections, I suppose—or to make up for the fact that he wouldn't let my mother take me with her, though somehow I don't think she tried very hard. Anyway, my father was determined to get custody—he really wanted me with him. I hated David's presents. I used to make Dad give them away.'

'And how do you feel about it all now?' Nat asked carefully.

'I suppose,' she said slowly, 'when I think about it, I feel sorry for my mother. In a way, she gave up love for money. She isn't even with David any longer.' Her voice was very low. 'I promised myself I'd never make that mistake.'

Nat studied her in silence, and then he said, 'Do I take it that all your comments about rich men earlier apply to David?'

'Not entirely. I did make my own mistake about someone. Once.'

'Do you want to talk about it?' he asked gently.

'No.' Gerald was very much the past. He had taught her a lesson she hadn't forgotten, but the real pain of it had long died.

Nat continued after a pause, 'Even if what you say is true of David—and this other guy—it doesn't have to apply to everyone else above the breadline.'

'Perhaps.' She knew from the tone she used that he would understand that she wasn't convinced.

There was another silence, then he gave a fleeting grin. 'You're quite stubborn when you want to be, aren't you?'

She wasn't ready to be teased. It had been an effort to give such an apparently dispassionate account of something she had rarely discussed with anyone. 'I just happen to believe that money, and wanting money, isn't a good thing, that's all!'

'All right, honey, don't get so uptight about it. I understand why you think as you do—but I still feel sorry for all the other poor rich guys who haven't got a chance. And what are all these "real things in life" you mentioned, that they don't know anything about?'

She wanted to say 'love' but she hesitated; the answer would sound too simple and stupid for someone as intelligent as Nat. She knew life wasn't as simple as that—of course it wasn't . . . And yet, when she thought of her father and stepmother, and the quiet contentment they now had with each other, and the happiness they were able to contribute to the lives of others, she knew she was right.

'They don't see people any longer in the right way,' she said at last. It amounted to the same thing. 'And it's the way you think about other people that really matters in life. Isn't it?'

'I entirely agree with you. But let's get back now to what started us off on this discussion, shall we? You want to spend your life married to a man who thinks of you in the right way—is that it? And what did you mean by "nice", Suzie? That sounds a bit tame.'

She was beginning to feel helpless and angry all at once. He was deliberately driving her into a corner, but she couldn't see why.

'I meant someone I loved!' she said defensively. 'Which means someone who isn't rich and who doesn't want to go on making more money—and then I could be sure I loved him for himself, and he loved me for myself.' The conversation was becoming agonisingly personal, and she didn't know how to change the topic, and divert him into a less dangerous course.

'So you won't let me persuade you into being a model?'

She shook her head, not trusting herself to speak.

'Come here.'

She looked at him doubtfully, but he was looking at her with no hint of that teasing grin on his face. With some hesitation she got off the end of her bed and approached him. He reached out and took her by the wrist.

'Sit down.'

Gingerly, she sat in the space he indicated, made by the curve of his body. He reached up and began to take the pins out of her hair, one by one. The heavy twists of hair fell to her shoulders and began to uncoil. Nat let the pins lie on the floor where he had dropped them, and loosened the rest of the plait, spreading her hair on her shoulders and down her back. She was acutely conscious of his physical closeness, and of the fact that he was probably naked under the covers, and concentrated all her will on keeping her head still, staring at her hands in her lap. Her heart was thudding so loudly, she was sure he must be able to hear it.

'Now look at yourself.'

She got up slowly and walked to the heavy gilt-framed mirror. The image that stared back at her was not so very different from the one she saw every day, but then, for an instant, she saw herself through new eyes—Nat's. The light fell sideways on her, highlighting the fine bones of her face and neck, and when she smiled at herself, a little embarrassed, the lips of the image curved mysteriously and the blue eyes changed with new lights. Her eyes looked enormous, and her skin, in the illumination of the bedroom, pale and translucent. The fine silk of her kimono fell sheer to her feet, except where the soft peaks of her upturned breasts lifted it. The image was at once remote and slightly seductive. She turned away, holding the edges of the silk together at her waist.

'Take that silk thing off,' Nat said suddenly.

Suzie stared at him in horror. 'I can't!' she protested. 'I haven't got anything on.'

'Yes, you have.' His reply was curt and dismissive of argument. There was no way he could see through the fabric, she knew that, but it meant that he had been studying her closely.

'Come here.'

'I wouldn't want to be the sort of model who strips,' she argued desperately, 'even if I did want to be a model.'

'Which you don't. I know.'

Despite her, her feet were taking her back to the side of the bed.

'I'm not asking you to strip,' he said. 'Sit down.'

She sat facing him, half off the edge of the bed, one foot tucked up under her, the other on the floor. He had moved back a little in the bed, and the distance between them was greater than before. He stretched across and gently slipped his fingers under the neck of the kimono, pushing it back from her shoulders. His touch awoke indefinable sensations across her skin. She held the front together with both hands, so that it revealed no more than the first hint of the swell of her breasts.

He looked at her in silence. 'It's a pity,' he said at last.

'What's a pity?' It was an effort to keep her voice steady.

'That you're not going to be a model, and all that is going to be wasted on a two-bedroom flat, two kids and the washing.'

'You've left out the husband.'

'Ah, yes. Love in a garret. Well, Suzie——' his voice suddenly deepened '—something tells me you don't know very much about garrets, despite what you've told me about the early days of your parents' marriage—and I'd be willing to swear you know even less about love.'

She was silent.

'Where's your boyfriend, that he's let you come gallivanting off like this to find yourself in bedrooms with strange men?'

'I haven't got a——' she began, and quickly decided that was a mistake. She knew he thought her inexperienced, but there was no need to give him even more ammunition. She thought of Duncan—it was certainly true he was a friend. They still corresponded. 'That is, I have, but I don't see him very often.'

'Why not?'

'We've—both got things to do and it's not very easy to meet. Anyway, I've known him for years. We don't have to see each other all the time.' She knew she was gabbling with nervousness, each attempt to explain making her list of excuses less plausible.

'No, I don't suppose you do. When *did* you last see him?'

Suzie couldn't remember offhand, but she didn't want to let Nat know that she couldn't. She said the first thing that came into her head. 'Easter.'

He grinned. 'Liar. I saw you making that up. It sounds very much to me as though things have been cooling off, and I rather wonder if they got very warm?'

She stared at him helplessly. Something was making it difficult to breathe evenly. She felt acutely nervous and full of a frightening certainty that something inevitable was going to happen. She seemed to be incapable of making any decision.

He touched her chin with his thumb, and ran it in a slow line under her jaw and down her throat to the space between her breasts where her left hand was clutching her kimono. She didn't resist when he loosened her fingers and gently pushed both her hands away, so that the silk slithered down from her shoulders to lie round her hips, partly revealing the lacy edge of the briefs that were now her only garment. The sleeves of the kimono still lay across her forearms.

She saw him looking at her breasts, at the rose-brown nipples and the creamy swell of the soft flesh, at the moulding of her ribs just under the pale skin, and at her narrow waist and the contours of her slim hips. He didn't touch her. At last his eyes sought hers.

'Lie down, sweetheart,' he said softly. 'I promise I won't do anything you don't like.'

Their eyes held for what seemed like an age, while her longing and her indecision held her paralysed beside him, and then she got off the bed to let the silk fall to the floor. He stretched out and took her hand, interlacing his fingers with hers, and drew her towards him.

Her mind was in a trance, while her body seemed to be functioning totally independently. She lay down beside him, on her back, shivering slightly; she wasn't cold, but she couldn't control the slight tremor in her limbs. She didn't know what she felt. She wasn't afraid, but she didn't think she felt desire, either. She had never experienced such sensations before.

She heard Nat's voice through a kind of haze. 'Relax.' And then she realised she had had her eyes shut. She opened them, to find his grey-green eyes watching her. He was smiling slightly and raised her hand, still clasped in his, to kiss her fingers laced through his own. Then he released her to put his hand flat on her body, just below her ribs, and gently moved it to and fro across her almost as she herself would have stroked a child, before his fingers began to explore the contours of her flesh, slowly travelling upwards between her breasts to trace the lines of her neck and shoulders. He was propped on one elbow, casually, head resting on one hand, watching her face.

Every movement was lighting little fires deep in her body, but she managed to lie without making any obvious response until he touched her breasts. She saw his eyes flick to watch the nipple harden under the slow, circling caress of his thumb, and she gave a little groan as it sent signals down her body in a way that was totally new to her. Her hips moved almost involuntarily as she repressed an overwhelming desire to arch towards him. He seemed so casual, so detached about it all, she was ashamed to show him how much he was making her feel—perhaps she wasn't supposed to react in any way like this?

He shifted his position to lie closer to her, his lips now taking over from the teasing thumb, while his hand slid down past her waist, and she couldn't repress the shiver that ran through her when he began a feather-stroke up and down the inside of her thighs. He was making no attempt to remove the lacy briefs, but seemed content to caress her gently. She wondered innocently if he felt any real desire for her. At last, half ashamed of her own all too obvious responses, she whispered, 'Stop, Nat, please. I can't bear it.' Instantly his hand was still and he raised his head to look into her eyes.

'Are you sure you're asking me to stop?' he asked quietly.

She looked at him desperately. 'Yes—I don't know. I just can't——'

He touched her face thoughtfully with one finger, and then kissed her cheek lightly. He said at last, 'If I had to make up your mind for you, I'd think you probably do mean yes—even though you mean no as well.' He was smiling at her, his eyes full of amusement.

The fires he had evoked seemed to be eating her away mysteriously, from inside. She looked at him through a cloud of longing. 'Kiss me, Nat.'

He brushed a thumbnail across her mouth. 'I just have.'

'I mean properly.'

He looked down at her. Slowly his eyes changed. There was

a desire in them that was now quite clear. 'Suzie, if I kiss you properly, then not all the yeses and nos in the world are going to stop me from taking you.' His voice sounded strange, and he gave an unsteady laugh. 'I never thought I'd be in this position—that I'd want a girl as much as I want you, and then be afraid to take her.'

'Then you do really want me?'

He brushed a strand of hair away from her face, but he didn't laugh at her. 'If you weren't so adorably innocent, you'd have found that out by now. It seems to me that that so-called boyfriend of yours wasted most of his time in your company. You've never felt like this before, have you?'

'No.' Her answer was scarcely above a whisper.

'Then I would be taking advantage of an incredibly sweet, innocent girl who's never had a man touch her like this, and doesn't know whether she wants it or not—which means, as far as I'm concerned, that she doesn't. And now I'm going to send you back to bed.'

Her whole body protested against it. She didn't know how she was going to spend the night apart from him, craving their physical contact with every nerve awake.

'No, Nat,' she begged. 'Let me stay—please! I promise I won't try to tempt you or anything——'

His laughter was an unexpected as it was genuine. 'Sweetheart, you're wonderful! You're temptation personified—and only someone as totally unaware of herself as you are could make a remark like that and mean it.' He looked down at her, the laughter lines still etched round his mouth, and put a hand on the curve of her slender waist.

Suzie couldn't know just how persuasive the mute appeal in her own eyes was.

'All right,' he said, 'Stay here—but one sexy wriggle and you're out on your backside. There's a limit to everyone's endurance, and even Sir Galahad must have had his breaking point.'

She sighed as he gathered her into his arms, fitting her body to his. Then she knew the proof of his desire, and the feel of his nakedness against her, knowing he wanted her, did nothing to quieten the turmoil in her blood—but then it seemed to her that nothing would, and at least he hadn't sent her away.

She tried to lie without movement, and to savour every precious second she was in his arms.

He spoke once more, unexpectedly, a few minutes later, his lips against her hair. 'Suzie?'

'Mm?'

'You are allowed to breathe, you know.'

CHAPTER SEVEN

SUZIE woke up suddenly and sneezed. There was bright sunshine in the room. Which room? She shut her eyes again, dazzled. Her hair was tickling her nose. She put up her hand to brush it away and heard a low chuckle beside her. An arm slid under her back and she smiled, keeping her eyes shut.

She was surprised to find that she had been asleep at all. She could only remember lying awake for hours and hours, achingly tired, and not wanting to waste one minute of the time she was in Nat's arms, her body still so strangely unsatisfied. She had thought he had fallen asleep quickly, his breathing even and deep against her. She had found herself wanting to kiss him and touch him, letting her fingers learn the texture of his skin and the contours of his body, but she had lain still. If she moved and woke him, he would send her away. Now she kept her eyes resolutely shut. If she opened them, he might get up and leave her, and she wasn't ready for that yet.

Nat . . . A finger traced the line of her lips. She didn't open her eyes. The finger travelled down the side of her face and down her neck, over the contours of her breast until it reached her thigh, and then the arm under her back and the hand under her thigh exerted a pressure suddenly that she couldn't resist and she was being rolled over towards him and pulled half on top of him. She opened her eyes to find herself staring down into the enigmatic sea-changing depths of his, and her hair was spilling down over his chest.

He was smiling. 'Good morning.'

She stared down at him, an answering smile slowly curving her lips.

'Aren't you going to say anything?' he asked plaintively.

She buried her face in his neck. 'I'm hungry.'

She could feel his laughter against her as he kissed her hair.

'If I'd known you were a vampire last night, I'd never have let you get into my bed.' Then he moved so that her head was on the pillow and he was looking down at her. 'You don't regret finding yourself in my bed, do you, Suzie? Sometimes things look a bit different in the cold light of day.' He put a finger quickly over her lips. 'I know what you're going to say, and jokes about the average Jordanian August temperatures at dawn are not what I was looking for.'

The sparkle of mischief in her eyes changed to something else, and she said seriously, 'I don't regret a single second. I'm surprised you can ask. After all, I *made* you keep me in your bed last night! I didn't leave you much choice.'

'No, sweetheart. It was I who didn't leave you much choice. I'm quite a lot older and wiser than you, and I should have known better.'

The light suddenly went out of her eyes. 'I'm sorry,' she said. Her voice was no more than a whisper.

His arms instantly tightened. 'Darling, I didn't mean I regretted it—it was what I wanted, much more than you. But you're very young, Suzie, and very sweet, and I don't want to take advantage of that.'

She kissed his chin, astonished for a moment by the roughness of the new growth of beard against her lips, and then said slowly, 'Yesterday, in the rocks, what did you think when I almost fell into your arms?'

'You *did* fall into my arms—there was no almost about it.' His voice was light and teasing again. 'I wanted to kiss you.'

'I didn't know that. But I wanted you to. Only I wasn't sure.'

'I guessed.' His lips touched her neck. 'I regretted my self-restraint afterwards, though! But shall I tell you what I'm contemplating at this very moment?'

Suzie couldn't help hoping it was kisses, but wasn't going to say so. 'What?' she asked innocently.

'Breakfast. We could have it sent up here, or we could go down to the dining-room. Or . . .'

She looked down at him speculatively. It was so wonderful being with him like this, she didn't want to get up. On the other hand, it would be embarrassing to have a waiter coming into the bedroom; it didn't occur to her until afterwards that everything could be left in the next room. 'What's "or"?' she asked hesitantly.

'Know what I'd really like to do?'

She was beginning to recognise the gleam of an idea when it appeared in his eyes. And he sounded so like a wistful boy that she was prepared to go along with anything he suggested.

'Let's ditch the luxury for a while and go and look for the cheapest breakfast we can find in the town.'

She was amused, but puzzled. 'Why? Are we just being lent the room and paying for the food, or what?'

'It's all being given to us, if you'll excuse the expression, on a plate.'

'Then why are we worried about money?'

'We're not,' he said firmly. 'I bet you I could earn the cost of a breakfast here in an hour if I had to. But all this is a bit too easy, and at least that offers some sort of challenge. It appeals to my sense of the ridiculous—and the opulence of hotels has only a limited fascination.'

'Don't you like it here?' she asked, disappointment in her voice.

'My sweet, I've never enjoyed a luxury hotel so much in my life.'

He sounded perfectly sincere, and she said in a tone of mock accusation, 'That sounds as though you've stayed in dozens. I thought computer engineers were supposed to be poor!'

'We get expenses,' he said non-committally, and then countered, 'I thought you were the one who wasn't supposed to be interested in what money can buy! And just how many luxury hotels do you think you're going to get to stay in when you're married to your garret and two point four children?'

She wouldn't answer. She couldn't tell him that it was not the hotel that mattered to her—it was him. But she wasn't so naïve as to imagine that, just because he had taken her into her bed, he had fallen in love with her.

He watched her eyes, and then lifted his head briefly from the pillow to touch his lips against hers. 'Think about it, sweetheart,' he murmured against them. And then lay back for a few moments, watching her, before he rolled her over on to her back. 'Come on. It's still very early. Let's get up and have my breakfast, and then if you're still hungry we'll have yours and order everything they've got on the menu.'

Idly, one hand had been sliding up and down over the line of her hip to her thigh in a leisurely caress. It was already having its effect upon her, but she was too unsure of herself to ask him to stay with her any longer. Instead she smiled up at him. There would, after all, be another night.

Both of them dressed casually in jeans and shirts, Suzie with hers hanging loosely outside her waistband and her hair all over her shoulders, wandered through Aqaba until Nat found some likely looking back streets. There he also found a grey-bearded Arab making a pot of coffee in a room stacked with crates, boxes and battered items of household furniture, and entered into conversation with him.

It wasn't long before they were offered small cups of the thick, dark, aromatic blend favoured by the Arabs, and some bread and goat's milk yoghurt were produced for them. Then an elderly transistor radio appeared from underneath a pile of cardboard boxes, and predictably Nat had the back off it, and was doing things to its insides. He looked up to catch Suzie's eye and winked, and she thought of the bedouin tent, and the way they had worked together over the sewing machine, and then how, with uncharacteristic daring, she had sewn his cuffs together afterwards. There was no interested audience now; only the old Arab producing bits of wire and a soldering iron on request from the jumbled confusion of his back room.

By the time they took their leave, with smiles and exchanged courtesies in Arabic, Nat had parted with no money. He took her hand.

'Know what I want to be when I grow up?' They were making their way through the back streets again.

'I couldn't possibly guess.' She couldn't repress a smile.

'A tinker. Wandering about mending things. It seems to be a very good life. Beats a lot of what I do now, anyway.'

'I thought you liked being a computer engineer.'

'The engineering bits, and the travel. But that's not all there is to it.'

She looked at him, but said nothing. Then after a pause, she began, 'You know, that breakfast *did* cost something.'

'What?'

'Your time, for one thing.'

He laughed. 'You see? You have got a business brain lurking there somewhere. But it doesn't apply at the moment. I'm on holiday.'

She tried another track. 'How much does Arab bread cost?'

He shrugged. 'A few pence.'

'And yoghurt?'

'The same.'

'Then it was a very expensive breakfast—much more than the hotel. Your training and skills are worth a great deal more than a few pence, whether you're officially working or not.'

'Ah, but that was fun, not work. It didn't count.' He stopped and put an arm round her waist, turning her to face him and tilting her chin. He was grinning at her again. 'It's worth it just to have you arguing with me.'

'You mean you like to see the wheels grinding round behind my eyes?'

'You're not going to forget that, are you? No, I just mean you're full of surprises. You look so beautifully meek and biddable most of the time, but you're really quite stubborn once you get an idea into your head, aren't you? What you're really telling me is that I lose the breakfast competition, and you want to go back and have another one.'

She grinned back at him. 'Not exactly—but I do like their orange juice.'

On the way back to the hotel he bought her a necklace of roughly cut beads of local white coral from a street stall. When she protested, he argued, 'It cost the equivalent of *one pound*. You can't say that's extravagant, even if it is our joint survival fund I'm spending.'

Somehow the topic of money stayed with them, until Nat was reminded of his earlier boast and couldn't resist the challenge

'I bet you I *could* earn the cost of a hotel breakfast. Want to take the bet?'

'Nat, you couldn't!' She didn't intend it as a challenge, but he certainly wasn't going to interpret it as a prohibition.

'If you win, I'll . . .' he paused for thought '. . . take you to the best restaurant in London when we get home. And if I win you can give me a kiss.'

'But that's ridiculous!' she exclaimed. 'There's no comparison between them.'

'Oh? I thought I was getting off quite lightly—and you don't know yet what sort of kiss I have in mind. You'd better hope that you win!'

They set no time limit on it, and the only condition was that she shouldn't wait around to watch him do it: he insisted he had to feel free to explore any opportunity. She made her way slowly back to the hotel to wait for him, no longer worried by the thought that she was alone in hostile territory. The very thought of Nat's existence gave her a confidence she had never felt before.

She decided to sunbathe on the balcony of their suite until he appeared. She scanned the beach once or twice, in case he had thought of selling ice-cream, or minding deckchairs—she wouldn't now be surprised to see him doing either—but there was no one even remotely resembling a tallish, sun-blonde Englishman in stonewashed jeans and a striped shirt.

It was lunch time before he returned. Suzie, in a yellow bikini and a loose shirt draped over her shoulders, was lying on a sun lounger half asleep. She started when he balanced a pile of coins on her bare stomach. He stood back, hands on hips, watching her.

'How did you get it?' she asked. She couldn't deny he had won the bet, but counted it ostentatiously on to the table beside her, wondering if he'd ask for immediate payment. Just the thought of it caused a tiny tremor of anticipation to run through her body. But he seemed to have forgotten it, and ignored her question.

'Let's have lunch, and this time we'll indulge your newly discovered taste for luxury and eat in the hotel.'

It was later that she found out how Nat had spent the morning. He led her by a devious route to the beach, and she guessed the instant the boatman greeted him as an old friend. No money changed hands, but almost immediately they were clambering into a little fibre-glass craft, and Nat was starting up the outboard and heading them away from the shoreline. The boat, to Suzie's delight, had a flat bottom, into which was fitted a huge sheet of glass material.

'It was too easy, really,' Nat explained. 'I persuaded him he wanted an assistant, and agreed to work for half the fare. He has two boats with an outboard motor fitted, and a few old tubs with oars. He doesn't trust the tourists with these, and his boy had knocked off for a few hours. Between the two of us we did quite a trade with a party of American tourists. I even offered myself as an English-speaking guide, and then gave him the tips. In gratitude, he's lending us this for the afternoon.'

Being in the boat was like floating over the sea in a diving mask, once Nat has switched off the outboard and let them drift. The water was a translucent turquoise, and between them and the sea was a layer of thick Perspex which enabled Suzie to lie at her ease, on her stomach between the thwarts, staring straight down into the sea. The dinghy was too small for her to stretch out fully if she wanted to look through the glass, and she lay casually tapping her heels together, propped on her elbows. The bottom of the boat was cold against her stomach and thighs, and her back felt hot in the sun. She had taken her shirt off, and was thinking of making it into an impromptu pillow across her forearms, so that she could lie there staring straight down into the sea.

Nat was sitting in the stern, and at last prompted by her enthusiastic comemntary got up to join her.

'Come on, move over. I've decided to abandon trying to control this thing. If we bump into a tanker, lying on the bottom of this like a couple of stranded sardines in full view of the crew, it'll be your fault for distracting me.' He gave her a playful smack on the bottom, and when she moved sideways lay like her on his stomach with his feet in the air, forehead resting on his folded arms, staring straight down.

Below them, the colours of the fishes were like all the hues of the sun—golds and yellows glinting as they twisted lithe bodies through an element as clear as air. The coral grew in white-branched forests, like stunted trees, dead and still as the fish darted in and out like curious, aquatic birds.

Suzie was only too aware of Nat beside her, and of the fact that as yet they hadn't mentioned the loss of the bet. She had been too shy to suggest paying him the kiss earlier, and he had made no reference to it during lunch. Since their intimacy of the night before, he seemed to have reverted to treating her with his former casual playfulness, and had made no attempt to follow it up.

They started to play 'I Spy', Suzie indulging in the silliness of the game almost as a distraction from Nat himself. The boat drifted gently, and he lifted his head to glance up occasionally to check their position, in between sessions of mutual cheating. Then once, when she protested that she couldn't see anything like an angel-fish in the blue world under them, and that 'a' wasn't fair, he put a hand on the back of her neck, pretending to turn her head so that she could see it clearly. The contact sent something once again like an electric current running through her body—he had only to touch her to ignite the little atoms of fire that had been floating through her veins ever since the night before. She tensed slightly, and he obviously sensed the change in her.

'What's the matter?'

'Nothing.' Her breath came suddenly much less easily, and when he moved his hand lightly down to caress the back of her neck it wasn't just her neck but her whole back, her whole body that was nerve-rackingly alive to his fingers. Every thought of their silly game flew right out of her head, and she was aware only of the sensation of his fingers at her nape, and when he trailed them absently down her spine it took every ounce of control left in her body not to shiver with anticipation.

She stared fixedly down through the bottom of the boat, seeing nothing, and determined not to let him know what he was doing to her.

'Suzie?'

'Mm?' She still couldn't trust herself to look at him. He would see her desire in her eyes too clearly.

His fingers had reached her waist, moving gently over the contours of her spine. 'There's a little matter of a debt since this morning—remember?'

'Mm?' She still couldn't look up.

'Well, I've decided to collect it now, with half the crew of the tanker we're just about to bump into watching us.'

She did look up then, with a little squeak, to find that they were some way out the bay and still a long distance from any of the dark shapes at anchor further out to sea.

Then she looked at Nat. There was the inevitable amusement in his eyes and a speculative smile on his face as he watched her, but behind the humour there was something else—a look she hadn't seen previously, even in bed when he had let her know that he wanted her.

Then, with an assurance she had never shown before, she reached out to touch his face, turning on to her side and letting her fingers trace the line of his cheekbone. 'I don't like being in debt,' she said unevenly. 'Even to people who play tricks on me and don't deserve to be paid.'

They were very close. Slowly he propped himself up on one elbow and reached out to touch her shoulder, and then, as she lay back again on the bottom of the boat, half turned towards him, very slowly so that she was aching for the moment his lips touched hers, he bent his head. Gently, he brushed her cheek with his mouth, and then her forehead and then her closed eyelids. Apart from the light touch of his lips and his hand on her shoulder, there was no contact yet, but she felt her limbs melting, and a strange, pleasurable warmth invading her thighs and beginning to pulse through her body.

His hand slid from her shoulder down her side to her waist, and as he leaned towards her, his body making contact with hers, she could feel the glass cold beneath her. The boat rocked slightly and she reached up to slip one arm round his neck and the other round his back to draw him closer, caressing his smooth, naked flesh, heated by the sun.

They were both lying full length now, their feet under the thwart in the stern, and it was as though they were lying on the sea itself; there was nothing below them but depths of blueness and the weird forest of corals with their silent birds flitting to and fro in the branches. Suzie felt as though she was floating in another world, as the man she now knew she loved—crazy, teasing, unpredictable Nat, now driving her into an agony of desire with every touch of his lips—traced the contours of her face and neck with his mouth until she thought she would cry with longing.

His lips met hers at last, almost hesitantly, as though he were testing for her reaction, and then their subtle movement became more insistent, and she felt his hand slide up between their bodies, over her breast to the column of her throat. The pressure of his thumb on the side of her face caused her to turn to him yet more invitingly, parting her lips to admit the gentle thrust of his tongue. She felt him pulling the strings of her bikini top behind her neck to loosen them, and then he moved his hand round the fastening under her back. The clasp slipped apart easily in his fingers, and she felt them trail in a tantalising caress across her skin to push aside the flimsy material that covered her breast. Within seconds she was almost naked in his arms, half crushed by his weight. She could feel the contours of his body against hers—the moulding of his ribs, the taut flatness of his stomach and the powerful thighs against her own.

She wanted the kiss never to end, and when he shifted his weight away from her she slipped her hand up his neck, into his hair, to keep him from drawing apart, only to find that the renewed caress of his hand moving gently down her body was awakening further sensations in her, making her want to writhe in his arms. When his hand slid under the thin fabric of her bikini briefs, she shivered and pressed against him, responding to the sudden urgency of his kiss.

Then, without warning, he broke away from her, severing the contact between their bodies. Suzie wondered what she'd done, and half sat up, dazed, her body taut with desire.

'Nat?' she said tentatively.

He too was half sitting, partly turned away from her so that she couldn't see his face. He was breathing quickly, and ran a hand through his hair as she spoke. 'Consider the debt paid,' he said, and without warning stood up and dived over the side. The boat rocked violently, and Suzie, realising she was only half-clad, felt for her bikini top and sat up to put it on. She felt dizzy with the sudden switch from an almost total abandonment of desire.

A long-fingered hand appeared over the gunwhales, and then Nat's head and shoulders emerged beside the boat. He pushed back the wet hair from his eyes and looked at her, unexpectedly serious.

'I'm sorry. I shouldn't have done that. Come for a swim—only mind the coral. It's bloody sharp.' Without waiting for her to make up her mind, he dived again and she watched him swim under the boat to tap on the glass panel and pull a face at her before swimming away. She hesitated, and then dived over the side to join him.

The cold water was a shock to her sun-heated limbs, and the tension between herself and Nat quickly ebbed away as they alternately dived towards and floated over the banks of coral some way beneath them. Once or twice he swam up under her, and tugged at her ankle, pulling her down suddenly to come up spluttering beside him. Then once she turned underwater to swim to the surface only to find him looming over her, his eyes looking straight down into hers, and she twisted to slide out from under him. She was too close to the coral for much manoeuvring and grazed her arm along one of the still white branches as she slipped away. The water instantly clouded with a thick dark stain, and she shot to the surface to find the blood streaming scarlet from a shallow cut down the side of her forearm. The wound looked far more dramatic than it felt, although it was undeniably painful, but Nat instantly surfaced and climbed into the boat, to pull her up over the side.

'I don't seem to be doing very well today,' he said, his face full of concern. 'That was my fault for creeping up on you. Here, wrap that round it until we get back to the hotel.'

Suzie looked at his shirt in consternation. 'That's far too good to get covered with blood—I'll use mine.'

'Wear yours,' he said, and then gave her a sideways smile. 'That bikini'll be the undoing of more men than me. We'll probably have to run the gauntlet of the entire hotel staff in their concern for you.'

He had already put on his jeans over the wet trunks and had started the outboard. Reluctantly, Suzie slipped on her own loose shirt, dripping blood dramatically as she did so, and then wound the fine cotton shirt round her arm.

Their appearance in the hotel was met with concern by the receptionist, and a few interested attendants, while Nat asked for a medical kit to be sent up to their room, but they managed to avoid further publicity. One of the staff operated the lift for them, a little unnecessarily, and accompanied them to the door of their suite where Nat firmly dismissed him, declining all further offers of assistance.

'He was hoping you'd faint from pain, and I'd faint from the sight of blood, so that he could leave me lying in the lift and carry you into your bedroom,' Nat joked, pushing her into the bathroom. 'You could see it written all over his face.' He unwound the shirt carefully, and put her arm under the tap so that the water streamed down a dark pink, and Suzie thought if anyone was going to faint from the sight of blood it would be her. She already felt slightly sick.

The first-aid kit arrived with commendable speed in the hands of one of the hotel guests who claimed to be a doctor. He was charming and efficient, and persuaded Suzie that it was no trouble to him to be whisked into the lift as he passed the reception desk on his way to the beach, to bandage the arm of a charming young lady who might be pale from shock, but couldn't yet be pale from loss of blood. The cut, despite appearances, was indeed superficial.

She had never been prescribed brandy before as a treatment —nor, of course, had she ever been treated by an Arab doctor in shorts, who, by the time he left, had invited both Nat and herself to dine with him in the hotel that evening.

'It's your talent for making friends again,' she accused Nat weakly when the doctor had gone, but he shook his head.

'Not guilty this time. That was all your doing. It's your big blue eyes—he couldn't resist them. Now go and put some clothes on. I'm not going to let you drink brandy half-naked. Goodness knows what ideas it'll put into your head.'

The brandy made her feel tired, and she spent the rest of the afternoon, respectably dressed in jeans and an unbloodied shirt, sleeping on her bed. Nat stayed with her until she fell asleep. He looked unusually serious, but he didn't say anything. She was alone when she woke.

The prospect of dining with the Arab doctor didn't fill her

with as much apprehension as it might have done. She had rather liked him, and with Nat there as well the evening might be very enjoyable. In a way she couldn't fully explain to herself, she preferred it to the prospect of another intimate dinner alone with Nat. After what had happened in the boat, tension would inevitably build up between them and she didn't now know what to expect from him.

By the time Nat returned, she had showered and washed her hair somewhat cautiously, taking into account her bandaged arm. She had put on one of her only two dresses, a plain black sleeveless cotton jersey with a low back, and her high-heeled sandals. She had decided to put her hair up, hoping to make herself look a little older. She was standing by the window with a magazine in her hands when he opened the sitting-room door. He made no comment on her appearance but crossed slowly to the window to stand beside her, taking the magazine from her to toss it on a nearby table. He raised both hands to her face, and ran his thumbs along the line of her jaw, tilting her chin. She met his eyes, a question in her own.

'Are you all right?' He sounded full of concern. 'You were very pale when I left you.'

'I was asleep.' It was no sort of explanation, but he smiled.

'You were still very, very pale.'

He didn't touch her again, and, even after a friendly and very successful dinner with their new doctor friend, he kept his distance from her on their return to their hotel suite. It was late, and Suzie wondered if she ought to go to bed. She stood for a while on the terrace, but Nat didn't join her, and after some time she went back inside, closing the doors behind her. She wasn't tired—her afternoon sleep had effectively dealt with her fatigue. Nat was sprawled on the sofa with a two day old copy of the *Financial Times*. He glanced up at her.

'Your turn for the bathroom first tonight, only mind where you drip the blood.'

She smiled, but didn't have the courage to argue about his suggestion and went into the bedroom to change. She took as long as she could over undressing and washing; there wasn't much point in having another shower and risking the bandage getting wet again. She combed her hair and put on her kimono. She no longer felt shy about Nat, even though he had never seen her completely naked, but she didn't want him to think that just because they had shared a bed the previous night—and whatever he said she *had* virtually forced him into it—she expected the same thing to happen tonight. He had shown her twice that although he desired her, he wasn't prepared to make love to her. Not, of course, that the boat had been ideal—she couldn't help wondering what would have happened if they had been in a more private place, the hotel bedroom perhaps.

She got out a nail file to smooth the edges of nails that were already perfect, and then decided to retrieve her magazine from the sitting-room. At least if she had to lie awake in bed she could have something to read. She regretted having slept that afternoon. It wouldn't make things any easier to know that Nat was in a bed only a few feet away from her, and that the previous night she had been lying there with him. She debated on the wisdom of going back into the sitting-room, and then decided that he surely couldn't think she was trying to entice him if she just went in quickly for her magazine and then left. The alternative was to get into bed and pretend to be asleep—and he would know she wasn't.

Nat didn't look up as she entered, but as she bent to pick it up she heard him shake the pages of his newspaper and fold them. Only that morning she had thought that what was going to happen was somehow inevitable, and that there was no way they could avoid the ultimate expression of the desire that had been created between them, like a magnetic force ever increasing in strength to draw them together. Now it was as though he had switched into another gear. He seemed reluctant to touch her, and although the attraction was still there, it was overlaid by a certain restraint—almost a withdrawal—that she was finding hard to bear. On the surface he was as friendly as ever, but since the episode in the boat it was as though he had deliberately distanced himself from her. When she turned round he had put the paper down and was looking at her. They were almost on opposite sides of the room, and it somehow expressed the gulf that seemed to have opened between them.

She was astonished then, when he said matter-of-factly, 'You know what nearly happened in the boat today. If you and I are in the same bed tonight, it *will* happen. Are you sure it's what you want?'

Her heart seemed to skip a beat. She had been telling herself that he didn't want it; and now his offer was almost cold-blooded.

'Yes.' Her voice was scarcely audible, but she was determined to match his detached sophistication if she could.

'And what about love in a garret, and your two point four children?' he insisted.

She knew she couldn't expect men like Nat to marry her—she wasn't that naïve. He had had women before, and, although she knew nothing about the relationships, she had understood that some of them had been pretty casual. But for her, no matter what the consequences, there had to be a basis of truth between them. Perhaps you didn't tell someone as sophisticated and experienced as he was, no matter how nice, that you loved him, but she was honest and she wasn't a coward. She felt an ache in her throat and swallowed hard. He must know how she felt anyway; he wasn't stupid. He was also kind and perceptive, and he wouldn't want to hurt her.

Her heart was pounding against her ribs, but her face, although she didn't know it, drained of all colour. She took a deep breath.

'Nat——' It was so hard to say what she had to with that terrible distance between them. She felt ridiculous—he had been so cool about it—but she had to go on. 'All that—my ideas about what you call the garret and the washing—it hasn't changed, but it's in the future. It may never happen . . .' She faltered, and then nerved herself to continue. That had been the easy part. 'It's you I want now. Not some unreal man who's still only a dream and might never be anything else. I love you.'

Perhaps the curiously dispassionate tone of her words or the unexpected pragmatism of her views surprised him. He stared at her across the width of the room, and for what seemed an eternity neither of them moved. Oh, God, she thought, perhaps he doesn't like what I've said. He doesn't want schoolgirl declarations—it was stupid to tell him.

At that moment she reached some sort of emotional crisis. The strain of his silence was more than she could bear, and it had taken more than she knew to nerve herself for that apparently calm, rational declaration. She did nothing to stop the tears sliding down her face, but turned away in a futile attempt to hide them.

She didn't quite know how it happened, but within seconds she was being lifted in his arms and held against him with such strength she could scarcely breathe. Then she was being carried and gently put down on a bed. She clung to him, desperately needing the reassurance of his touch, but he seemed to have no intention of leaving her.

It was the second time she had cried in his arms, but the first had been the aftermath of fear, and relief, and had been no more than a child's grief in comparison. This time the pain of her tears was gradually mingled with something else as he held her against him, gently caressing her, kissing her face and her neck with half-articulate endearments that she was scarcely aware of. The silk kimono fell apart under his hands, and what had at first meant no more than the comforting that could be given to a child became the adult caresses, perhaps unconsciously but skilfully given, to arouse desire. The recent emotion was slowly engulfed by a renewed and terrifying physical need, so that when he broke away from her suddenly, the torment in her veins forced her to plead, 'Don't stop, please, not this time . . .' She was scarcely aware of him pulling the kimono from under her, and then the bedcovers, so that she was lying stretched out on the sheet. When his body finally covered hers, he was naked and the feel of his limbs against hers told her that this time his lovemaking wasn't going to end the way it had before.

Afterwards, as she lay in his arms, he stroked the hair back from her face and asked, 'Did I hurt you?'

She turned her head to look at him. The grey-green eyes were full of such concern she was tempted to lie. Instead, she smiled and put her finger against his lips. 'Sssh,' she said. 'I love you.' Yes, it had hurt, but in a way she had desired. And the latent fires were still there in her body, although for the moment strangely appeased.

His arms tightened round her, and he pulled her down to lie with her head buried in his shoulder. He was silent for a few moments, stroking her back almost absentmindedly, and then he said slowly, 'Suzie, I wanted to tell you something before we made love, but everything happened so quickly just now, I couldn't. We've got to talk about this——'

Again she laid a finger against his lips, and raised her head from his shoulder to look at him There was a half-anxious expression in his eyes, and suddenly she felt much older than him, and protective in a way that was almost maternal. It didn't matter that he didn't love her, if that was what he felt he had to say. He hadn't promised her anything, or lied to her, and perhaps love was always unequal. It didn't matter just now. And whatever he had to say wouldn't change the way she felt about him; she knew now she would always love him, and if that mythical garret didn't one day hold Nat, then it would hold no one. But it was too soon to break the spell they had just woven together.

'Not now, Nat,' she said gently. 'Now everything's perfect. We don't need explanations yet—don't let's spoil it. Wait until later.'

And later, much later, when everything in her life suddenly seemed to have fallen to pieces, Suzie remembered those words, and couldn't believe she had ever said them.

CHAPTER EIGHT

ON HER own, Suzie would have arrived at the airport hours too early, irrationally afraid that she would miss the flight, but being with Nat changed everything. Somehow, he managed to alter his own flight arrangements so that he could travel with her. His casual attitude dictated as late as possible a start, so that the bags could be checked in straight away, and very little time need be spent idling in a relatively small and unexciting terminal.

They had stayed at the flat until the last possible moment after tidying the rooms they had used and packing. Suzie had watered the plants and then wandered about aimlessly, looking at her watch, until Nat had pulled her down on to the sofa and teased her and tantalised her until she forgot all about the time, and their flight. Then a ring at the door had called her reluctantly back to reality and the realisation that it was probably Fahad, ready to drive them to the airport and to recover his jeep.

She was still pinning up her hair when Nat showed him into the sitting-room, and his knowing smile as she shook hands told her that he had guessed what the relationship between herself and Nat had become. Her hand went automatically to finger the coral necklace that Nat had given her.

Once at the airport, they delayed going through to the departure area. The flight had been announced as over half an hour late, and it was more amusing to sit and chat with Fahad than to wait with the other passengers. Looking at Fahad she wondered how she could ever have been scared of him. His once predatory features were now handsome to her, and there was no threat in his smile or his eyes, just friendliness and good humour. It was strange the way fear could influence judgement: it seemed incomprehensible now that she could ever have mistaken Fahad, let alone Nat. Petra and its remembered threat was a world away from her. She was going back to London, to her friends and to her job, with a whole new context to her life. She wasn't even going to spend the night in her own flat, but in Nat's. She wondered what Katrina would say when she phoned her from there.

She was smiling at Fahad, only half listening to what he was saying, aware all the time of Nat in the chair he had pulled up beside her, his knee touching hers, when a young man, obviously English and wearing a well-cut business suit and dark tie despite the heat, approached them. He was carrying two briefcases, one rather larger than the other. His manner suggested urgency, but there was a certain deference also as he approached Nat; it was something she only identified later.

'Mr Laird? Thank goodness we've traced you, sir. I'm sorry, but we've had to cancel your arrangements. We tried to get a telex through to you, but no one knew for certain where you were.' He smiled vaguely at Suzie, his mouth suitably curved into a meaningless greeting.

Nat's expression was one she had never seen on his face before, and his eyes sparked with an unfamiliar light. His glance was not directed at Suzie, but it caused her to catch her breath as a cold little shock registered through her—it was like a sudden warning, a very effective bursting of her little bubble of complacent security. It told her that she did not yet know Nat, despite the fact they were lovers. It scared her a little. She hoped fervently he would never have cause to look at her like that.

The young man, obviously cowed by Nat's reception of him, produced a computer print-out which he handed to him.

Nat flicked his eyes over it quickly, and then crushed it into the pocket of his short leather jacket, getting up as he did so. He moved away from herself and Fahad, but despite the precaution was still partially within earshot. It was the first time she had heard him swear.

There was a brief exchange, too indistinct to follow, and then she heard him say, 'Why the hell can't you send someone else?'

The young man's reply was painfully apologetic. 'That takeover bid really has put the cat among the pigeons, sir.

And they can't do a thing without your decision. The whole situation is pretty delicate and needs careful negotiation. We've got a plane waiting.' He cleared his throat nervously. 'Whenever you're ready, sir.'

A curt instruction from Nat caused the young man to withdraw, discretion written all over him. She didn't see where he went, because her eyes were now wholly on Nat. There was a tension in his athletic body and a steely look in his eyes she had only ever glimpsed before.

She didn't know what was going to happen, but it was obvious that something had gone wrong. A tiny butterfly was fluttering somewhere in her stomach; she didn't know how to react to this new Nat, and was glad his anger, if that was what it was, wasn't directed against herself. But when he put his hands on her shoulders, giving her a brief kiss, and then drew her into his arms, she told herself she had been imagining things; mixed with the inevitable responses of her body to his was something like relief.

'Darling, I can't fly back with you,' he was saying, his lips in her hair. She could smell the woody tang of his aftershave. He kissed her ear. 'Something has cropped up with the damned company. I've got to go on to Dubai first, and then I'm flying to Washington tomorrow. I don't know how long it's going to take, but I'll ring you as soon as I can.' He held her away from him to look into her eyes. 'This is just about the worst time, as far as I'm concerned, that anything like this has ever happened. I hate leaving you.'

'Don't be silly, Nat,' she said more positively than she felt. 'If the company sends you somewhere, you have to go. It's your job. I understand.'

He started to say something. 'Suzie, it's not——' And then he broke off.

She gave a warm smile. 'I'm perfectly capable of getting home on my own, you know!'

His lips twitched. The sea-change eyes were enigmatic. 'Are you indeed?' His words were teasing, but his voice had an unsteady roughness to it that she was beginning to recognise. Their eyes held for a moment, and he said quickly, 'I'll ring you.' Then, her lips parting eagerly under his, he kissed her with the kind of urgency he had let her know only the last time they had made love. It scared her and excited her all at once; it was too easy to lose herself. He could melt her body and weld it to his so easily, and his touch instantly created for her their own private world. For a moment she forgot where she was.

Then he was gently disengaging her clinging arms and, holding her casually against him while he spoke to Fahad over her shoulder, gave her time to recover the poise he knew very well he had just destroyed.

'Look after her for me, Fahad. See she gets the flight—she's too young to be trusted out on her own! We'll both see you in London before long—if not sooner.' He pushed Suzie away from him, quite gently, and shook hands with Fahad, who was smiling and making some suitably light-hearted reply.

The young man reappeared, and was now hovering at the entrance to the passport control and hand baggage check. Nat slipped a hand round Suzie's waist and brushed her cheek with his lips, before giving her a mischievous grin.

'Something to remember me by,' he said, and pinched her bottom. Before she had time to react, he was gone.

Blushing, she caught Fahad's eye. He had seen all too clearly Nat's parting gesture, and was laughing at her openly.

'I think perhaps you've changed your mind since Petra?' he asked good-humouredly.

She gave a half-smile. 'Nat's a rather unusual person.'

'Crazy,' Fahad agreed, pointing to his forehead in the traditional gesture. 'But clever crazy. There's more to Nat than meets the eye—as you say in England.'

'What do you mean?' she asked, her mind only half following the conversation. She was thinking of an Arab market, and the first time Nat had kissed her.

'He's not just an ordinary engineer. I know some, and they are not like Nat. What was he talking about just now—when the guy with the briefcase turned up?'

'I'm not sure. The man who was with him said something about a takeover—and about decisions. I don't think I understood.'

Fahad shrugged impatiently. 'Neither did I—if he's a computer engineer. They are like the men who come to mend your television. Are they the people who make decisions about their company? The people who do that are the directors, and the majority shareholders.'

Suzie laughed, and didn't pursue the topic. She had no idea what Nat had been talking about, although Fahad's words seemed to make sense: a mere computer engineer's decision on a takeover bid? But why should Nat lie about himself? It didn't make sense. With half her mind she was already trying to work out how many hours it would be before she would see him again.

Fahad took her hand when they eventually said goodbye, and kissed it with elaborate courtesy. She waved to him as she was clear of the baggage check, and sailed through passport control on a cloud several inches above the ground. Suddenly her world seemed full of romance; the holiday that had very nearly been a disaster had turned out to be the most eventful few days of her life.

On the flight back to London she went over again and again her last twenty-four hours with Nat. They had started the long drive back to Amman quite late, so that they could spend as long as possible in the hotel suite, and far away from the reminder that the holiday, for both of them, was about to end. He had shown no impatience this time with the luxury of his surroundings, nor any desire to find interest outside the four walls of thier bedroom. They had slept late and ordered up breakfast to please Suzie, and eaten what little they had wanted of it while still in bed. Nat had not made love to her again then, but had held her in his arms, and kissed her and caressed her until they had both forgotten the time. Suzie remembered her romantic daydreams about being in bed with him; the dreams had fallen far short of the reality.

It was late when they had finally returned to Amman, and Nat had insisted on picking up take-away hamburgers on the way back to the flat.

'You can cook when we get back to London if you're that keen on it,' he had replied to her protests. 'And anyway, we'll have them in memory of our first meal together.'

She had thought of the way they had eaten their hamburgers in the street that first time, and of offering him hers to finish, enjoying the casual friendliness that had existed between them at a stage when she was still unsure of him, and more especially of herself. She was glad that he had thought it worth the memory.

Now, as she thought about the unique combination of humour, kindness, intelligence—and unexpected passion—that had stolen her heart, she knew, with a sort of detached certainly, that she could never love anyone again as she loved Nat.

He still had all her Jordanian money, but she had a return ticket from Heathrow to central London, and enough change to get home on the tube. She and Katrina shared a top-floor flat in an old town house in the Chalk Farm area. The houses had once been impressive, but the district had become run-down, and the rows of four-storey terraces, all with paint peeling from their walls, was depressing to come back to. Still, Katrina had originally been lucky to find a two-bedroomed flat for which the rent was not too high.

It was no surprise to Suzie to find a collection of dirty dishes on the kitchen table, and a clutter of ashtrays and a couple of wine-glasses in the living-room when she finally got home. It meant at least that Katrina was back from wherever it was Bob had whisked her off it. Suzie had cleared away everything before they had left for Jordan.

Katrina was probably at work, and Suzie secretly felt relieved. She was still caught up in an unreal dream, and had to force herself to concentrate on the chores in front of her. Also, with one part of her mind she was already hoping that she might hear from Nat. She knew it was too soon—he was probably caught up with whatever crisis had taken him from the airport—but she kept wondering. She had given him her telephone number written on a large piece of writing paper when they were packing.

The likelihood that he would ring her later that evening forced her out to do some shopping, after a quick, depressing survey of the fridge and cupboards. She didn't linger over it, and spent the rest of the day washing her holiday clothes and cleaning the flat, doing Katrina's ironing for her in the process. She didn't feel like eating, and it helped to have something to occupy her; at the back of her mind there was always the thought of Nat. She wasn't sure of her calculations of the time difference, but guessed there must be at least two hours between London and Dubai, if not more, and when she started watching television later that evening was aware, with every hour that passed, that in Dubai it must be even closer to the time he would ring her.

She thought idly once or twice of her conversation with Fahad, and wondered what it was that had taken Nat away from her so unexpectedly. She wondered too about the deference the dark-suited man had shown in addressing him; perhaps Nat was more important than she had realised. Then she smiled to herself as she thought of her first sight of him, in Arab head-dress—or later in a bedouin tent, letting her make a fool of him by sewing his cuffs together.

It was half-past eleven when she heard Katrina's key in the lock. There were no voices—for once Katrina was alone.

'Suzie, is that you?' Katrina came in backwards, a large cardboard box in her arms, an expensive handbag perched on top. 'Be a darling and shut the door, would you? I nearly dropped this on the stairs.'

Katrina was about Suzie's height, with straight, blonde, shoulder-length hair and wide hazel eyes. She had undeniably striking looks, and, although a little more heavily built than the younger girl, dressed and walked to show off her figure to advantage. She usually contrived to acquire a tan, even in winter, either by carefully spaced holidays, or judicious use of a sunlamp, and her looks, combined with her open effervescent manner, ensured that she was never short of interested young men.

Suzie was very pleased to see her. She had been feeling more depressed with every passing minute; whatever his reasons, Nat's failure to ring her was a disappointment.

'What on earth have you got?' she asked, extracting Katrina's keys from the front door before she closed it. Their lobby was about three feet square, and took one line of clothes hooks and no more.

'It's an ice-bucket—Bob bought it for me in Harrods today.

Oh, Suzie, he's *so* nice! He just never stops buying me presents. That sounds awful—but you know what I mean. I've just been out to dinner with him.' She was unwrapping the packaging as she spoke. 'Gosh, this is gorgeous. You know, Bob's so funny—he thinks Harrods is the only shop in London. I suppose it's the only one he's heard of, being an American. That and Burberry's.'

Suzie remembered a conversation she had had with Nat about Arab bathrooms, and wondered what he would make of Katrina.

'Where are we going to put this?' Katrina went on. 'We'll have to give a drinks party so it'll get used. Did you have a good time? You look quite brown.'

Suzie smiled to herself. Katrina's interest in her holiday would probably be superficial; her own concerns were usually what absorbed her. Suzie didn't mind. She wasn't sure how much she wanted to say about Nat anyway.

They put the ice-bucket on a table in the living-room, pending further inspiration.

'What's the matter with your arm?' Katrina asked, catching sight of the bandage when Suzie absentmindedly pushed up the sleeves of her jersey.

'Oh,' she tried to sound offhand, 'I cut it on some coral. It's OK now—it doesn't hurt at all.'

'Did you go to Aqaba? Bob took me there. I thought the back streets were a bit tatty, but the swimming's fun. We stayed in a fabulous hotel—it cost the absolute earth, but Bob didn't mind. We had breakfast in bed and ordered drinks up the whole time.' She picked up a white linen jacket from the chair on which she had dropped it. 'I'd better hang this thing up before it gets any more creases—it's hopeless. I'm almost sorry I bought it. By the way, thanks for doing the ironing. You are an angel.' Her voice became muffled in the interior of her bedroom wardrobe. 'What did you do after Bob and I left you? Did you get to Petra? Bob and I went there the next day. We had a fantastic time climbing the rocks and watching the sunset and things.'

'Yes,' said Suzie.

'And what did you do after that?' For the moment, Katrina

sounded genuinely interested. It was one of the endearing things about her—her attention span was never very long, but there was a warmth in her that made it difficult to dismiss her as wholly self-absorbed. Suzie always responded to Katrina fairly uncritically; she could take no really dispassionate view of her family and friends. But, despite responding to Katrina's interest, she felt disinclined to tell her anything about Nat; he was very special to her, and as yet she didn't want to share him with anyone.

'Oh, I met somebody, and spent most of the time with them,' she replied vaguely.

'I knew you would,' Katrina said comfortably. 'Bob was a bit worried about you, and if it had been for any longer I wouldn't have left you, but it was only a week, and we always meet people, don't we?'

Suzie smiled and didn't answer.

When the phone rang after midnight she and Katrina were drinking tea in the kitchen, Katrina still enthusing on the subject of Bob. Suzie jumped visibly, but before she could move to answer it Katrina flew to the living-room.

'It's probably Bob—he said he'd ring.'

The conversation which followed proved her guess correct, and soon after that Suzie went to bed. There was no point waiting for Nat's call now. She didn't think somehow that he was the sort of person to ring at inconsiderate times when he knew she shared a flat with someone. She went to sleep telling herself she would hear from him first thing in the morning.

But if Nat rang the next morning, it was after she had left for work. She was almost late, hanging about nervously, alert for the telephone bell. She was working in an accountant's office where her agency had sent her just before the holiday, and a familiarity with her surroundings did little to keep her mind off Nat. The routine of the day seemed exceptionally tedious, and she thought half-past five would never come. At first it was difficult to believe in the reality of the office, with the clicking of typewriters, the telephones, the occasional chatter of the typists, and the general to-ing and fro-ing of personnel.

Katrina returned to the flat that night not long after Suzie,

who had decided to have a bath to spin out the waiting time
between the first possible moment she could reasonably expect
Nat to ring, and the moment he actually did call. She was
expecting Katrina's usual impatient 'Hurry up! I've got to go
out again in half an hour', but it seemed that Bob was busy for
the evening, and Katrina had nothing else lined up.

Suzie offered to make supper for them both and, after
concocting an elaborate salad, merely picked at hers when the
time came to eat it.

'So who was this person you met in Jordan?' Katrina asked,
after a somewhat one-sided conversation about the day's
events. 'He or a she?'

'He.' Suzie resigned herself to the inevitable questions.
Katrina would probably lose interest pretty soon. Nat couldn't
compete with Bob in any way in Katrina's terms.

'What was his name?'

Suzie smiled, remembering her first meeting with Nat.

'Ahmed,' she said.

'*Ahmed?* You mean he was an Arab? Suzie, that sounds
incredibly adventurous for someone like you!'

Suzie explained briefly about the events in Petra. 'He really
was an Englishman. His name is Nat.'

Katrina's eyes widened with curiosity. 'It's all amazingly
romantic! Nearly raped in a ruined city and then rescued by
two Arabs on horseback, one of whom turns out to be an
Englishman in disguise! What does he do in real life?'

Computer engineering didn't impress Katrina much, but
she evidently felt that the situation had had some potential.

'Pity he has such a boring job,' she said at last, 'but he
sounds quite fun himself. Was he handsome?'

Suzie gave a reflective little smile. 'Yes. Very.'

Katrina reverted to the topic again later that evening. 'This
Nat character—are you seeing him again?'

Suzie, her eyes on the television screen, her mind miles away
in a hotel bedroom in Aqaba, looked up vaguely. 'What?'

'Are you seeing Nat again, or was it all just a holiday fling?'

'Who said anything about a fling?' Suzie countered, and
wondered if she would give the game away by
blushing—surely Nat must have cured her of that, if he had

done nothing else! But she had carefully omitted all reference to any of the events that might lead Katrina to suspect any sort of romantic involvement with him.

'Oh, come on, Suzie. You've had stars in your eyes ever since you came back, and you're even dreamier than usual.'

There was no point arguing it. 'Yes,' she said slowly. 'When he comes back from Washington.'

'And when will that be?'

'I don't know. He had to leave suddenly.'

'Well, don't build too much on it. I know all about these things, and leaving suddenly isn't a very good sign. I suppose he got some mysterious message at the airport . . . You don't need to say anything—I can see that he did. They're all the same. I even wonder about Bob sometimes.'

'Nat's not like that!' Suzie said hotly. Katrina's casual pigeon-holing of a man she'd never met—especially Nat—she thought very unjust.

'Why not ring him?'

'I don't have his number.'

'Not even his flat? You never know—you might find he hadn't gone away at all.'

'I don't have that, either. He's going to ring me.'

Katrina looked at her pityingly. 'Well, if he doesn't call in a couple of days I'd forget about him if I were you. Don't expect too much.'

She thought of Nat's kiss at the airport, and his teasing parting, and the fact that he had included her in his words to Fahad about seeing him in London, and shook her head. 'Nat's not like that,' she said again. 'If he doesn't ring me, he's got a good reason for it, and I'll see him when he gets back.'

She was sure of him—then. But she remembered the conversation, and it became increasingly ominous as the hours passed, and several days later there still had been no call.

The gradual change from tense but certain expectation to miserable doubt, and then to a kind of conviction that Katrina's words had been close to the truth, took four achingly long days.

At first there were plenty of excuses to be made: Nat was

very busy—he couldn't get to a phone at a time when he could reach her—he had mislaid her number—he was coming back sooner than expected and wanted to surprise her. But gradually the doubts began to creep in. She refused her parents' invitation to spend the weekend in Cambridgeshire, thinking that the long-awaited call was most likely to be made then, and subsequently spent two unhappy days in the flat, unable to settle to anything.

Again and again at unguarded moments, Katrina's cynical remarks came back to her. Perhaps they were true of a lot of men—she had no way of judging and Katrina probably spoke from experience—but surely they could not be true of Nat? Why should he lie to her? He had had no need to involve himself with her, especially once he had dropped her safely in Amman. He had been careful to preserve the 'uncle and niece' fiction for her sake, even when he'd wished it otherwise—the episode climbing the rocks had proved that. He had invariably been careful and protective of her, and, far from persuading her into bed, he had given her a choice right up to the very last.

Nat had a way of cutting through pretences, and she had thought that at least there was honesty between them. Then she remembered how she had stopped him talking to her after the first time they had made love. What had he been going to tell her? Now, her former confidence undermined by so many nagging doubts, all stemming from the fact that he seemed to have made no effort to contact her, she began to construct a whole new background to the romance that for her meant total commitment.

Perhaps Katrina had been right when she had described it as a holiday fling, because, as far as Nat was concerned, that could easily have been what it was—but she had been aware of that at the time. He was well travelled, quite a bit older than she, and had had other lovers—he had made no attempt to hide it. Perhaps, had she given him the chance, he would have told her that it didn't mean that much, because underneath she still thought he was honest and had been very aware of her vulnerability.

Perhaps that was what he had wanted to say before they had

made love, but, as he had said, everything had happened so quickly that there was no time. Afterwards it might have been only too easy to fall in with her wishes. She didn't suppose it would be easy for a man to tell a young woman who had been a virgin until he took her to bed that she mustn't imagine that what they had just done meant any sort of commitment—especially if he had any real friendly concern for her. And Nat wasn't callous.

She thought again and again of Katrina's cynical comments. Then Fahad's words at the airport as they talked idly about Nat came into her mind. He had seemed to think Nat was no ordinary engineer. Well, perhaps he wasn't. But what did it matter? Except that he must have been lying about himself. Why tell her he was a penniless engineer when he wasn't?

When she came to think of it, despite his apparent lack of affluence, they had spent a remarkable few days together. Of course, Nat had the knack of making friends easily, and perhaps he was a useful business contact. That might account for the generosity of his hosts. Then she thought again of the young man at the airport. He had called him 'sir', and the urgency of the business that had taken him away had had nothing to do with the sort of installation problems he had once told her about. So he couldn't have been wholly honest.

She found herself with another disquieting image: an expensive gold watch on a bedside-table. She saw herself turning it over to look at the initials N.L. engraved on the back. So what if he did have an expensive watch? It could have been a present to him. But then there was the fine tailored shirt she had been so reluctant to get covered in blood the day she had cut her arm. She had recognised the name of the tailors, and had known from Katrina that such shirts were made to order and didn't come off the shelves in chain stores. None of it added up to the image she had formed of Nat—the image he had presented of himself.

The next week became an ordeal to get through, and the office work was almost torture. She made far too many typing errors, her mind forever preoccupied with the same thing, and several times made an excuse to go to the ladies' room where she could cry without being observed. She even took to wearing eye make-up as a sort of tear-deterrent, but it didn't often work.

It was half-way through that week that Katrina came home unexpectedly one evening and found her curled in an armchair, crying as though her heart would break. She had thought that Katrina would be safely out for the night. She didn't want to show her real feelings in front of Katrina, who with her worldly wisdom could apparently dismiss things so lightly.

But in some ways it was a relief to confide in her. She could offer ready sympathy when it was needed, even if it didn't go very deep.

'Suzie, darling, whatever's the matter?' she exclaimed, switching on the living-room light.

Suzie had been grateful for the summer dusk that was even deeper in rooms that were not well lit at the best of times.

'Is it something that's happened at home?'

Suzie shook her head, unable to speak for the deep sobs that racked her. In an unusual fit of motherliness, Katrina sat down beside her and took her in her arms. She petted her, and stroked her hair.

'Don't cry, darling. It can't be as bad as that.'

Suzie tried to sit up. 'It's all right—it doesn't m-matter . . .'

'Of course it does! I've never seen you cry like this before.' Then, 'It's not that dreadful engineer character, is it?' she asked with sudden acuteness. Suzie with boyfriend trouble was something she wasn't used to dealing with. 'That idiot who called himself Abdul?'

'Ahmed.'

'Same thing when the man's a lunatic. Oh, Suzie, I'm sorry! What *was* his name, anyway?'

'Nat.' Suzie was half upset by Katrina's attitude, and half relieved to be able to talk about him at last.

'What kind of a name's Nat, for heaven's sake?' Katrina sounded utterly dismissive. 'You are not, absolutely *not* to shut yourself up here pining for that no-good opportunist. You're much too sweet and good to waste yourself on someone like that, and it's no good telling me how amusing he was.' She paused, and then asked with uncharacteristic hesitancy, 'You didn't sleep with him, did you?'

Suzie nodded, unable to acknowledge it in words.

'Oh, darling! No wonder you're so upset. I know you think it's awfully special—and, well, I suppose it is—but men do have a different way of looking at it.' There was another pause and then she added anxiously, 'You don't think you could be pregnant, do you?'

'No.'

'Thank goodness for that,' Katrina said matter-of-factly. 'Now promise me to forget all about him for the next twenty-four hours. There's half a bottle of brandy that Bob brought round here somewhere, and we're going to get very drunk. That is, you're going to drown your sorrows, and I'm going to get drunk in sympathy. And if that Nat character rings up after all this time, I'm going to give him a piece of my mind.'

'Nat's not the sort of person you think he is, Katrina—he's different from anyone I've ever met. It's just that . . . I was so sure he'd ring, and there doesn't seem to be any reason why he can't——'

'Well, I think he's behaving very badly, so drink up and forget about him for a while.'

Suzie's subsequent protests were without energy. The long days of suppressed tension and the fit of crying had exhausted her. By the time Katrina had forced a claret glass half-full of Courvoisier into her hand and stood over her while she took a few sips of it, the acuteness of her unhappiness seemed to have subsided into a dull ache, and without listening to Katrina she let her mind drift. She was seeing a tanned face, with high bones and hollowed cheeks, changeable eyes, a wide, smiling mouth with a quirk at the corner, and a broad forehead shaded by an untidy mop of sun-bleached brown hair. Nat.

CHAPTER NINE

'I'VE been invited to a party tomorrow night, and you're coming too,' Katrina announced on her return home the following evening. 'It's Friday, and time to start the weekend as you mean to go on.'

Suzie at once protested. 'Honestly, Katrina, I'm no good at that sort of thing. It's very sweet of you to ask me, but you'll enjoy it much more on your own with Bob.' Her heart sank. When Katrina was in this sort of mood, she didn't stand much of a chance of resisting the pressure.

'Nonsense!' said Katrina encouragingly. 'Anyway, you can't back out. Bob's got an American friend who needs an escort for the evening. I've met him—he's not wonderfully handsome, but he's young and nice and quite well-off. Just what you need after that no-good Nat creature.'

'No, Katrina.' She had no real hopes of Katrina accepting her denial, but ideas of arranging to go home for the weekend occurred to her. Then she realised she'd have to deceive her stepmother's all too perceptive eyes, and pretend the kind of quiet contentment she was far from feeling.

It would be easier not to go home, and then to pretend she was ill when it came to the Friday night party. That way she would have a perfect excuse to stay behind at the flat and spend the evening alone.

In the event, she found herself sitting in front of Katrina's bedroom mirror putting on make-up that she hoped would make her appear less washed-out, and more sophisticated.

Katrina, spectacularly dressed in scarlet taffeta, had put her hair up. It made her look older. Suzie felt childish and insignificant beside her. Inevitably, Nat crossed her thoughts. When she had been with him, he had managed to make her feel as thought it didn't matter how she was dressed. And he had had a way of passing on his confidence to her. He had once told her that she underestimated herself, and the very fact that he had thought that had encouraged her to meet and talk to people in a way she had never done before.

As always, the thought of Nat tightened that little knot of pain inside her that never went away. Determinedly, she confronted her wardrobe and opened the door. The first thing she saw was the dark blue skirt and top she had worn that night in Amman. Katrina had followed her into the bedroom.

'Wear that,' she had said at once. 'It suits you and it's just right for this sort of do.'

Suzie hesitated; it had too many associations for her. But she could think of no reasonable excuse not to wear it, and it was the most suitable thing she had. Without allowing herself to weaken, she took out the dark blue. Pulled in at the waist by a gold belt that matched her high-heeled shoes, it looked different from the other time she had worn it. She put on more jewellery than she was accustomed to, with a thin gold choker and a pair of heavy gold ear-rings of Katrina's that almost matched her bracelet.

'You look fantastic,' Katrina assured her. 'Sort of beautifully remote and interesting. I'm glad you decided to wear your hair down. It looks more sexy that way.'

Suzie didn't reply. She needed the confidence the clothes would give her, but it was all only an act. Her appearance was something for her to hide behind.

They caught the tube together to Piccadilly, Katrina chattering most of the way. Suzie only half listened. She didn't quite believe in herself; everything seemed unreal. She felt numb inside, and stared into the darkened glass of the windows as the train rattled along, seeing none of the images they reflected. She heard Katrina say that they were going to a kind of business drinks party to be held in one of the hotels. Bob was to be there for business reasons, and most of the guests would be fairly high-powered.

I told Bob he'd better be careful!' Katrina was saying. 'Introducing me to a lot of glamorous millionaires isn't the best way to keep me!'

'I thought Bob *was* a glamorous millionaire,' Suzie said vaguely.

'Well, mildly glamorous and half a millionaire—but very sweet. But there's going to be a couple of guys there from really big companies—one started his company himself and it's making millions, and the other one runs a big multinational in the States. Bob's definitely got competition!'

Bob met them at the entrance to the hotel. The quiet opulence of the surroundings, liveried doormen, and the hushed atmosphere of wealth would have overawed her in the past, but now she followed Bob and Katrina without interest, as Bob guided them towards the suite reserved for the party. She was introduced to a tall, pleasant-looking American called Tim. She smiled, and tried to look interested in the preliminary skirmishes of conversation for Katrina's sake, and accepted the drink Bob handed her without even asking what it was.

Katrina alternately flirted with Bob, and showed concern for Suzie.

'Aren't you feeling well?' Bob asked kindly. Too long-jawed to be good-looking, he nevertheless had an attractive face. His smile was good-humoured and flashed a set of white teeth perfect enough for any advertisement, and his skin had that sort of Californian tan that marked him as an American.

She smiled at him. 'It's just a headache,' she lied. 'I'm fine.'

'You look pale,' he commented. 'What happened to all that Jordanian sunshine? Katrina looks as though she spent a year in the tropics!'

Katrina laughed, and Tim said, 'Come on, Bob! Where's all that famous gallantry and charm? You sound as though you're criticising the girl. Looking the way she does, Suzie should set a new fashion.'

Tim too had clean-cut American looks, without being in any way handsome. She should have been flattered by his obvious interest in her, and if it hadn't been for Nat she might even have found him interesting herself. He was certainly one of the nicer escorts Katrina had produced.

'Tell me about this amazing holiday of yours,' he was saying. 'What happened to you when Bob whisked Katrina off on his white steed into the desert sunset? Can't say I think much of Bob leaving you like that!'

If anyone had been whisked away on a white steed, it had been Suzie herself, not Katrina. Again she put the thought of Jordan from her mind—and if she had learned one useful art with Nat it was how to handle a conversation, even when she was out of her depth.

'It's Katrina who had the amazing holiday—you ought to ask her about it,' she smiled, evading a direct reply. 'But what do you do, Tim? What brings you to London?'

Tim seemed only too happy to tell her about himself, flattered by her interest. She looked up at the tall American and smiled from time to time, and told herself to ask the right questions when he paused for some reaction.

It occupied only half her mind. Concentrate! she kept telling herself. Don't let your thoughts wander—don't remember. Don't think of anything that will remind you. It's over. Finished. You had a wonderful time while it lasted—maybe he never meant to see you in London, or maybe he did . . . but not in the way you'd hoped. That man deserves your attention; he's making an effort to be nice to you and the least you can do is listen. Oh, Nat . . .

She found herself staying with Tim after that. He showed no inclination to look for other company, and when he was introduced to someone he made sure that she was introduced too. She knew one or two of the women by sight—some of them were acquaintances of Katrina's—and there was a kind of shifting dance of meaningless introductions, smiles, and preliminary exchanges of information, none of which she retained. It could all have been a dream.

Once or twice there was a stir of interest as a new arrival of evident importance made an entrance, but it meant nothing to her. When could she go home? Katrina would probably want to go on somewhere afterwards and that would mean she couldn't escape for hours. Perhaps it would be better to make her move now, before she got entangled in any further plans.

Tim was talking to her when Bob moved behind her and touched her elbow.

'Tim—Suzie—I'd like you to meet Nathan Laird.'

Suzie turned to find herself looking at someone in a dark businessman's suit. He was wearing a discreet, expensive-looking tie. He was tanned. His hair was sun-bleached. The split-second impression suddenly focused—his eyes were grey-green, changeable as the sea, and he was staring at her.

The introductions were going on. 'Katrina, this is Nathan Laird about whom you've heard so much. Nathan—Katrina Liddell . . .'

He was taller than she'd remembered him, and more impressive; undeniably important, and coldly remote. Even his hair, recently trimmed, was smoother than before. He was wearing one of his favourite striped shirts, but he also wore gold cuff-links.

Nat.

For a moment's heart-stopping silence Suzie saw and heard nothing. Wherever else he might have a reason for being, he had no excuse for being in London—*London!*—without contacting her, if anything he had once said to her had been true.

But this man, with his executive suit and his expensively linked shirt cuffs wasn't Nat, the scruffy, unpredictable Nat she knew. And now, without consciously trying to recall the information, she knew too that he was one of those men Katrina had been talking about—did it matter which?—who made fortunes for themselves and for others, running a multinational company or building up his own little empire before he was thirty.

No, it didn't matter. Because this wasn't Nat. Not her Nat—because Nat had never really existed, except in her own imagination. She couldn't have fallen for this remote tycoon, not after the lesson Gerald had taught her about the values of the people in his world. Then with a pang she thought of her own mother—and realised that in trying to avoid what her mother had done, for very different reasons she had nearly made the same mistake! Nat, it seemed, was no exception to the rule: he hadn't even told her the truth about himself—he had been acting a part all the time!

Those eyes she had been thinking about, and trying not to think about for what seemed a lifetime now, were looking into hers, but he wasn't smiling, and as far as she was aware he hadn't said a word.

Scarcely conscious of what she was doing, she handed her glass to Bob who was beside her, and fled. She heard then Nat say abruptly, 'Suzie!' but didn't wait, even to retrieve the light jacket she had left with the cloakroom attendant.

There was a taxi at the door as she ran out into the street. Without hesitation she stepped into it and gave her address. She had her purse with her, and there was more money at the flat if she didn't have enough for the fare. Her one thought was to get away. She didn't care what anyone thought of her now—Bob, Tim, Katrina. But perhaps Katrina would understand once she realised who 'Nathan Laird' was.

From one instant to the next her whole world had shattered. She knew then that she'd merely been persuading herself that she'd given up hope; she hadn't really. She just hadn't been able to believe it was over until now.

Nat had told her nothing that mattered about himself. In fact, he had lied to her. She had been a fool ever to think he had cared for her beyond the immediate romance of their holiday together—he hadn't even told her he loved her. Of course he had no intention of continuing the relationship between them—how could he? He had been playing a game all along to amuse himself. He was probably tired of the sort of girls who chased after men with yachts and fast cars; he had even wanted something different, and had found it in her. He had even told her as much.

He might have rung her again one day, of course, even to take her out when he was tired again of his other girlfriends. She couldn't forget the look on his face—the coldness, almost boredom—as Bob introduced them. He had scarcely even been looking at her. Her mind replayed that last split-second as she had looked at him, knowing she couldn't stay to face him, to hear his polite evasions or, even worse, his greeting her like a stranger. His expression had changed—but not to anything she wanted to remember. It had been of astonishment, almost shock, at the sight of her, and she hadn't waited to see more. She had seen the way men looked when suddenly confronted with unwanted girlfriends. She didn't need Nat's version to remind her.

Her self-control lasted until she had paid the driver and

bolted all the way up four flights of stairs to her own front door; then she leant against it without even the desire to take out her key, sobbing helplessly.

After a while she heard a telephone ring and wondered if it was Katrina phoning to find out why she had run away so suddenly. At least Katrina would be good at finding excuses for her—if there were any plausible excuses for running out of a party when you'd just been introduced to somebody who happened to be one of the most important men in the room. By the time she had the door open, it had stopped ringing.

She lay for a long time on the sofa, hurting too much by now even to cry. Her world was suddenly without purpose. She had never realised until now just how much she had built on that relationship.

She had had brave words for Nat when she had thought she knew what she wanted. What was it she had said? 'It's you I want now. Not some unreal man who's still only a dream, and might never be anything else . . .' But Nat himself had been her dream, and her future, and she had made that foolish distinction between them as though she could be the kind of person who could live from day to day, and change with the changing circumstances.

She had of course been clinging to the hope that Nat would ring her, from some outlandish place probably, with every good excuse for his silence, and a request perhaps for her to meet him off a flight. It wouldn't have occurred to her to doubt whatever he told her, and they would have gone to his flat together, and their whole little world would have been recreated, just as thought there had been no interruption.

Seeing him in London, in a context in which he could not possibly have expected to meet her, had destroyed every last deluding hope. He could have been in the city for days. There was no need to find any complicated explanations for his silence.

The telephone rang again after about fifteen minutes. She was tempted to leave it, but the thought that Katrina might genuinely be worried and start a hunt for her forced her to pick it up.

'Suzie?' it was Katrina's voice. The pang she felt told her

that, despite everything, she still hoped—and feared—it would be someone different. 'You idiot!' Why didn't you tell me that your Nat was Nathan Laird?' She sounded excited, but her voice was hushed. There was a murmur in the background that might suggest she was still in the hotel. 'Don't you know he's the whiz-kid of the electronics world? Everyone's after his company! If you don't come back here this minute, I'll be after him myself—Suzie?'

'I'm . . . not coming back.' She could hardly put her thoughts into words; her voice wouldn't seem to obey her. She sounded husky and indistinct. 'I'm sorry. Please make my excuses to Tim—and Bob.'

'Don't be silly!' Katrina was firm. 'Nathan wants to see you. He's coming round to the flat as soon as he can get away. He phoned you earlier but you probably weren't back.'

So he did have my telephone number, Suzie thought dully.

'Don't you dare leave until he comes to fetch you!'

There was a click, and Suzie put the phone down.

The thought of facing Nat—no, not Nat—*Nathan* on her own doorstep in a few minutes' time terrified her. He was a stranger. What could he want with her? There was nothing they could say to each other now. It was pointless to ask him why he had lied to her about himself. She didn't want to hear excuses. And she didn't want to see him—not now, not ever. But she couldn't wander the streets of Chalk Farm all night to avoid him.

She undressed quickly and put out all the lights. If he did come, he would think she had gone out again, despite Katrina's warning. She lay in bed with the covers over her head and her fingers in her ears. She didn't want to hear the doorbell.

But shutting everything out didn't mean that she could shut out her thoughts. The image of him, so persistent in the past weeks, couldn't be banished so easily.

Of course, he was used to staying in luxury hotels; no wonder he hadn't been impressed by anything. He had shown her again and again that he liked a challenge; how stupid of her then not to see that she herself must present something of a challenge to him—he had even told her in so many words. It was humiliating to think of herself as a novelty, a sort of toy for a rich man who was so bored with his wealth that he played games, pretending he was as penniless as the foolish girl he had picked up to amuse himself with. But she must have proved a disappointment to him—she hadn't given him much of a game; she must have appeared too naïve, too ready to allow herself to be won by him.

But what hurt most of all, when she tried to look at it rationally, was that, despite everything they had said to each other, there had been no basis of truth for their relationship; all the while she had thought he meant it, she had known nothing about him.

She was almost certain he was only coming to see her now because Katrina had badgered him. She wasn't going to let a rich man slip through her fingers—or the fingers of a friend. And Nat—*Nathan*—was much more of a catch than Bob: younger, more glamorous, better-looking, and of course, a great deal richer.

She heard the bell, despite the bedclothes and the closed bedroom door. She even heard the repeated knocking, and Nat's voice saying, 'Suzie—Suzie! It's me—open the door!'

The sound of his voice, without the hostile image of the stranger before her, made her heart thud unevenly, and for just one second indecision paralysed her. It *was* Nat, her Nat, not the man at the party—but then she knew what she would find if she opened the door. Not the smiling, relaxed, unpredictable computer engineer, who made her laugh and took her breath away by turns, a man who worked for his living like other ordinary, unpretentious people and who didn't think he was paid enough, but the owner of an electronics company whose personal income per annum was probably more than she'd earn in years of her working life, and whose personal assets probably ran into millions. A playboy, who got his amusement out of pretending he was somebody else and making other people believe it too. She turned on her face and cried silently, every tear wrung, it seemed, from her soul.

*   *   *

There were two phone calls the next morning. The first she ignored, and, since there was no response from Katrina, she deduced she must have spent the night with Bob. The second time the phone rang just as she had finally pulled herself together sufficiently to go out shopping. She picked it up in case it was for Katrina. 'Suzie, I've got to talk to you——'

It was Nat. Her limbs seemed to melt, and her hands turned to ice. She put the phone down without a word, and cried.

There was no point staying in the flat any longer. After several hours indecision, she rang her stepmother, and told her to expect her home by an afternoon train. She would have to be picked up from a local station.

'Are you all right, darling?' Louise had asked straight away. 'You sound a bit depressed.' The suddenness of the decision was uncharacteristic of Suzie; perhaps it been that that gave her away. She thought she had managed very well to sound bright and normal. Home therefore was going to be no solution to the problem, but at least it would get her away from London and everything—everyone—in it she didn't want to see.

She left a note for Katrina, and walked to the tube station, nerving herself for a weekend of tactful reticence from her parents once they saw that something was wrong, which was inevitable. She had never been good at hiding things; she hadn't succeeded over the phone.

To her surprise, the time passed more easily than she had expected. Her sister was away for the weekend staying with a schoolfriend, for which she was grateful. Her parents, guessing her present rather sad, abstracted mood might have something to do with her holiday, were tactful in their enquiries on the subject, whereas Judy would have pestered her unmercifully.

Her father drove her into Cambridge to catch an early train to London; Sunday connections from their local station were erratic. They spoke about general subjects on the way, her father always initiating the conversation. It wasn't until he turned into Station Road that he asked, 'Everything is all right, isn't it, Suzie? You would tell us if anything was really wrong?'

She knew he was watching her out of the corner of his eye, and nodded, not trusting herself to speak.

'All is well with Katrina and the flat, is it? Still got a job?'
They would be pulling into the car parking area any minute.

'Honestly, Dad, everything's fine.' It sounded hollow, but it
was the best she could do. She knew he wouldn't believe her
anyway. He drew the car up in front of the station building,
and leaned across her to open her door.

'You know you can always count on Louise and me, don't
you, love? Whatever it is.'

Again she nodded. She couldn't speak this time. It was
true—she knew that whatever she did her parents would
always give her the same loving support. They wanted the best
for her, and worried about her so that sometimes it was almost
wiser not to tell them things, but they would never judge her.

Her father gave her a peck on the cheek, and slipped his arm
round her shoulders to hug her. 'If it's boyfriend trouble, you
just send him along to me! And remember—boyfriends are like
buses, there's always another one along any minute.' It wasn't
just a shot in the dark; her father had always been good at
assessing the cause of her depressions. She blinked quickly
to clear the glint of tears from her eyes, but she knew he would
have already seen it.

'Thanks, Dad.' She gave a watery smile. 'I'll probably be
back next weekend, if that's all right?'

'We'll put out the red carpet. 'Bye, love. Take care of
yourself—I've been instructed to tell you not to forget to eat. I
don't suppose you'll take any notice, but at least I've cleared
myself!'

Her grin was fleeting, but at least it was genuine this time.
She and her father had often seen themselves as conspirators
against Louise's anxious concern. 'Saving her from what she
didn't know,' as her father expressed it.

'I won't. 'Bye, Dad.'

He didn't wait, and she had little to think of on the platform
but the dreary inevitability of Monday morning.

There was a huge bouquet of flowers lying in the middle of
the floor when she got back to the flat. Katrina was washing
her hair.

'They're for you!' she shouted as soon as Suzie had got
through the door. 'They're from your devoted admirer,

Nathan Laird. I looked at the card.' There was splashing and the sound of water draining away.

Suzie stood staring at the acres of cellophane packaging, bedecked with ribbons, and containing a superb arrangement of hothouse flowers. They hadn't left much floor-space.

Katrina came in with a towel round her hair. 'Well, aren't you going to open them?' she demanded. 'They must have cost a fortune. I did put them in water when they arrived yesterday, but I thought you'd want to find them as soon as you got in.'

'Well, I don't,' said Suzie with an uncharacteristic lack of grace. Her throat was aching with the effort of keeping bakc the tears. A terrible wave of longing had suddenly swept over her, only to leave her with a sense of despair. Oh, if *only* . . .

She picked up the bouquet and dropped it into the waste-paper basket, and without a word went to her bedroom and shut the door.

When she emerged later, Katrina was waiting for Bob to collect her. She had retrieved the flowers and arranged them in the ice-bucket. The card was propped up against it.

The ice-bucket somehow associated the whole thing with Bob, and millionaires, and money, and all the things that were wrong with Nathan Laird. Those flowers now had nothing to do with Nat. They were a rich man's present; they had cost him nothing except money. He had probably asked his secretary to phone the florist.

'Honestly, Suzie, don't you think you're taking this a bit too far?' Katrina accused, catching her glance at the arrangement. 'After all, all the guy did was forget to ring you. And he'd only just got off a plane when he turned up at that party with a whole troop of top executives in tow. He could hardly hold up everything while he rang his girlfriends! Aren't you expecting too much?'

Suzie turned to her, eyes full of misery. She didn't want to discuss it—now or ever—but Katrina had none of her father's tact.

'Katrina,' she said slowly, 'just for once will you believe what I'm saying? I don't mind about the phone call—I'm sure he could explain it. I don't even mind that I made a fool of myself rushing out of that party. But I do mind, I mind . . . very very much——' she took a breath to steady her voice '—that the man you know as Nathan Laird is completely different from the man I know as Nat. When you put those two things together . . . all they amount to is a rich man's game . . . Nothing Nat and I did together meant anything at all to him.'

Katrina stared at her in silence for a moment, registering the words, then she protested, 'That's silly, Suzie, and you know it! He's besotted with you! The first thing he wanted to do when he got back to England was to see you.'

'All right then, let's go back to the phone call.' It was the first time she had voiced any of her thoughts, and now she had started she was gripped by a kind of anger she had never felt before—a resentment against the man who was making her so miserable. 'Did he ask you for my phone number on Friday night when he rang here?'

Katrina looked puzzled. 'No. He had it with him.'

'Then he could have rung me any time from the States! But he didn't—that's just how besotted he is. And it doesn't matter, anyway. That man you met with his—his executives and his private plane is a stranger as far as I'm concerned!' She was really upset now, caught up in a kind of intense and furious misery. She could feel her cheeks burning. 'I don't want to talk about it any more!'

Katrina shrugged. 'I'm going to wait for Bob downstairs. You're being impossible.' And she had gone.

Suzie stared at the square of white board propped up against the ice-bucket. It was a typical florists' card with a spray of flowers on one side, and was covered with writing. The greeting, in large letters, she could read even from where she stood. It began, 'My Darling Suzie', after which the handwriting became minuscule. Resisting the temptation to read the rest, she snatched it off the table and threw it into the waste-paper basket. Then she took the ice-bucket into Katrina's room.

CHAPTER TEN

NAT didn't give up. The following morning, and the next, there were increasingly large bouquets delivered to the top flat and left by the florist for either herself or Katrina to find propped up against the door. The messages, in contrast to the size of the bouquets, became shorter and shorter, culminating in the curt instruction: 'SUZIE—READ THIS! I MUST SEE YOU. NAT.' She *had* read it before she had a chance to throw away what could, after all, only upset her.

'What's the matter with you, for heaven's sake?' Katrina demanded, exasperated. 'There's one of the nicest men in London sending you a hothouse full of flowers every day just to beg you to talk to him for five minutes! What more could anyone do?'

Suzie looked down again at the card in her hands, in an agony of indecision. She didn't know herself any longer. She didn't know what to do, and in an awful way it was easier to go on doing nothing.

Inside she was a turmoil of confused, conflicting emotions. One part of her desperately wanted to see him, and to be told that it was all no more than some dreadful mistake—that none of what she had discovered was true. But at the same time a cold, detached little voice was telling her that it *was* true: there was no Nat, only Nathan Laird. No amount of explaining from him was going to change the facts. He was a very rich man; everyone, except herself it seemed, had known that. And as such he must also be very successful in a world where only the ambitious and the ruthless got to the top. The people he mixed with professionally and socially were the people she actively avoided, and his true aims in life must surely be those she despised.

She said reluctantly, as though the words were being dragged out of her, 'It doesn't cost him anything. When he was Nat in Amman everything was different—you wouldn't understand! He would never have sent anyone expensive flowers like this—it just wasn't the way he looked at things. he'd be much more likely to send someone—well—a *buttercup*, for a joke!' And she burst into tears.

Katrina put an arm round her shoulders in instant sympathy. 'Hey, honey—wait a minute. Aren't we getting a bit confused here? It's the same guy—Nat, Nathan—remember?'

'But he's *not*!' Suzie protested hopelessly. 'When I saw him at that party he was so—so rich—and powerful and everyone seemed to think he was so important because he had a lot of m-money . . .' She was sobbing so much, Katrina could scarcely catch the words. 'N-Nat was just ordinary!'

'Suzie, that man could never be ordinary! And you never even waited to see what he was like at the party. He's made an absolute fortune by the age of thirty—no wait, you haven't heard what I was going to say—and Bob says he doesn't give a damn about it. Imagine that! He could lose it all tomorrow and he wouldn't bat an eyelid, just find something else to start up. You're too busy thinking he's a bad guy because he's so rich.' She hesitated, and then continued with unusual seriousness, 'I know you think I'm wrong to go chasing after people like Bob—although he's a bit different from all the men I've known before. But that's not what I'm trying to say. I know it's wrong to think that money's the only thing in the world, but you're just as one-sided in your point of view. You're saying money's bad, therefore anyone who's got money must be bad too. But that's nonsense—of course money can change people, and even corrupt some of them, but we're not talking about some of them. We're talking about Nat.'

'It's not just the money,' Suzie sobbed, 'it's everything! He's not the same. And he never told me the truth—he pretended he was this ordinary engineer—he even said he wasn't paid very well, and none of it—*none* of it was true!'

'Well, if he wants to explain it, don't you think you owe it to him to listen? After all, he did give you a wonderful time. And whatever you say about money, Suzie, all that fun you had in Jordan was paid for by somebody. Maybe it wasn't Nat, and maybe he is brilliant at improvising things out of nowhere, but money does a lot for romance when you're in big flats and luxury hotels.'

Suzie shook her head. She would have felt the same about Nat if they had had to spend the six days together in her scruffy little hotel room in Amman. Nat. Not Nathan Laird, with his power and his money and his minions. No wonder he had had such private amusement out of teasing her about garrets and washing and poverty-stricken husbands. He knew nothing of such things; they were just a game to him.

There were no more flowers the next day when she got home, and Katrina was preparing to go out. She emerged from the bedroom waving her nails just as Suzie closed the front door.

'I had lunch with Mr Nathan Laird today,' she announced offhandedly. 'That's Ahmed the Gnat to you.'

Suzie was silent, struggling suddenly with a tangle of emotions.

'Well, say *something*!' Katrina demanded. 'Aren't you even interested?'

Suzie walked past her into the kitchen, and dumped a carrier bag of groceries on the table. 'I don't want to hear about him, Katrina—please! I just want to forget all about him.'

Katrina looked slightly piqued. 'Well, maybe he just wants to forget all about you, too. He's asked me out to dinner tomorrow night.'

For the first time in her life a stupid, irrational jealousy stabbed Suzie. What was happening to her? She'd never even imagined such an emotion before, and now to be jealous of Katrina who was so wrapped up with Bob, anyway! But she couldn't help feeling a little betrayed. It was true that she had said she wanted nothing to do with Nathan Laird and all his power and money, but it hurt to think, however fleetingly, that Katrina might now be playing for higher stakes than Bob. And that she thought nothing of making Nat her object. Nat . . .

She'd got herself into an impossible situation, and she knew it. If she had rejected Nat, then surely Katrina was free to go out with him if he wanted her to. On the other hand, what was Nat doing taking Katrina out at all when he said he loved *her*? Rationally she shouldn't care if he went out with half the girls in London—but she did care; she cared so much, she didn't know how she was going to bear it.

She felt wretched all the next day, and by the evening had decided to ring her parents to confirm her weekend visit. If she didn't think she could face London again by Sunday afternoon, then she would say she was ill and have a week off work or something. Katrina didn't come in until very late, and she went to bed early to avoid seeing her. She didn't want to have to hear about dinner with Nathan Laird.

On Friday morning as she was packing for the weekend before getting dressed for work, there was a ring at the door. She listened to see if Katrina was stirring, but there was no other sound. The bell rang again, and thinking it was the milkman she pulled on the silk kimono over her underwear, grabbed the money from the milk-tin on the living-room sideboard, and opened the front door, making careful adjustments to keep herself decently behind it.

There was a small boy on the threshold. He was wearing a grey prep-school suit, and a typical House tie and cap.

'Special Delivery,' he said solemnly, and handed her a large, rather bedraggled yellow chrysanthemum.

Suzie looked at it in astonishment, and then at him. He had round blue eyes, a pasty face, and freckles on his nose. She had never seen him before.

'Are you sure?' she asked. 'I think you must've got the wrong flat.'

He looked at the number on the door. 'Nope,' he said firmly. 'It's the right flat.' And then stood staring at her.

She looked at the whiskery flower so unceremoniously thrust into her hand, and then down at him. 'Have you any idea who it's from?' she asked.

At that moment there was a hiss from somewhere beyond the bend in the stairs, and then a loud stage whisper. 'Simon—come *on!*'

The boy turned to address whoever it was crossly. 'I'm coming! Wait just one minute.' He turned back to Suzie and examined her unwinkingly. ''Bye,' he said, and then disappeared round the bend in the stairs.

Suzie stared at the flower in bewilderment for a few

moments, and then quickly shut the door and ran to the living-room window. By leaning out over the sill she could see clearly down into the street.

After a minute, the boy appeared, his scarlet and black cap bobbing along four floors below her. He was clearly arguing with someone followinghim. A nondescript black car was parked by the pavement, and the passenger door was opened as the boy approached it.

Then a girl emerged in the wake of the boy. She was tall and angular with long strands of brown hair down her back. She too was clearly wearing school uniform. As she reached the railings that separated the area in front of the house from the pavement, she turned to look up. She looked straight at Suzie. They stared at each other for a moment, and then the girl smiled. Her face, like the boy's, was pale, but thin and bony-looking. When she smiled it became alive with energy and a sort of eager interest. Suzie noticed that her dark skirt was fashionably, but unsuitably, long for a school one, and she wore a pair of dangling silver ear-rings. A moment later she was in the car, and was driven away.

Suzie gazed at the flower she held, mystified. She could think of no plausible explanation for the extraordinary visit—except that the children must have got the wrong house. They had, though, shown a certain amount of curiosity about her.

She noticed that a piece of paper had been wrapped round the flower stem, just beneath the head of the bloom, and ineptly secured by a bit of Sellotape. She unrolled it, a faint suspicion beginning to dawn, and found the words: 'This didn't cost anything but a lot of effort!' There was no signature, and no doubt as to who had sent it.

'Katrina!'

There was no response, so she pushed open the bedroom door. Katrina, her blonde hair tousled, looked up from the pillow as she entered.

'Whaddyouwant?' she asked sleepily. 'Is it time to get up?'

Suzie didn't waste words. 'Who were the children who brought this?'

Katrina turned her face into the pillow, her voice becoming

muffled and even more indistinct. 'Go back to bed. It's not time to get up yet.'

'Yes, it is!' persisted Suzie, her heart suddenly beginning to sing; somewhere there was a person called Nat who had sent her a ragged yellow flower. 'Come on, Katrina—don't pretend you know nothing about it! You told Nat what I did with the other flowers, didn't you?'

'Mmm. Go away.'

'And when you had lunch with him you told him what I said about the buttercup—and all that business about having dinner with him and trying to make me jealous was because you were plotting something with him! Who *were* those children?'

Katrina opened a bleary eye and regarded her in silence. Then she said, 'You look very different all of a sudden! Could it be that you're seeing sense at last?'

Suzie evaded her. 'You still haven't told me—who were they? I'll even get you some coffee in exchange for the information!'

'His nephew and niece. He's got a brother who doesn't live far from here. The girl's called Ali, but you weren't meant to see her. Apparently, you've heard quite a lot about her, and he didn't want you to put two and two together too quickly.'

Suzie laughed, her heart, after what seemed like years, absurdly light. 'Why all the secrecy if you're telling me this now?'

'Because you didn't want to listen before, that's why. Am I going to get any coffee? It'll be time to go to work before you've even boiled the kettle.'

She took the flower into the kitchen and looked at it while she waited for the kettle. Perhaps it had been she who had been wrong—not Nat—although it still hurt that he hadn't told her the truth about himself from the first. Perhaps she should forgive him for that initial encounter, though—that had been part of an eleborate game which even Fahad had aided and abetted. And what about Fahad? Had he known all the time who Nat was, or had he been just as mystified as Suzie? She thought about their conversation at the airport. He had clearly been puzzled—or was it all put on for her benefit, to prepare her for some new ideas about Nat?

But there was a time when it had become dishonest to play with her feelings in the way he had. Why hadn't he told her the truth? Perhaps he had been going to tell her that night in Aqaba; but what difference would it have made? It was impossible to say. It might have spoiled what was wonderful between them, or maybe the very fact of his presence, his physical closeness to her, would have done away with all her subsequent ideas about power, and wealth, and the way he was using it—and her. She longed now intensely to see him again.

When she brought her coffee in, Katrina was still in bed. 'I'm glad to see you've come round to a reasonable frame of mind at last,' she said reprovingly. 'I was beginning to despair of you. I've had to stop that man breaking into the flat—he wanted to climb a drainpipe and smash a window when I wouldn't give him the key the night of the party.'

Suzie laughed. 'That sounds fairly typical. Nat's nothing if not resourceful!'

'You haven't heard anything yet. He's had plans to kidnap you from work, bribe your agency to send you round to his office as a temp, and lie in wait for you among the dustbins when you got home at six-thirty . . . So I'm glad you've come round at last,' she repeated. 'But it's a bit late.'

Suzie's heart missed a beat, and she stared at her, wide-eyed. 'What do you mean?'

'He's going to America for at least three weeks. I don't know where he is now, or what he's doing, but I do know he looked pretty fed up with the whole thing when I last saw him—and I'n. not talking about the States.'

If she had thought she felt despairing before, it was nothing to the blackness that swept across her now. Just as she had thought she had found Nat again, she had lost him. She could at least have been prepared to listen to him, even if she had been unwilling to accept what he would say. She hadn't given him a chance, and she had to admit he had tried hard enough to see her. If he had grown tired of trying, she couldn't blame him.

She thought of him now, not as she had seen him at that disastrous party—a virtual stranger with a cold, hard expression—but as he had been in Jordan, sitting with the bedouin in the light of a fire; climbing the rocks with her in the early morning; saying wistfully, 'Know what I want to be when I grow up?'

She could not yet combine the two images: the successful businessman in his expensive suit, and the unpredictable idiot she had fallen in love with, in his Arab scarf and faded jeans. The man she loved hadn't sent her those armfuls of expensive flowers wrapped in florists' cellophane, but a battered chrysanthemum. But was it a greeting, a sort of farewell?

There was nothing more to be got out of Katrina. All the way to work, and all through the day, she wondered whether she shouldn't postpone her weekend in Cambridge, and try to get some sort of message to Nat before he left for the States— if he hadn't gone already. She hoped he would try to contact her, but the day dragged to an end and there were no messages for her. He must know where she worked! He had been in constant communication with Katrina since the party.

In the end, she caught the Cambridge train because there had been no word from Nat, and she didn't want to disappoint her parents.

Her sister, ready for bed, jumped on her the moment she came through the front door. 'Hello, Suzie-Woozie! I bet you forgot to bring me a present from Jordan!'

'And I bet you I didn't!' Suzie laughed as she disentangled the nine-year-old's bony arms from round her neck. Judy was clinging to her like a monkey, legs wrapped round her waist. 'You're too heavy for this—get off!'

'Dad says you're going to take me to Cambridge tomorrow and we're going to have lunch and tea there, and then we're coming home on the bus.'

'Oh, we are, are we? And who's paying for lunch? You, I suppose?' It seemed that half her weekend had been planned for her. At least she wouldn't have trouble filling in the time with Judy around—she'd scarcely even have a moment to think of Nat.

Judy let go of her suddenly and danced across the hall to the staircase to begin leaping up it, only to hop down again step by step. As she watched her, Suzie thought how much she had missed her little half-sister. There was too great an age gap for them to be companions, but she found that her feelings for Judy were almost maternal, and she had much of the fun of her company with none of the responsibilities.

Her father drove them into the city the next morning, Judy proudly wearing a narrow bracelet of Arab silver Suzie had bargained for, with Nat's help, in her first Arab bazaar.

The Saturday traffic in the centre was slowing to its usual dead march by the time he dropped them in a side street.

'I'll get tired of the great metropolis long before you two, and I'm going home for lunch. Catch the five o'clock bus. Judy's got the money, but don't spend it all in one place or people will get suspicious.'

It was an old joke—her father had been saying it ever since he had given her her first pocket money. Suzie smiled, and gave him an affectionate kiss.

'Thanks, Dad. Does that mean if Judy gets caught for shoplifting you won't bail us out?'

'Get along with both of you. I'll be paying a parking fine in a minute!'

Tradition dictated that they went to one restaurant for coffee, a second for lunch, and then ended up at a tea shop in King's Parade at about four o'clock. By then Suzie was exhausted. She felt as though she had been dragged round every stationery shop, clothes shop, record shop and toy shop in Cambridge.

'It's much more fun with you,' Judy had encouraged. 'Mum only wants to buy food!'

Suzie thought sympathetically of her stepmother, and her loathing of big supermarkets where she had to shop for the whole week ahead.

Now she stared unseeingly at the sticky cake in front of her, bought to please Judy, but destined for her sister rather than herself. She sipped her tea, and wondered if she should ring Katrina to find out if she knew anything more of Nat. She had brought the chrysanthemum home with her—it would only die over the weekend in the flat, she had told herself—and it was now in a narrow vase on her dressing-table.

If Nat really wanted to contact her, of course, he could find

out her phone number from Katrina—or even Directory
Enquiries. There weren't that many McClarens in the book.
But perhaps he was waiting for her to make some response. He
had sent her the flower, after all. Now that it was too late, she
saw what she should have done: Katrina had said she had no
idea where he was, but at least she would have known his
office number, or his flat. She could have sent a message, or a
letter—anything to show that she was ready to listen. No, more
than that. She wanted desperately to see him.

Judy's high, petulant little voice broke across her thoughts.
'There isn't enough *jam* in it. I don't want that bit.'

An unsatisfactory doughnut had been dissected on her
sister's plate, and there were crumbs all over the table.

'Have my sticky cake. I don't want it and it's got lots of jam
and icing and things on it.'

Judy eyed it doubtfully. 'I can't remember if I like that
kind.' She was tired, and dangerously close to that mood in
which she wasn't prepared to be pleased by anything. It was
another three quarters of an hour until the bus.

'Just try a little bit,' Suzie coaxed. 'You can leave it if you
don't like it, and get another doughnut. But please, darling,
brush those crumbs off the table. Nobody will want to sit here
ever again.'

The voice that answered her was as unexpected as it was
heart-stoppingly familiar. 'Oh, yes, they will. In fact,
somebody wants to sit at this table right now!'

Suzie forgot to breathe. Everything in front of her eyes
suddenly blurred with shock. Somewhere, in the part of her
mind that was still functioning, she wondered if she was going
to faint.

'Come on, Judy. Move over. Your sister's forgotten her
manners.'

Suzie's vision cleared, and she saw both the casually dressed
man in jeans and a navy sweatshirt standing by the table, and
Judy's blank expression under her dark page-boy haircut as she
gazed up at him.

'How do you know my name?' Judy demanded suspiciously.

'I've heard a lot about you. And especially that you like
whale jokes.'

'Oh, those are *ancient*,' said Judy, with all the crushing dismissal of a nine-year-old.

'Nat!' Suzie's voice didn't seem to be working any more and she wasn't sure she'd ever known how to breathe easily. Half the restaurant must be able to hear her heart thudding.

'Does Suzie know you?' Judy asked.

'Well, I certainly know her, but I'm not sure if she wants to know me any more.' There was that familiar quirky smile in the corner of his mouth, but his eyes, which were on Suzie, were serious.

'Oh,' said Judy, and without comment moved on to the chair beside her, taking her plate and glass of milk with her. Nat sat down in front of the scattered remains of the doughnut.

'What's *your* name?' Judy reached out for the sticky cake.

'Actually, I've got three names,' Nat said conversationally. 'The one I prefer is Ahmed.'

'What are the others?'

'Most people call me Nat. Suzie calls me Nat.'

Judy giggled. 'That's a stupid name—it sounds like a fly. What's the third one?'

'My real name. Nathan.'

Nat transferred his gaze from the nine-year-old beside him to look very directly at Suzie.

'My name is Nathan Laird,' he said slowly, 'and I run a very big company which makes computers and which I started nine years ago. Sometimes, when there's a crisis and I can get away, I do the jobs my engineers should be doing—because I enjoy it. I know how much an engineer earns, but I don't know how much exactly I earn a year. And even if I did I probably wouldn't tell you, because if it matters to you—and it shouldn't—you've got your priorities muddled somewhere.' He sounded unusually tense; almost—except that it was hard to believe it of Nat—really angry.

Suzie swallowed nervously, and opened her mouth to say something, but Judy, deliberately provoking, cut in, 'Are you Suzie's boyfriend?'

Nat turned back to her, but not before he had given himself time to watch the blush that flooded Suzie's face. She was just beginning to recover from the shock of numbness that had paralysed her since she had registered the appearance of the man beside their table.

'I'm too old to be a boy,' Nat said firmly. 'And before you ask, I'm thirty-one and I deserve some respect.'

Judy gave a reverential whistle. 'Whew. That's old!'

'Judy! That was very rude!' Suzie sounded agonised.

Nat caught the look of acute embarrassment on her face, and seemed to relax a little. He turned to the child at his side.

'How would you like to help me spend some of my millions, and buy yourself another cake? I'll tell you some more of my life history when you come back.'

'Are you really a millionaire?'

'Yes. I'm filthy rich. Stinking rich. Now go and get your cake before I change my mind about giving you thirty-five pence or whatever it is.'

Judy got up and wriggled past his chair. 'I'll have to wait in the queue. And the chocolate cakes are forty-five pence. Each.'

Nat pulled a comic face. 'I can see you've got more of an interest in the realities of finance than your sister. Come to me if you ever want a job.'

Judy examined the coin in her hand, glanced from Nat to Suzie and back again, and then went to stand at the end of the long queue. The tea shop was filling up.

'Doesn't miss a trick, your sister, does she? Hello, Suzie.'

Suzie stared at the crumbs on the table as though her life depended on remembering the exact position of each.

'I'm—I'm sorry she was rude to you . . . She's very spoilt,' she said at last.

'I like kids, and I'm used to Simon—who's met you. He's a lot worse than Judy in his own inimitable fashion. You told me about Judy in Jordan. She's a very pretty little thing.' Nat's words were casual, but there was still an indefinable tension in him.

There was a silence. Suzie's heart was beating so fast she could hardly breathe; she felt dizzy and there was a sort of rushing in her ears. One moment she had been thinking of Nat with longing as a vague and unreal dream, and the next—there he was, standing by her table.

'Look at me.'

She swallowed nervously. Her mouth felt dry. Slowly she raised her eyes, wondering what she was going to find, and remembering how she had fled from their last meeting. *Was* he angry? She had thrown away his flowers and refused to see him. She didn't yet know Nat in all his moods, and he had frightened her before with an intensity of anger she had sensed in him, although it had not been directed against herself. Perhaps the man was a stranger, after all. She clenched her hands in her lap.

'Don't I even get a hello?'

He was looking at her. His eyelashes were darker than she remembered, and his eyes unexpectedly green and intense. But he was her Nat—not the man she had met in London; the faded jeans, and striped shirt under the navy sweatshirt was familiar, and he was just as tanned as he had been in Amman. His hair, though a little shorter, still had that fair look of the sun as it flopped across his forehead. But now it seemed as though those last three interminable weeks, only a short time in reality, had created a gap between them wider than she could ever have imagined.

'How—why are you here?' she faltered.

'To see you. I've tried just about every other way.'

'But I thought you were going to the States . . . and how did you know I'd be here?'

'Your stepmother told me. She said you were a creature of habit.'

'My . . . my *stepmother*?'

'Don't look so horrified! She didn't tell me anything about you that wasn't one hundred per cent complimentary—except that you can be stubborn when you get an idea into your head. Katrina gave me your address when I found out you'd gone home for the weekend. I had hoped,' he said carefully, 'that the flower might have kept you in London. I suppose it went the same was as all the others?'

'If you've spoken to Katrina, you must know it didn't.' Her reply was so low, he had to bend forward to catch it.

'When I asked her about it she couldn't find it, so we naturally assumed the worst.' He hesitated, and then continued showly, 'If it didn't, does that mean you've forgiven me for not phoning you from the States last time?'

'Nat, it wasn't the phone call!' Suzie burst out. 'I was sure you had some good reason! At first, anyway . . .' She trailed off, uncertain what to say next.

Nat put his elbows on the table, and then began to trace a pattern in the crumbs with one long finger. For a moment he seemed to be wholly absorbed in what he was doing.

'Katrina tells me you see me as a sort of Jekyll and Hyde character—and more especially Hyde. Is that right?'

It was an effort to speak. Suzie twisted her hands together nervously in her lap. 'I . . . don't know what you mean.'

'I think you do. I'm a bad guy because when you met me in Jordan I was an engineer and I hadn't got any money, and then you met me again in London I seemed to have lots of that filthy lucre which I know you despise, and I owned the company I was pretending to work for. You thought I deliberately misled you in order to seduce you and amuse myself for a few days. Isn't that it?'

Suzie was utterly silent this time. It would cost too much to speak. Nat looked up again from the table, and the green of his eyes blazed into hers. 'I never lied to you, Suzie. I know what I did and said was misleading—I meant it to be, but it was just a game which had noting to do with you at first. After a while it became—well—important for me to keep it up.'

Suzie said desperately, 'Nat, if you . . . if you *care* about someone, you tell them the truth. There wasn't any truth between us!'

She felt a tear slide down her cheek, and her eyes were stinging. She looked down to find a handkerchief in her sleeve, and saw that his hands were clenched as they lay on the table, and his knuckles were white.

'Oh, God,' he said, 'we can't talk here.'

Suzie leaned forward so that her hair partially hid her face, and then surreptitiously wiped her eyes and blew her nose. Once she really started to cry, she wasn't sure she'd be able to stop.

'I have to take Judy home soon. We're catching the five o'clock bus. There isn't another one until seven.'

'No, you're not,' Nat said quickly. 'You're coming with me. I told your father I'd bring you back if I managed to track you down here. My car's in the central car park.'

'Oh, but——'

'No buts. I have an official parent-given invitation to supper, and after that I'll have only just over thirty-six hours to make you see sense.'

Suzie could see Judy at the cash desk, holding what seemed to be a plateful of chocolate cake in one hand. It would be impossible to talk once she returned to the table.

'What do you mean—thirty-six hours?' she asked quickly.

'I'm flying to the States on Monday morning. I thought Katrina told you?'

Of course, she should have remembered he would be leaving so soon.

'Suzie, this isn't the place to talk and we haven't even started yet . . .' He hesitated, and then went on, 'I've been to see your parents—looking for you—and had a long talk with them. They've agreed to give you up for the rest of the weekend.'

She stared at him in bewilderment. 'What do you mean?'

'I'm taking you down to a cottage in Sussex where I live when I'm not working. You're free to refuse if you don't want to come, or to leave any time once we're down there—but please, Suzie, say you'll come. I've got to talk to you.'

Suzie, suddenly in a turmoil of conflicting emotions, stared at him, unable to say a word. It was as though she was losing all control over the direction of her life, and agreement—as she had known once before among the rocks in the desert—would mean abandoning all the paths she knew. And she hadn't yet fully come to terms with the man sitting opposite her.

Then, as she stared into Nat's eyes, she understood what it was she could see in them. She hadn't been able to read him up to now, but in them, quite clearly, she saw an intensity of longing and unhappiness that mirrored her own. It shocked her.

'Yes,' she said.

CHAPTER ELEVEN

THE DRIVE down to Nat's cottage took over three hours, and, although they set out soon after supper with her parents, it didn't seem long before the summer dusk was thickening over the landscape, intensifying the powerful beams of the car's headlights.

Nat had joked about the car when they had first approached it in the city multi-storey. It was a very new silver-sprayed BMW.

'I know you'd prefer a beat-up old Mini with rust problems and years of unfaithful service behind it, but oddly enough I can't afford it. One ill-timed breakdown could cost the company millions—and I mean that literally.' Then he had given a fleeting grin. 'Of course, you haven't yet seen the Rolls in the garden shed and the gold taps on the kitchen sink.'

She had been saved from the need to reply by Judy claiming his attention, and now, as she sat back beside him enjoying the comfort and smoothness of the journey, she could appreciate his need for a fast, reliable car that would cut down the strain of driving long distances. She wanted to tell him that she understood why he had made his earlier comment, but the atmosphere between them was still too highly charged.

Although the reference to the Rolls and the gold taps had clearly been an attempt to restore some of their former relationship, it hadn't succeeded. The terms of the joke were too close to all the differences still unresolved. Several times she glanced across at him, before it grew too dark to make out any fine detail clearly, and noted the shadows under his eyes, and the lines of strain about his eyes and mouth. His profile, strong and determined, gave little hint of his true mood. The slightly winged eyebrows could have been drawn into a frown.

Once, when he was aware of her attention, he looked quickly across at her and smiled, but the smile was tense. Once or

172

twice he raised his hand to the back of his neck, and eased his shoulders, and she wondered if he had a headache. At first, unsure of how to approach him, she made no comment, but later, when she saw him smother a yawn and check his watch with the digital clock on the dashboard, she asked hesitantly, 'Are you very tired?'

He had turned on the radio when they set off, the music providing more of a background to their thoughts than something to listen to. Now he switched it off, his eyes still on the motorway ahead.

'I had a lot of phoning to do so that I could get away today. In the end I didn't get to bed last night.'

'You mean you haven't slept at all?' she asked, horrified.

'Things are pretty hectic at the moment—which is why I have to go to the States. I can't just ignore it all, much as I'd like to. I have a responsibility to the other directors and shareholders in my company, and to all the people who work for me. And to the banks and private investors who finance my projects. Just at the moment, I'm the person who can do my job best. That's not a boast, and it doesn't necessarily say anything special about me.' His tone was matter-of-fact; there was no conceit in Nat. He genuinely believed what he said.

She thought of Katrina's words about him—that he was the 'Whiz-kid' of the computer business world; and she thought of the deference with which men older than him like Bob treated him.

'It's just one of those inconvenient facts,' he was saying. 'And when I'm tempted to pack it all in sometimes and become—oh, I don't know, a tinker for example—I have to think of all the people who depend on me. But jobs like mine have a way of making very ill-timed demands.'

There was a slight pause. Suzie wasn't sure how to reply; she needed time to think about what he had just said. Then he went on, 'That was what happened in Jordan, after I had failed to make contact with my office when—as it turned out—I should have done. I honestly didn't think there was anything in the pipeline they couldn't handle, and I thought I needed a break—very much on the 'change is as good as a rest' principle. I've done it before. I really do enjoy the engineering side, and part of the challenge is seeing how I can get along with virtually no money and no identity—none of the credit card back-up I have to cart about on my usual business trips. And I didn't lie about my name; I just relied on people not making the connection. The hotel manager did, but only because I'd used some company links in the first place.'

'And Fahad?'

'I think he got a bit suspicious towards the end, but as far as I know he didn't guess.'

No, thought Suzie, but he'd been right to see in Nat 'no ordinary engineer'.

'What about the phone call?' she asked. It seemed like the time to mention it.

'You mean the one I didn't make to you? It all goes back to what happened at the airport.'

'Katrina said you had my telephone number,' she said, very low. 'I thought you must have lost it.'

'You sound as though you expect me to be making up excuses.' His reply was tense, almost like an accusation—as he obviously interpreted her remark to be. 'No, I didn't lose it. But I didn't have it, either. When we packed in Amman, that piece of paper got into the bag that was checked on to your flight. You wrote it out for me when you were doing the luggage label, if you remember, and you were coming back with me anyway, so there was no reason to have it with me. Then I switched planes so quickly there wasn't time to retrieve any baggage. I tried to trace you through my office in London, but they said you weren't in the phone book.'

'No,' she said quietly. 'The number is in Katrina's name.' It had all been so simple. She should have trusted her first instincts, before any of those destructive doubts had crept in.

'One of my staff picked up the bag from Heathrow and delivered it to my flat. I had all the paperwork and stuff I needed in that briefcase John had brought with him to the airport in Amman. A couple of days later I managed to contact the guy in London, and told him to go to my flat and look for the number. The idiot couldn't find it, and then I did think I'd lost it. I couldn't do anything except wait until I got back to England, and then phone every temp agency in London for a beautiful, brown-haired, blue-eyed secretary called Suzanna McClaren.

'When I saw you at that party I'd already tried to ring you from my flat. I'd come straight off a flight from the States, and I only just had time to shower, change, and turn the bag inside out for the telephone number before I was expected at that damned hotel. I got there late as it was.'

She had run out of that hotel, without giving him a chance to explain, and she had been running ever since. But then—it had never been just a simple question of the phone call.

'I'm sorry I ran out on you like that. It was just that I . . . it . . . ' she faltered, unable to put that awful moment into words.

'It's all right. I think I understood how you felt. I was pretty surprised myself. I had been thinking of you, but you were the last person I expected to see. Then on my way to your flat I realised that my sudden rather casual departure in Amman might have started you wondering about me and interpreting the whole thing in a different light.'

'You didn't even have any clothes with you!' she exclaimed, struck by the unreasonable demands of a businessman's life. It was a relief, however short-lived, to hear him laugh.

'I'd like to leave you with the idea that I turned up at all the board meetings in jeans and a leather jacket, but in fact I have an apartment in Washington, and cupboards full of clothes I only wear in the States when I want to impress peopel. I know it's a disgraceful symbol of my capitalist wealth, but the company actually owns the apartment, so it's not as bad as it sounds.'

'You make me sound like a communist!' She was hurt that he should deliberately misrepresent her views.

'And I've sometimes wondered if you don't see me as the archetypal capitalist exploiting the underprivileged, grinding the faces of the poor and all that, just so that I can enjoy my power nicely cushioned from the realities of life by my money.' This time he sounded bitter, and his voice was hard.

'But I don't—I never said that!'

'No, you didn't. But you must think it, otherwise you wouldn't have reacted in the way you did at that party.'

'But it wasn't like that, Nat!' she protested. 'It was just that when I saw you like that, with all those people, it seemed you hadn't told me the truth, and that changed everything else that had happened. I couldn't bear it.'

There was a strained silence. She turned her head aside quickly, fighting the urge to cry. She had wanted to be with Nat, and thought about him and dreamed about him for so long, that now she was at last in his company the reality was nothing like her imaginings. It was all going so wrong.

Then he said, 'I'm sorry. I'm too tired to do two things at once—talk to you the way I want to, and concentrate on driving at the same time. Perhaps we'd better wait until we get to the cottage.'

They drove in silence for a long time then. Suzie, tired and tense at the same time, let her mind drift. She thought about Jordan: Petra with its pink rock tombs and bedouin tents, far away as a dream, and Nat kissing her for the first time in a crowded market, surrounded by Arabs. And Nat arguing casually about her garret and two point four children.

Then she thought of the conversation she had had with her stepmother only a few hours ago. She had learned something from it—a lesson vitally important to her relationship with Nat, but she was no longer sure she was going to get the opportunity to put it into practice. And there was still something she had to know from Nat first.

She had a vivid mental image of her own hands, holding lettuces under a tap in the sink. She saw her own slim, polished nails, and the green soft leaves of the lettuces as she rinsed the earth from them. She had concentrated on them as though washing them was the most important thing in her life, ne₁vous about what her stepmother would say concerning her sudden decision to spend the rest of the weekend with Nat—someone they'd never even heard of before. But Louise's attitude had been entirely unexpected.

'He's very nice, Suzie.' There had been no attempt to lead up to the subject; no careful soundings taken first. 'Is he the reason you've been so unhappy lately? Want to talk about it?'

She had shaken the water off the lettuces with exaggerated care.

'I'm not sure,' she replied cautiously. Nat was in the garden with her father. She wondered if it hadn't been deliberately contrived between her parents so that her stepmother could talk to her, but it had seemed to happen so naturally. She was surprised, too, to see how well Nat got on with her father; it was almost as though they had known each other for years.

'Mum, I honestly didn't know Nat was going to turn up here,' she said awkwardly. 'Things have been . . . a bit difficult between us.'

Her stepmother had smiled. 'I know. He told us. I gather you didn't altogether approve when you found out he wasn't the penniless vagabond you always hoped to marry.'

'He said that?'

'Not in so many words, but knowing you, darling, I can guess that's what it amounted to. I know why you think as you do, but much as I admire your unworldliness, I think it's a case of not seeing the wood for the trees—or whatever that silly proverb is.'

'What do you mean?'

'That you're letting some rather cloudy ideals get in the way of what you really feel. If you love him, Suzie, and you want to marry him, don't let all those ideas you used to have get in the way of reality.'

Suzie stared at her hands. 'I'm not sure any longer how I feel,' she said rather desperately. 'And he's never said he loves me or that he wants to marry me.'

'Why don't you give him the chance to talk to you, and then you might find out?'

She turned to face her stepmother—still a young-looking woman with hair as dark as Judy's, only faintly threaded with grey at the temples. Her eyes, brown like her own daughter's, showed her concern, but as always there was a placid smile on her face. Suzie leaned against the sink, and took a deep breath. 'You don't mind him wanting me to go off with him tonight, just like that?'

'You're old enough to make up your own mind, and I can't stop you. I suppose I should be very grateful it's someone as nice as Nat appears to be. But if you're really not sure about him, darling, don't let him persuade you into it. Your dad and

I worry about you a lot, you know.'

She wasn't sure. But in thirty-six hours he would be a whole continent away, and there would be an ocean between them, and if she refused him she might never see him again.

There was a pause, and Louise had said, 'You're very young to get yourself seriously involved with anyone, Suzie. If you do change your mind about him, don't feel that anything's irrevocable, no matter what's happened.'

She knew what she was telling her, and it gave her the courage she needed. It also told her something she needed to know.

Nat had teased her once, telling her she knew very little about love. In many ways, that had been true. At first, she had been overwhelmed by his sheer physical power over her, and that had been love. Then, when she realised he was offering her a reality very different from—but in some ways beyond—her schoolgirl fantasies, she had accepted him for what she had thought him to be at that time, setting her dreams aside, and that had been love. But when she thought of her stepmother, and the love she had always offered—so entirely unselfish, unconditional—it was in every way what love should be. Without conditions . . .

'Would you like to hear some music, or are you going to sleep?' Nat's voice cut across her thoughts, and she realised with a start that she had hardly been aware of him for some time.

'Do you need to be kept awake?' she asked, remembering a drive through the desert at night, when he had asked her to talk to him and had ended up doing most of the talking himself.

'It's not much further now. There are some tapes in the compartment on your left, but don't feel you have to play them. They're sounds of my youth—or to be more exact, my older brother's youth. I was only just waking up to pop music when he used to play these.'

Suzie opened the dashboard and took out a handful of cassettes.

'Actually,' said Nat, 'in my old age I'm getting to prefer Rachmaninov piano concertos, but don't feel you have to listen to one of those. I'm willing to admit they might be something of an acquired taste.'

'I like Golden Oldies,' she said. 'Especially the sort of thing you've got here. But I don't mind listening to Rachmaninov, either. It's probably much more effective for keeping people awake!' She hoped to make him laugh, but there was no response. Then she wondered if he wasn't deliberately trying to emphasise their age difference.

It was too dark to see much of the cottage when they arrived. For some time they had been driving down country roads, narrow and high, hedged in places. They had crossed a humpbacked bridge over a stream, and then turned down a one-way track that seemed to be going nowhere. It wasn't until they had no option left but a dark field that Nat pulled up alongside a hedge with a gate in it.

'This is it,' he said. 'You'll have to get out my side. I'm too close to the hedge, but there isn't any room for manoeuvre.'

She slid across the front seat, and scrambled inelegantly out of the driver's door. Nat was already taking two bags—one the light weekend one she had packed—out of the back.

'The gate comes off its hinges. You'd better wait for me,' he instructed, and she watched him while he half lifted it open. A narrow path, long grass either side, led up to the front door. They seemed to have come to a long, low cottage. Small paned windows were set into a wall of timber and brick, and there was a wooden porch over the door, which was a solid, unpainted oak.

Nat fitted a key into the lock, and Suzie followed him inside. It was very dark. 'You realise you could be sampling all the luxuries of my London flat right now instead of this, don't you?' He turned to look at her as he slipped the key into the pocket of his jeans, and switched on the light. She couldn't read his expression.

'No, I didn't—why aren't we?'

'Because I've got something to prove to you, and this is the best way I can think of doing it.' They were in a small hallway, with a stone floor. A narrow wooden staircase, evidently new, but carpetless, rose in a single flight behind his back. 'After you.'

He opened the door to her left, and she found herself
stepping into a long, low-ceilinged room with a bare wooden
floor, covered in front of the fire and between a couple of
comfortable sofas by dark coloured rugs. There were large
bookcases, filled with books, and a couple of low wooden
tables. There was no pictures on the walls and no ornaments of
any kind, but, despite its spartan appearance, in the warm
glow of the lamps the room looked inviting. The heap of ash,
the charred end of a log in the big open fireplace, and a pile of
old Sunday supplements stacked on one side of the tables
made it look lived-in.

'Are you hungry?'

She shook her head. It seemed hours since they had eaten
with her parents, but she was too tired and tense even to think
of food.

'Then I'll make some coffee. We have to talk,' Nat said
abruptly. The archway facing her at the far end of the room
evidently opened into the kitchen. 'Take your bag upstairs if
you want to. The bedroom at the end on the left is the guest
room—the other one's full of builder's rubbish. The
bathroom's upstairs first left.'

The implications of his directions only struck her as she
reached the top of the stairs. There had been another door
opening off the hall downstairs, and when she had glanced
through it, the room, a future dining-room or study, had been
empty except for a step-ladder and an array of paint tins. But it
meant that there had to be another bedroom above it. Nat
wasn't expecting to sleep with her. Then it occurred to her
that he hadn't even touched her.

She sat down on the end of the chintz-covered bed,
wrapping her arms round her, hugging herself. Her stomach
felt as though it had tied itself in knots, and she had to stop
herself shivering, although she was not cold. She stared at the
bare boards of the bedroom floor.

Perhaps he was going to tell her that the whole thing
ultimately amounted to no more than a friendship. It was
possible; he had had affairs before, and what had happened
between them in Jordan couldn't have meant as much to him
as it had to her. He had never said anything about loving

her. And Katrina, for all her little chats and conspiracies with him, could have been wrong about his motives for wanting to see her again. The bouquets didn't have to be a declaration of anything except his guilt: he now felt that he had in some way taken advantage of her. Perhaps he was going to tell her that it had been no more than a holiday romance after all, but that he still wanted them to stay friends.

She had to know just what he thought and felt before she could commit herself to anything, but she would have given a great deal not to have had to face him again that night. She would have liked to stretch out on the bed there and then, and, giving in to the exhaustion that underlay her present attack of nerves, fall asleep. But she owed it to him to listen to what he had to say. She hadn't given him the benefit of the doubt before, and now he had gone to the trouble of finding her the least she could do was accept what he said, however painful.

When she at last went downstairs, she found Nat squatting on his heels in front of the fire with a piece of wood in his hand. Dense yellow flame streamed upwards from the heaped logs in the hearth.

'There's nothing like fuel oil to start a good blaze,' he said. 'The coffee's in the kitchen if you'd like to fetch it. This all happened more dramatically than I'd planned.'

She watched the flames for a few seconds, glad of the life they brought to the room. It wasn't cold, but there was a hint of early autumn chill in the night air.

When she returned with the mugs to set them on one of the low tables, he had abandoned the fire and was sitting, half lying back, on the sofa with his eyes shut. She was shocked at the signs of fatigue clearly visible in his face.

There had been no relaxation of the strain between them since they had arrived, and she nerved herself to speak.

'Nat, you look very tired,' she said at last, trying only to let her concern show, not her nervousness of him. 'Don't you think it'd be better to sleep, and talk in the morning?'

He opened his eyes and looked at her. His eyes were grey-green now, like the sea.

'No,' he said slowly. 'I thought once I got you under this roof I'd be able to leave it, but I can't. I keep thinking that there might be a phone call telling me to put forward the flight, or meet someone in London tomorrow at a moment's notice. I can't take that risk. We've got to talk about what's gone wrong between us before I go to the States again, and time's running out.'

With an obvious effort, he pulled himself upright and then sat, elbows on knees, with the coffee-mug in his hands. His hair had fallen across his forehead in the familiar way, but he seemed unaware of it. He was staring, apparently unseeing, into the mug in his hands.

Despite his last words, there was a long silence. Then he said, 'Tell me what you feel, Suzie. What you think right now. I don't mind what you say, so long as it's the truth.'

He didn't mind what she said . . . The words came as something of a shock. If they were true, he couldn't be so very concerned about the difficulties in their present relationship. They almost amounted to telling her that he had no feelings for her——

'It isn't I who haven't told the truth, Nat, it's you!' She hadn't meant to sound accusing, but the thought of his indifference hurt her more than she could bear—especially now, when she was prepared to make any concessions if only he loved her.

'Now you're making it sound as though I deliberately tried to deceive you.'

'But you did!' She took a deep breath, and then said more gently, 'You knew how I felt about . . . about money, and lots of things! You didn't have to tell me you were an engineer, or to go on pretending you were after we—after we . . .'

'After we what?' he demanded brutally. 'Got into bed together? Does that amount to saying that you didn't think it meant anything to me? That I was just doing it to pass the time?'

She didn't know how she could bear any more. This wasn't Nat, it was some stranger—but someone more alien to her even than the man she had run away from in London. She knew he was deliberately trying to hurt her. She could see it in his eyes. They were suddenly filled with a cold, hard light.

Abruptly he put down the coffee-mug on the table, and had

reached forward to grasp her wrist before she was aware of his
intentions, pulling her towards him so that she fell on the rug
on her knees. She stared at him, too surprised to react.

'Supposing it did mean something to me, Suzie? Only in a
way you obviously haven't thought of—what then?'

'Nat, please, let go of me—you're hurting me!' She glanced
down at the strong fingers on her arm. Her sleeve had been
pushed up and she caught sight of the end of a long pink scar
that ran up the side of her forearm. Then she saw him looking
at it, too. There was a second's pause that seemed like an
eternity, and then his fingers relaxed. It was the first
time—and the thought now twisted in her like a knife—that he
had touched her.

She saw him pass a hand over his eyes in a gesture of utter
weariness. 'Oh, God,' he said. 'I didn't mean to do that. I just
don't think I can handle this now—there doesn't seem to be
any way of approaching it without . . .'

'Without what?' she faltered, when he was silent.

He shook his head, and said nothing.

She had stayed kneeling where she was, on the rug, in front
of the fire. Somewhere, irrelevantly, in the back of her mind,
she knew she had seen a rug like it, and that it came from the
East. She didn't know what prompted her to ask, 'Is this like
the one in that flat in Amman?'

But the question, interpreted as implied criticism, triggered
an angry response from Nat. 'Why? Because it's expensive—is
that what you mean?' Then his voice became dangerously
quiet. 'You won't give up, will you? You're determined to see
me as the bad guy because my name's Nathan Laird and
sometimes I wear a suit and go to board meetings, and make
decisions about large sums of money. I can't be made to fit into
your romantic ideals of garrets and unreal poverty.'

'Nat——' She wanted to tell him that that hadn't been what
she meant—far from it—but he didn't appear to be aware of
her interruption.

He no longer sounded angry, or even annoyed. Just bored
and tired. 'Your friend Katrina might have some persistent
notions about money, but at least there's a grain of sense in
them. Yours might be very sweet, Suzie, and understandable,

but they're also very silly.' The sudden rather frightening flash of temper had burned itself out apparently, but what had replaced it was harder to endure.

'I brought you here to show you something, but up to now you seem to have missed the point: this is the way I would choose to live if I could. Not because it's a challenge, or a stunt—or even some sort of rich man's trick you might think I'm playing on you. This place has all the things in it that mean something to me—rugs, garden spade and all—and it's mine because I like it.' After a second's hesitation he went on, 'If you're tired, you can go to bed almost one minute from now, because I've nearly finished what I was going to say.'

She looked at the deep shadows under his eyes, and at the hollows under the high cheekbones, and the grim line of his mouth. She felt as though she was silently weeping inside, because there was such a distance between them, and she didn't know how to cross it.

He was still speaking. 'We don't seem able to talk the way I'd wanted, and I know the fault's partly mine. I can't find a way to ask you what I want to know, or to tell you what I think. So all I am going to tell you is this: I'm not Jekyll and Hyde, Suzie, whatever you imagine. The two sides—or however many, I don't know—you think you've seen in me are one person and you have to accept that whole person, not just the bits you like. I'm going to the States for a month, and I'm not going to call you or write to you while I'm there. If you make up your mind you want to see me when I get back, that's fine. You've only got to ring. And if you don't want to, that's fine too. It's up to you.'

If he had loved her, surely he would have said so then. Never, never had she felt so empty inside. It was just as though he had taken away the whole reason for her existence. He was going away, and it didn't seem to matter to him whether she saw him again or not.

The flames had died down now, and there was just a warm, steady glow with the occasional flicker of yellow licking round the edges of the logs. Even from the misery of her former doubt, she had come to think in the last twenty-four hours that he must care for her in the way she wanted—ever since that ridiculous chrysanthemum in fact. Even half an hour ago, although she didn't understand his mood, she had still suspected that he might have brought her here to tell her so. But surely no man who loved her as she loved him could make a speech so dismissive.

There was an interminable silence.

Then he said, 'Suzie? Do you know what I'm saying?'

She hadn't realised that there were tears on her cheeks. She kept her face to the fire and didn't answer.

'You're not angry with me? Look at me?'

'No, I'm not angry,' she said at last. 'I just don't understand.' She watched a flame flicker and die, and then another flare up in its place. The edge of the log was black and charred where the flame licked round it, and scored with patterns. Her mind registered the details independently. She heard Nat get up behind her, and without touching her he came to stand by the fireplace, one hand against the horizontal beam that supported the wall directly above the hearth. The other hand was thrust into the pocket of his jeans, and he was staring into the fire. His stance was apparently casual and relaxed, but when she looked up at him she saw a muscle twitch in his cheek.'

'I promised your parents I wouldn't try to pressure you, or use any unfair means to influence you,' he said, without looking at her. 'You're very young. You should be free to choose what you want to do for the right reasons. Before I came along, you had a lot of dreams and ideas that you believed in, for understandable reasons, and then I tried to change them. I even had another go at them just now. I'm sorry. I had no right to do that—maybe you're not ready for it. I think you still do believe those things underneath, and you reject a lot of what I stand for. Because of that, I don't want to persuade you into anything that's only going to make you unhappy in the end.'

'Nat,' she said desperately, 'I don't reject what you stand for! I thought I did, but it wasn't just you who made me see that my ideas weren't very realistic. It was my stepmother—and even Katrina . . .' She hesitated. 'And it was thinking I wasn't going to see you ever again.'

There was a long silence.

Nat didn't answer her. He leaned his head against his forearm and stared directly down into the fire. His face was hidden by the angle of his arm, and by shadow.

'Nat?'

He didn't move. His voice when he spoke sounded rough and unsteady. 'There's nothing I can say to you, Suzie. You're so young and vulnerable. I feel guilty even talking to you like this, because all the time I'm loading the dice against you and I wanted to leave you free to make up your own mind.'

It wasn't until that moment that something became clear to her—something so obvious that she should have been convinced of it from the first if she hadn't been so stupidly confused about her own feelings. Katrina had been telling her so for days; even her stepmother who had known nothing about it had guessed. Of course he loved her. But love once declared imposed constraints, and he was afraid he would leave her no freedom. She would be forced to make a choice, and naturally she would choose him.

Slowly, she got up from the rug and turned him to face her. She was shocked at the lines of pain drawn on his face, dark with shadows, and his eyes were full of exhaustion that was more than physical tiredness. Could this be the same man she had known in Jordan—friendly, casual, laughing? He said he had tried to change her, but without ever intending it she had altered him, or perhaps brought out something that had always been there—something serious and passionate that lay too far below the surface to be detected in a casual encounter.

And he had tried so hard, against everything she was now sure he so desperately wanted, to put her interests first. He did want her—as much as she wanted him. There would be now no doubt for either of them, and no question of choice. The kind of love they had for each other didn't allow that freedom.

He had called her young, but unexpectedly in that moment she found herself years older than him. As Nathan Laird, he had scared her with his authority and his power; but now he was just like a little boy caught in an impossible situation—longing for something for which he couldn't ask.

She felt now for him as she did sometimes for Judy, and a
wave of tenderness flowed through her. She wanted to stop
him hurting, to take all his pain away, on to herself if need
be—anything so long as she could put that look he had lost
back into his eyes. Love, if it was to be love at all, had to be
without conditions.

She put up her hands to his face, and slowly drew one finger
along the line of his cheek. 'Did I ever have any choice from
the moment I met you?' she said unsteadily. And then, 'Nat,
I'm so sorry.'

'What for?'

'Because all this has been my fault. I made you unhappy
because I didn't trust you enough—and then I blamed you for
not telling me something I'd stopped you from saying. If only
I'd listened to you then, or even understood what you were
telling me when you spoke about your job. You gave me
enough hints—I was just too stupid to see them.' She paused,
and then went on more slowly. 'I know that because you've
spoken to my parents you feel that you can't say anything
that'll give you an unfair advantage, but Nat, I'm not being
persuaded by anybody when I say that I really do accept
everything about you—the way you live, the way you work,
the way you think. If you don't want me, you've only got to
tell me you don't love me in the way I love you.'

He didn't respond immediately, but she was sure of him
now, and of herself. In the last few hours she seemed to have
grown up. Nothing about him could ever intimidate her
again—not his anger, nor his ability, nor his power and the
respect he commanded in a world which was entirely alien to
her. She reached up, smoothing the hair back from his face. 'I
want what makes you happy,' she said simply. 'You told me
when we first met that I had to trust you, but now you've got
to trust me—that I'm old enough to know what I want, and
that I've made up my own mind.'

Then she was caught up against him, almost crushed against
the hard, muscular planes of his body. His face was in the dark
cloud of her hair, and his arms wrapped so tightly round her
back and ribs that she could hardly breathe.

She found herself half laughing, half crying as she gasped

for breath. 'Nat! Let me go!'

The tension in his arms eased only a fraction, and he said against her hair, 'Not now. Not ever——' His voice was gruff and indistinct. 'Oh, Suzie . . . Suzie . . . Suzie . . .'

They stood as they were, their bodies locked together, for long minutes saying nothing. When she tried to disengage herself from him gently, he merely shifted his hold on her, and tilted her chin with his thumb so that she had to look into his eyes.

'You're everything I've ever wanted,' he said slowly. 'You're sweet, and you're beautiful, and somehow you still manage to surprise me.'

'You mean, I'm enough of a challenge even for a Nat?' she teased, smiling up at him. 'But I thought I must be so predictable! How can I possibly surprise you?'

His finger traced the line of her cheek. 'As I told you once before, you look so meek and biddable sometimes—but you're not entirely, are you? I'm never quite sure of the way you're going to react. I knew I had to marry you from the moment you sewed my cuffs together in that bedouin tent, but I didn't know how I was going to get you to say yes to a man who had all the filthy riches you despised.' His voice suddenly deepened. 'Earlier tonight I was afraid I was going to lose you—but there was no way I was going to let you go for good, even if it took years.'

It had all been so simple, so obvious, if only she'd had the wit to see it. He had been frightened to lose her. The deception had been quite innocent at first—Nat's characteristic way of finding a challenge—and then there had been too much at stake. He had hinted the truth to her several times, and had even been going to tell her when she had stopped him. The consequences would scarcely have mattered if they had returned to England together, or if she had had more faith in him after that party.

'And you do forgive me for being so stupid?' She slipped her arms round his neck. 'You can't imagine how I felt—miserable, and then angry—and even jealous of Katrina who was only trying to make me see sense! And you tried so hard . . . we could just have gone on being happy if it hadn't been for me.'

His kiss was infinitely loving and infinitely gentle, and when at last he raised his head to smile down at her the message in those grey-green eyes was utterly clear to her.

Then he said, 'The nearest I can offer you to a garret is upstairs. There isn't a carpet and I haven't put in the central heating yet.'

'I know. I've seen it.'

'No, you haven't.'

'Does that mean——?'

'It means whatever you want it to mean. You can still sleep in the guest room if you really want to.'

Her lips touched his cheek, then the side of his mouth, and then his lips, asking to be kissed in a way that could leave him in no doubt about her decision.

Eventually he said, 'I'm worried about point four.' There was a smile in his eyes.

Another Nat joke? 'What's point four?'

'Of a child. Couldn't we make it three?'

She laughed, and he released her only to turn out the lights, and taking her by the hand, pulled her after him.

'You know,' he said, as they climbed the stairs, 'there was a time when you'd have blushed when I said something like that.'

He sounded quite regretful.

HOW FAR CAN LOVE BE CHALLENGED?

REDWOOD EMPIRE *By Elizabeth Lowell* £2.95
The best-selling author of *'Tell Me No Lies'*, creates a bitter triangle of love and hate amidst the majestic wilderness of America's Northwest empire. 19-year old Maya Charter's marriage to Hale Hawthorne is jeopardized by her lingering feelings for her former lover – his son, Will.

CHERISH THIS MOMENT *By Sandra Canfield* £2.75
Senator Cole Damon is Washington's most eligible bachelor, but his attraction to journalist Tracy Kent is hampered by her shocking past. If their love is to survive, he must first overcome her fear of betrayal.

BEYOND COMPARE *By Risa Kirk* £2.50
When T.V. presenters Dinah Blake and Neil Kerrigan meet to co-host a special programme, the only thing they have in common is their growing attraction for each other. Can they settle their differences, or is their conflict a recipe for disaster?

These three new titles will be out in bookshops from March 1989.

W❀RLDWIDE

Available from Boots, Martins, John Menzies, W.H. Smith, Woolworths and other paperback stockists.